$\mathcal{F}$ORTUNE'S
DAUGHTERS

ALSO BY CONSUELO SAAH BAEHR

Three Daughters

One Hundred Open Houses

Softgoods

Nothing to Lose

Best Friends

Report from the Heart

Thinner Thighs in Thirty Years

FORTUNE'S DAUGHTERS

a Novel

CONSUELO SAAH BAEHR

LAKE UNION
PUBLISHING

Text copyright © 2017 by Consuelo Saah Baehr
All rights reserved.

Published by Lake Union Publishing, Seattle

www.apub.com

Amazon, the Amazon logo, and Lake Union Publishing are trademarks of Amazon.com, Inc., or its affiliates.

ISBN-13: 9781477848364
ISBN-10: 1477848363

Cover design by PEPE *nymi*

Printed in the United States of America

For Andrew, Nicholas, and Amanda (again).

Heartfelt thanks to my editor, Jodi Warshaw, for finding me, the needle in the great haystack of Amazon.

Fame, love and fortune on my footsteps wait . . .
I knock unbidden once at every gate!

—*from* Opportunity *by John J. Ingalls*

Author's Note

This is a work of fiction. While it is based on historical events, liberties have been taken for creative license.

Prologue

At the turn of the twentieth century, the Hempstead Plains, fertile and halcyon, bordered by the great Atlantic, blessed by God with every source of outdoor pleasure, broke off from Queens and became Nassau, the sixty-first county of New York State.

America's bankers and industrial tycoons built castles along the rolling North Coast and manicured the rough virgin woods from Great Neck to Lloyd Harbor. J. P. Morgan, Frank Woolworth, Marshall Field, Harry Guggenheim, Frank Doubleday, and Asa Simpson. The names told the history of America's stunning growth. The unblemished county was only twenty-nine miles from the squalor of glutted lower Manhattan, where the millions were made on the corner of Broad and Wall.

Chapter One

Faith Celeste Simpson chose July 3, 1898, a day when everyone needed to prepare for the holiday outing, to push her way into the world. The housekeeper, Mrs. Coombs, had routed the first chauffeur from his Sunday dinner and, uncharacteristically coarse in her excitement, told him that Madame had had the "bloody show" and could deliver at any time.

The Daimler was parked and ready between the two marble lions that guarded the entrance to the main house, sixty-five rooms replicating England's Wilmington Castle. More than a century after the Revolution, America still aped the British, and the captains of industry sought security in the life of a country gentleman.

Asa Simpson was one of the first New York millionaires to build on the North Coast, an area made up of a string of villages along the shores of Long Island Sound. Asa chose Muttonville, a farming center with two canning factories by the railroad depot. He bought the entire easternmost acreage and knocked down thirty houses and three stores to get the land he wanted for his estate, which he named Seawatch. Muttonville reminded him of Troy, where he had spent eleven happy years before his parents were murdered by a hobo to whom his mother was feeding her best rabbit stew.

The northern border of the property had a half-mile frontage on the water. The western end of the beach was an inlet to a deep, protected tidal creek, whose banks were carpeted with flowering cactus, beach plum, and wild crab apples. Between the creek and the sea, Asa had constructed a bathing pavilion with open verandas that provided an unobstructed view of the opposing Connecticut shore. To the west was J. P. Morgan's East Island enclave.

The dairyman, Joe Stokes, wondered at the unusual activity in front of the house but didn't stop his routine. Sunday or not, the cows had to be milked and then weighed. Joe kept the cows in top-notch health and tested them for tuberculosis because the extra milk was sold in the village. The locals joked that Asa Simpson sold milk for one dollar that cost him three to produce.

The cow barn was one of the favored stops on Mr. Asa's early-morning walk before he headed off to Mott's Dock, where the steamboat took him to the foot of Wall Street. "They've never looked better, Joe" was all the compliment he ever gave. Sometimes Asa would ask Joe's opinion on some political issue, but Joe was too shy to offer more than a "yes, sir" or "no, sir." William McKinley, touting a prosperity platform of "sound money and high tariffs," had just succeeded the "greenhorn" Grover Cleveland in the White House. Asa and Joe both knew that the cows would be fine, no matter what went on in Washington.

There was no visit today from Mr. Asa, and Joe wondered again what was going on in front of the mansion.

◆ ◆ ◆

After a restless night, Alice Simpson allowed the maid to help her into the car but told the driver to wait. The labor pains had been steady and regular, but now they had stopped. She wasn't due for another three weeks, and if she got the doctor on his day off for a false alarm, he'd think she was a hysteric. She'd spare Asa, too. He was down at the pavilion with Billy watching the Hook and Ladder Company volunteers go through their drill. The plush back seat of the Daimler was as good a place as any to wait for the squirming infant inside to make up its mind.

In the cushioned silence, her thoughts turned to the social upstaging she had received at tea the previous day from Imogene Iglehart. As Imogene began to pour, the butler announced that Mr. Lucker had arrived to fit Junior for his Knickerbocker Grey uniform. It was gravely important for a boy to be admitted to the Greys' drill team, the same as making Skull and Bones at Yale.

"Make him at home," said Imogene, as if nothing momentous had happened, "and ask him to fit the drivers for new livery while he's here."

The news was like a slap, and Alice fixed her gaze on a pair of ghastly Foo dogs flanking the fireplace to hide her feelings. Mr. Harry Lucker of the Warnock Uniform Company had outfitted military men of every rank, and outfitting the Greys was his personal chore. Yet, even Mrs. Rockefeller regularly traveled to *him*, taking young John and all the male staff to Mr. Lucker's office. Alice hadn't wanted to visit anyone with her pregnancy so far along, but Imogene had coaxed and pleaded. Now it was clear she had staged this tea to let Alice know that Junior had not only made it into the Greys, but that Mr. Lucker, who never went to anyone, *had come to her*.

Alice's own boy, Billy, was just four but would soon have to pit himself against tiny Harrimans, Twomblys, Vanderbilts, and Burdens, vying for a place in society's little army. She had seen that band of boys in their white trousers and gray tunics marching up Park Avenue to the strains of "Saint Julien," armed for hell with rifles and swords, but only headed for the steps of Saint Bartholomew's. Each applicant and his mother had to be proposed and seconded by someone connected with the Greys. Suppose no one proposed her and Billy? Imogene was clever and always knew just the right person to flatter, but Alice didn't feel clever at all. There was always someone richer and higher up on the social scale to put you in your place or snub you and ruin your sense of well-being.

Alice missed her family in Brooklyn, where social life was open and simple. Of four children, she had been her mother's favorite. She always helped lace up her mother's corset, and they laughed as they struggled with it. She had never learned to be the mistress of a house or manage a social life. Now she was stuck in this huge, lonely place with people like Imogene always doing something that showed how lacking she was.

It was unfair because Imogene was the *parvenue*. Her money had been acquired in the past ten years, while Alice could count Thomas Murray on her father's side. Murray was partners with Thomas Edison and had been made a Knight of Saint Gregory and Malta by the pope.

Alice glanced out the window and realized the chauffeur was still standing by, waiting for her direction. There were no more pains. Was this baby going to be born today? Mrs. Coombs put an end to her indecision.

"Why hasn't Trevor taken you to the hospital?"

"The baby stopped coming," she said. "It's going to be an obstinate child. I can tell."

"We can't expect them all to be as angelic as Billy." Mrs. Coombs reached in to help Alice out.

Trask, the butler, approached the scene. As the ultimate custodian of the family's welfare, he wanted to know what was going on.

"She's had false labor."

"Who decided it was false? Has anyone told Mr. Simpson? Has anyone called the doctor?"

"Not necessary." Mrs. Coombs found his manner so off-putting, she did everything short of rebellion to challenge his authority.

"The father is entitled to know if his child is about to be born."

"Go ahead, then. Get him. Take him away from the drill that Billy's been talking about all week. He'll find his wife in bed reading a magazine."

Trask walked away, but he knew she was right. What would Mr. Simpson do anyway? It wasn't as if he and his wife were devoted. They didn't even sleep in the same room. Mr. Simpson was exclusively in love with two things: Wall Street and his son, Billy.

◆ ◆ ◆

The Hook and Ladder Company had dragged the rig across the beach by hand, and the men were now trying to best each other in scaling a twenty-foot ladder. After each attempt, there was polite clapping from the estate workers. For the finale, Chief Bailey moved a shack donated by a local farmer to the shoreline and was planning to torch and then rescue it, hoping to entice the audience into funding three hundred feet of new hose.

Asa Simpson, wearing a business suit and looking out of place in the July sun, sat on the upper floor of the pavilion, pretending enthusiasm. Four-year-old Billy Simpson had a toehold on the balustrade and was hanging over the top for a better look. Each time his son's blond curls dipped over the railing, Asa's heart lurched, but he controlled the urge to pull him back.

Asa was impatient with holidays that closed the financial markets. He would have preferred to be in his office with the cable line open for news of the naval war in Cuba, and the Edison telegraph ticker spilling out the quotes. The tape was all the entertainment he needed. It was news and drama all in one, and he watched it from morning until it stopped.

It had annoyed him to read in the *Times* a description of the average New Yorker as "a pushing person always trying to get ahead," as if it were a crime. He had started with less than nothing, and now he was listed as the ninth-richest man in the country. In actuality, he had no idea how much money he had. Just below him was a soap salesman from Philly named Wrigley, who had the entire country sappy over a candy-flavored novelty that you could chew all day. Above Asa on the list was Buck Duke, who had taken over his father's tobacco business and hired a French actress to promote his cigarettes. Buck had ten million Americans puffing away.

Getting ahead was the guiding spirit in America's current engagement in a war with Spain. Next to ambition, the other driving force was pride in the American identity. People hated change, and everyone was disgruntled to find unpronounceable names in their newspapers. Cuba, "Porto Rico," Philippines. Mr. Taft called the foreigners "the little brown brothers."

"Don't lean too far, Billy. You could go right over." Asa tried to keep his voice calm.

"Look, Papa. It's Fred Hatcher's turn up the ladder. He's too fat. He'll break it."

More likely he'll have a heart attack, thought Asa, *and close down the afternoon with a medical emergency.*

"Stand here with me so you don't miss it," said Billy, beckoning his father to get closer. "Chief Bailey has a surprise, but I can't tell you."

Asa stood and took his son's small hand. He couldn't help but think how the coming baby would change things. The tenderness he felt for Billy sometimes overwhelmed him. Looking at the boy's slim shoulders, he didn't think it was possible to make room in his heart for someone new. "Watch," commanded Billy. "I want you to watch with me."

"I'm watching," said Asa. "Nothing's going to pull me away."

At that moment, Asa saw his butler's bald head as he walked over the bridge that linked the beach and tidal creek to the mainland. He had a small boy by the hand. Asa had invited John Drury and his son to join them. He'd done so in part to surprise Billy but also to grill Drury—who was related to the secretary of the navy—on the details of the war. He was disappointed to see only the boy.

"Where's Mr. Drury?" he asked as Trask climbed up the steps.

"A call came before he arrived, asking him to return home. There's been a victory in Santiago. The war is all but over."

"Are you absolutely sure?"

"Yes, sir. I took the call myself."

Asa was surprised that such sensitive information was so easily had, but having heard it, he couldn't sit still. He wanted to be alone to consider the implications. The sinking of the *Maine* had proved disastrous for the stock market, but then in May, Dewey had sunk the whole damn Spanish fleet at Manila Bay, and the list had gone up. Stocks had been drifting down; this victory was sure to send them soaring, and he chafed at being unable to act on the news before it was public.

"Take the boys to Mrs. Coombs," he told Trask. "I'm going back to the house."

"Mrs. Coombs is with Mrs. Simpson. She's had symptoms that the baby might be coming."

"Is she all right?"

"She's resting. It was a false alarm. I'll keep the boys myself and let them watch the firemen."

When he reached the house, Asa looked in on his wife, who was asleep. He went to his study, sat at his mahogany desk, closed his eyes, and let the possibilities of the situation possess him. He made a list of the issues he would buy if he were able. Steel certainly, and copper, sulfur, oil, and tobacco for sure. The clock began to strike the hour. The chimes reminded him of Big Ben. The Fourth wasn't a holiday in London. If he could get to his Wall Street office, he could buy all the stocks he wanted on the London market at rock-bottom prices before the New York Exchange reopened.

He grabbed his hat and left immediately. It was almost dusk, and the last excursion train had left Oyster Bay station. The last ferry from Glen Cove had also departed, but he persuaded a commercial oyster hauler to take him to the foot of Wall Street. He arrived at midnight and walked from the dock to his office on Broad, only to find he had no key. He went out on the deserted street and found a group of home-less newsboys playing prisoner's base. He approached the tallest and thinnest boy and offered him twenty dollars to slip through the open transom and unlock the door.

For the rest of the night, the millionaire and the ruffian—who had never enjoyed three meals in any one day—worked as a team, sending cable after cable to London on a buying spree of steel, oil, tobacco, cop-per, and sulfur stocks. The boy, who had left the Mission schools after the fourth grade, rose to the occasion. They worked until the sun came up. Asa sent the boy out to buy them breakfast, and they put in three more hours. At ten in the morning, with the London market about to close, they finally shut down, and Asa went home.

Asa had the driver leave him at the gate; he walked down his driveway hoping the stiffness of the long night would work itself out. He passed the dairy barn, and Joe Stokes was smiling. "Morning, sir. Mrs. Stokes and I want to offer our congratulations." When Asa looked puzzled, Joe reddened. "We heard she was a fine baby girl, sir, and we wish her well."

The new baby had come during the night. He walked quickly to the house and went to the nursery. Asa lifted the netting on the bassinet. The tiny baby girl looked worried. Her brow was furrowed even in sleep. He would make it up to her. He would take the proceeds of the night's transactions and put them in trust for her. That would make up for his absence.

Chapter Two

The two negotiable traits Agatha Murphy received from her parents—a sublime complexion and stunning copper curls, fed by two centuries of pure Irish blood—she unwittingly diluted when she married Sen Lee, a railroad cook she had known barely four weeks, and bore him a mixed-breed child.

Sen Lee had cooked in the dining car of the Atchison, Topeka and Santa Fe on the stretch between Louisville and San Francisco. He had been the camp cook for gold miners, but mining had died down and he needed work. The railroad manager saw that he was clean and spoke English so let him apprentice at the railroad's showcase restaurant in Florence, Kansas. When he arrived home from a two-week stint, his parents told him they were returning to China, which was the dream of most immigrant Chinese. Sen begged to go with them, but they insisted he stay and earn money to send to the family. "Just a year or two," his mother promised. Her voice was stoic, but there were tears in her eyes. He was her youngest boy and her favorite.

Lonely and bereft, Sen couldn't stand to live in his old neighborhood, where the Chinese were despised. He took the train to Oakland and booked passage on the next boat for New York.

He landed in lower Manhattan, where the Chinese population lived in the glutted streets surrounding Chatham Square. He found a spot in a boardinghouse for Chinese sailors on Baxter Street with tiers of beds lining the large room. At any time of day, you could find the sailors lying about smoking opium or playing cards. He was ill at ease with the rough opium-dazed boarders and spent his time out of doors. There were days when he didn't speak a single word. If he was still, anguish overtook him, and he felt close to suicide. He walked the streets from dawn until dark, concentrating on the triangle created by Mott, Pell, and Doyers.

A man sold bits of candy on one corner of the triangle. Sen noticed a steady flow of customers throughout the late morning and all afternoon. The man was pocketing at least four or five dollars every day. It looked like an easy business to start and could provide an immediate income. It didn't require experience or storage space for the merchandise. Sen followed the man to a supplier and set up his own concession at Jefferson and Henry. From the very first day, he had a steady stream of customers. Once he had his business, Sen followed a routine that saved his sanity. He began the day with a bowl of soup from a nearby restaurant, took dinner at the boardinghouse, and visited a bathhouse twice a week. Sen had a pleasant, unlined face, but now he was cadaverously thin and very pale. The sight of him provoked a reporter to write about the rigors withstood by all the street peddlers: "The patience with which they stand at their posts day after day and in all weathers is touching." "They are dirty, dull, and hopeless," wrote the *Daily Forward*. Sen wasn't dirty or hopeless. He sold his entire stock by four thirty, when the children came out of the Seward Park Library. He cleared more than three dollars a day, more than enough to live on.

◆ ◆ ◆

Agatha Murphy had come from Ireland with her parents, but within two years her father died. Most of the Murphy men died young or were imprisoned young over what her mother called the stupid mistakes of the poor. The mistakes of drink, the mistake of illness gone untreated, the mistake of making do with dead-end jobs that the Jews and Italians would not take. Agatha's father had been a gravedigger, a job without hope. He didn't even have the dignity of illness to blame for his death. He fell, dead drunk, into an uncovered sewer hole and drowned in the filth of New York.

Agatha and her mother boarded with her mother's sister, Aunt Deirdre, her husband, and Deirdre's two boys. Six struggling people squeezed into three rooms on Baxter Street, Ragpickers' Row.

Agatha's mother was the only one able to work. The reverend at the Lander's Mission had a daily job sheet, and he sent Agatha's mother to work as a maid at the Astor House, which was across from the post office on Broadway. The Astor was *the* hotel. The Prince of Wales had been a guest.

The winter Agatha was fourteen, there was an influenza epidemic at the Astor. Half the staff got pneumonia and several died, including Agatha's mother. The papers were full of consumption news. Every week, someone would ask, "Where's so-and-so?" The answer would be "Oh, he got 'amonia' and died." Agatha found work as a button attacher to pay for her keep. Her undiagnosed nearsightedness made her ideal for the task of attaching silk buttons to a cardboard square.

There was no privacy in the apartment, and as she grew and filled out, her cousins' aggressive stares and roughhousing made her uncomfortable. She'd escape to church and pray with fervor. "Please, God. I want a room of my own. Hear me now. Quick." Then she'd turn the kneeler up and search the floor for a note from God.

One day, her uncle told her she had to go out with a stationery salesman who had lent him money that he couldn't repay. Her aunt overheard and became agitated. She took Agatha aside. "I don't want this on my conscience. You're my dead sister's child. Leave the house before the man comes. Go right away." She tucked a handkerchief with a couple of dollars and some change inside Agatha's blouse.

Agatha collected her few things and left. The first night she spent in a basement dormitory in Five Points, where the water from the river mixed with the wastewater in the house. The walls dripped with dampness, and filthy drunkards slept inches away. After that dark hole, the streets were like the Garden of Eden. In the morning, she walked down Jefferson with everything she owned draped over her arms.

She went skipping along the street taking deep breaths, scouring the neighborhood for a suitable boarding house. The relief of being out of doors and inhaling fresh air momentarily overrode her bleak circumstances. In her exuberance, she knocked over Sen's candy table. The merchandise went skittering over the sidewalk and into the rotting litter in the gutter. Agatha went down on hands and knees picking up the bits, but Sen dismissed the lost candy and gently helped her up. She was grateful but confused. No man had ever treated her with such courtesy. They talked for a while, and since he had no more candy to sell, Sen offered her supper and she accepted. Inside the restaurant, she stared at the items written on a card for several minutes, placing it almost at her nose and then putting it down on the table. "I can't see the words," she said.

He took the piece of cardboard and put it aside. "I can choose for you."

During the meal, she laid out the details of her predicament. "There were five of us in two rooms. It was six before my mother died. Lately the boys were getting too familiar, and some other things that were worse. But it's all right," Agatha added, fearing she was sounding self-pitying. "I know I can work. I can make my way." Sen listened as if every word were important.

Agatha put aside her problems and concentrated on the man before her. She liked Sen's face and his neat, full hair. He had a strong jawline and lovely, even teeth. His thin lips and calm bearing made him seem wise and safe. He hadn't reprimanded her for knocking over his merchandise and wouldn't allow her to pick anything up from the street. His gentleness and consideration were like an elixir.

It wasn't such an unusual pairing. The Irish and the Chinese lived side by side in those days and often married. In fact, Chuck Connors, an Irishman, had been the mayor of Chinatown.

That night, Sen took Agatha to a lodging house on Dexter Street and paid for three beds so she could rest without anyone crowding her on either side. In the morning, he greeted her outside the lodging house and took her to an eye clinic, where she was found to be severely nearsighted. The doctor shook his head. "You've been living like this?" She began to cry. "Hush," he said. "I'm not scolding you."

When he fitted her with the right lenses, she shrieked. She walked around the room with her arms in the air. "Thank you, God. Thank you, Jesus. Thank you, Mother Mary."

"Thank your husband," said the doctor.

As she and Sen went down the street, she kept stopping and grasping his arm. "It's wonderful. How can I thank you?" They had dinner again, and he took her back to the lodging house and again bought three beds. Sen, as it turned out, was Agatha's note from God. At least for a while.

◆　◆　◆

When he met Agatha, Sen was like a marionette brought to life. Agatha was full of energy, cheerful, and docile. He had been waiting patiently for his life to change. After a week of knowing her, he couldn't imagine living without her. She took inventory of his candy table and advised him to add toffees and chocolates that would appeal to adults. He liked her ambition. He was able to share thoughts with her without nervousness. She lifted his loneliness. He didn't know if she loved him. She was not yet eighteen and alone with no place to call home and no one to care for her. Sen filled both needs, and they were married at city hall on a balmy Saturday in January. By late May, Agatha was pregnant.

Soon after his marriage, Sen gave up the candy table for cigar making. He would buy remnants of tobacco from the dealers and roll cigars all night—as many as 180—which he sold the following day for four cents apiece. He could make more than fifty dollars a week if he worked every night. They lived in a rooming house run by a Scottish woman, and she complained of the smell every day. "Why don't you buy me out, Mr. Lee?" she'd ask. "Buy my house and stink it up as much as you want." With his new optimism, Sen felt capable of buying the house. He was amazed that by trading candy for cigars, he almost tripled his income, and he was certain there was some other commodity that could triple it again.

With new clear vision, Agatha's energy was boundless, and she pestered Sen to teach her how to cook. There was a woman who sold a tasty meat cake on the corner of Mercer and Broadway whom Agatha greatly admired. She was clean and tidy with upswept hair and a white butcher's coat over her clothes. She could dish out the food, make change, and trade "good-days" with ease. Agatha's dream was to have her own cart and sell wholesome food to hungry customers. After a few lessons from her husband, she perfected several Chinese-American hybrid dishes that she sold from a cart with an ingenious nest for warming stones that Sen made for her out of scrap lumber and discarded pram wheels. She kept her menu simple but distinct: dumplings stuffed with fish paste, diced vegetables and pork wrapped in a crisp pancake that was tucked up so the filling stayed inside. The hungry office workers in lower Manhattan who couldn't afford a restaurant bought lunch from Agatha. They loved her spicy finger food and her rosy good looks. She experimented with a variation of egg-roll skins shaped like a tart, filled with her own combination of shredded potatoes and chicken in lemon sauce. The food station was so successful she never gave a thought to how the baby would change her life.

Sen and Agatha had no extended family. They had no one to visit or invite to their room. Agatha envied the Jews their social clubs, *landsmanshaften*, where they could at least meet people from the same European hometown. Outside of the lively street life, she and Sen only had each other. Sometimes, in the evening, they visited the Educational Alliance, where they sat side by side, learning little life lessons, such as the importance of brushing your teeth, packaged in larger political lessons, such as the theories of Karl Marx. Most nights, the only activity after dinner was to count out the money each had made. They laid it on the table, smoothed out the bills, separated the coins, and counted everything twice. The money made them more hopeful and excited than the coming baby.

Agatha worked until the end. On February 15, she was rolling the food cart home at four in the afternoon when the first labor pain came. It had been a hectic and stimulating day because the newsboys were yelling that the USS *Maine* had been sunk in Havana Harbor and 258 sailors were dead. Agatha took the cart to the shed space she rented from the butcher, Teagle, and started up the street. By six, the landlady had called the midwife, who said they had waited too long. The baby was crowning, and the midwife barely had time to get a clean sheet under Agatha before the child was born.

The sight of the little girl silenced everyone. They had expected the inescapable features of the mixed breed, but the baby was pink and delicate with large eyes that only hinted of a tilt. She had wisps of copper hair. "Praise be to God," muttered the midwife. "You can't tell she's half from the heathen Chinee." Without much thought, almost indifferently, her parents named the baby Hope.

Chapter Three

For the first few months, the baby blended into Agatha's life. She kept the pram next to the food cart unless the weather made it impossible, in which case she left the baby with her landlady. On the corner of Broadway and Barclay from eleven until three, you could depend on the sight of the baby in the pram, gurgling or sleeping by her mother's side. When the baby was hungry, Agatha would let her suck on a rag soaked with sugar water until they went home and she was able to nurse her. The customers found Hope's dainty features and rosy coloring irresistible and took her for short strolls. Agatha, using her own precarious childhood as the norm, managed without much fuss. When they were alone, she kept up a running dialogue, as if Hope were already her companion. "Will you look at the patties. They're just right today, although the dough was the devil to roll out. I thought they'd be all tough, but they're as flaky as can be. Too bad you can't chew, sweet one. All you get is my milk, but I'll eat one for you. What shall it be, a little cod patty or the chicken? Lord, I'm thirsty. You dried me out this morning, Miss Sunshine, God's perfect darling. Mama's big girl."

When Hope was able to sit up, the passing street scene on Broadway provided lively amusement, and the baby clapped and pointed at everything she saw. Unlike the other Irish women vendors in quilted bonnets,

Agatha liked to imitate the young office girls who wore shirtwaists and serge skirts.

Store owners on the street urged Agatha to take the baby in the back to change or breast-feed her. Someone was always around to watch the cart for a few minutes. At three o'clock, Agatha pushed her cart and her baby home and made dinner for Sen.

Home was only one big room with a little cook stove and sink and a table, but it was warm and secure and scrupulously clean. In the early morning, Hope awoke to the smells of her mother's cooking and the sounds of her lilting babble. Agatha talked to herself and tried to say the rosary as she worked, but couldn't keep track of the Hail Marys and would start over and then give up. "Hail Mary, full of grace, the Lord is with thee . . . did I salt the pork? I ruined it. Oh Lord, don't tell me I ruined it." Words came out of Agatha in torrents, and that sound, together with the rustle of Sen's movements, was Hope's reality, as familiar and steady as her hands and feet. Life would be this way forever.

The little family was doing well. Over the first year, they were able to save $900, and Sen talked about buying the boardinghouse. The landlady wanted $10,500, and although difficult, it seemed a real possibility. Sen went to the bank to ask about a mortgage application. In the evening, he'd pore over the bank papers, as if struggling to make it work. Agatha broached the idea of remodeling the parlor floor to include a small restaurant. Sen laughed. Agatha knew his laughter meant he was marking time until he decided what to think. He laughed quite a while over Agatha's restaurant idea, and that knowing laughter haunted her in the middle of the night. Spring became summer and summer fall, and still Sen didn't finish filling out the bank papers.

It wasn't apparent right away, but Agatha slowly realized that Sen changed as Hope grew. After dinner, he would write long letters to his parents and relatives in China. Agatha was surprised that he had never discussed his relatives or their importance to him before.

She knew that Sen was up to more than sending news of his life, but she couldn't figure out what that purpose was. "I never knew you had so many on the other side," she would begin.

"Oh, many. Many," Sen would answer pleasantly.

Meanwhile Hope turned four, a happy active child. She was too restless to stay by the cart, so her mother began taking her to the Lander's Mission and Home for Little Wanderers to spend the day. She outgrew the day nursery and was put in the primary classes, where she learned her numbers and began to read.

The reverend from the Lander's Mission tried to persuade Agatha to work at the Astor as her mother did before she died, but Agatha was adamant. Her cart was all she wanted. Agatha gave Sen a daily accounting, and he wrote it down. "And you?" she would prompt, "How much?"

"I already threw it in with the other bills. Maybe a couple of dollars more than you. I'm too tired to add it up tonight."

He put all the money in a metal box that he kept under a loose floorboard. Agatha's unease grew. But, she reasoned, Sen was the man who had rescued her from a frightening future. And even if she were to question him, what would she ask? All up and down Broadway she spelled out her fears. *I don't feel right when you sit there night after night writing letters to people I never knew existed. We used to count our money together and talk about the future. That's finished. Now you take my money and lock it away.* "Oh, darling"—she'd end up talking directly to Hope—"your mama's gone daft. I don't know what's worse: your papa's new ways or my silly fears."

In any case, there was little she could do to change anything. She had to get up and cook by five, get her chores done, get Hope off to school, and be out with the cart loaded by ten thirty. There was no time to feel sorry for herself.

The letter writing stopped, but Sen was often moody and self-engrossed. He was impatient with his day-to-day life. Instead of the companionable exchange Hope was used to hearing from her parents, she heard bitterness and complaining. As a Chinese, Sen couldn't become a citizen, nor did he have the protection of the courts. Owning property was out of the question. With great resentment, he would enumerate his fate to Agatha. "As a Chinese man, I can have three careers. I can carry a sandwich sign. I can be a laundryman. I can roll cigars for the rest of my life."

"Maybe I could buy the house in my name," Agatha offered.

"And how would we pay for it?"

"If we could find a place for a little restaurant, we could make it work," said Agatha. "I know it."

This suggestion would provoke Sen to laugh in a hollow, mirthless way. Whereas before he had liked her ambition, now he reacted as if it were silly and too optimistic. In America, Sen knew he would always be disdained, and the disdain would spill over to Agatha. There were thirteen thousand Chinese living around the triangular space bounded by Mott, Pell, and Doyers. Ninety-nine percent of them were male, and many had wives back in China. They regarded themselves as sojourners and planned to return and buy land for their families with the money made in America. Agatha had to convince herself that her husband was different.

Hope watched the change in her mother. Instead of the former easy chatter, there was silence. When Agatha did the usual things like setting food on the table or folding up the bedclothes, a little vein at her temple would throb.

The Christmas before Hope's sixth birthday, Sen was offered a job that changed everything. A businessman, George Kamen, had a furniture store on lower Broadway, and Sen sold him five cigars every day. Like all small speculators, Kamen traded stocks on the New York Curb Market, which did business with chaotic informality on the curbstone of Wall Street. The traders had assistants perched on windowsills next to telephones. An order was then transmitted to the trader below with a shout or cryptic hand signals.

Kamen needed someone discreet and trustworthy to be his runner at the curb and make his transactions. He tapped Sen for the job and offered to train him.

"I'll give you one percent of my profits," he told him. "You can still sell your cigars. You'll find plenty of ready customers down on the Street." People like Sen didn't go into the serious room upstairs. They made deals on the sidewalk or in the public room downstairs. Sen was overjoyed to have this extra revenue stream from an enterprise that, thanks to the industrial revolution, had become explosive in America: the business of stocks.

America was becoming an industrialized country, and the stock market was now the vehicle for savvy citizens to place their bets on the growth of the new corporations. Bernard Baruch, who had started out as a young clerk, had parlayed his philosophy of contrarianism into a fortune, whetting people's appetite to try their luck on Wall Street.

◆ ◆ ◆

Kamen wanted Sen to keep detailed records, and he taught him to understand the information in the *Wall Street Journal* and how to chart the daily averages to see whether the trend was bullish or bearish. Kamen had made a little money on the price fluctuations of the railroad stocks, but trying to snatch a few points here and there was a ruinous operation because the manipulators were expert at luring the public to buy stocks they wanted to dump. The only way to beat the odds was to position oneself with the plungers, men like Ed Harriman, the railroad king, or Baruch, who was brilliant at predicting the market swings, or James Keene, whose expertise was reading the tape. Sen's job was to keep his eyes and ears open to see what big lots were being bought or sold and to spot the wash sales, which made a stock falsely appear in active demand.

Sen moved like a ghost among the shouting, agitated men on the curb. No one suspected him of wanting to gain an edge, so they spoke freely in front of him. Sen discovered where the brilliant speculator A. A. Houseman's runners hung out and where they went for a bite in between chores. Baruch's runner was proud to work for the "Lone Wolf," and often he'd hint around that his boss was going to cause some big uproar and they'd all see soon enough what it was. The traders' clerks and runners all liked to brag this way over deals executed for their employers.

Their facial and hand signals were complicated, but Sen soon figured them out. Winks, nods, thumbs up or down, fingers held up, an open palm—they all meant something. Sen began to bring Kamen precious information. Many days, he took Hope with him to further discourage suspicion, and he'd explain all the hand signals and call out the key players. For Hope, the drama of Wall Street was better than school, and she asked detailed questions that made Sen laugh with surprise. When they passed the First National City Bank on the corner of William and Wall and saw the bank's president, old Mr. Baker, in the doorway, Sen pointed to him and said, "There is the richest banker in the whole country. Only millionaires can put money in his bank."

When Sen was into his third month on the job, the Brooklyn Rapid Transit stock went from twenty to over a hundred in a short time. One morning, Sen watched a floor trader buy big lots of BRT. He saw a man whisper something that made the trader change course and unload what he'd just bought. Sen called Kamen.

"Baruch's man bought several big lots of Brooklyn Rapid Transit. Someone tapped him on the shoulder and whispered in his ear. He immediately sold what he had just bought."

Kamen took a moment before answering. "Something unexpected must have happened. I'll take a gamble. Short one thousand shares."

As it happened, the stock's promoter, Flower, had died of a heart attack, sending the market into a panic. The stock plummeted sixty points, making Kamen $60,000 in a matter of days. Sen's commission was $600. When Sen got home, he startled Agatha by taking her in his arms and dancing about the room, knocking over a chair. "This was a good day," he said, and told her the news.

It would be many months before anything even close to the BRT deal came again, but Sen continued making small amounts each week. He liked to get to the market early, read the previous day's quotes, situate himself where he could spot the important runners, and gather what information was there for the taking. He began putting up money of his own, betting along with Kamen. Even though he considered it gambling, he managed to amass $1,100 within six months.

As Hope grew and balked at going to the Mission School, Sen would take her with him almost daily. The sight of the tall Chinese man and the beautiful girl became familiar around Broad and Wall. Very little escaped Hope's eyes, and what she didn't grasp, she pestered Sen about until he explained it to her satisfaction. She knew the names of all the big players, especially the manipulators, and she knew the names of the stocks they had used to trick the "little guy." At night, she would reproduce all the hand signals for Agatha and tell her what they meant. An unexpected bonus for Sen was that she became an extra set of eyes and ears. She was thrilled when her papa asked her what she'd seen or heard, especially if she could tell him something useful.

As they returned home one late afternoon, she looked at the children going into the Seward Park Library.

"Where are they going?" she asked Sen.

"They're going to the library. To read."

"Why are they reading?"

"People read books. That's how they learn. You should be reading more."

Hope was mildly interested in reading, especially the Bowery Billy comic books, but nothing compared to the excitement she felt as she watched the drama at Broad and Wall. Soon it became as familiar as her cot at home or the sidewalk next to her mother's food cart. It was another playground.

◆ ◆ ◆

Like all traders who have early luck, Sen began to feel invincible. And like all invincible traders, he made a colossal mistake. In his defense, the struggle for control of Northern Pacific brought down the most experienced men, as well as neophytes, but for Sen, it was the end of his life as he had known it.

Morgan and Harriman were locked in a struggle for control of the nation's transportation system. The outcome of that tug-of-war affected the lives of both Faith and Hope.

Kamen sent Sen to buy three hundred shares of common stock of Northern Pacific at a price of $149, but by the time Sen arrived, the price was $350, and he became paralyzed. He had a check in his hand for $50,000 and couldn't find a free telephone. As if in a trance, he decided that nothing could support such a rise in price. Ignoring Kamen's order, he made a disastrous decision to sell short.

No one knew that Morgan's men had taken the shares off the market and put them into a vault. There was nothing for the short sellers to buy back.

◆ ◆ ◆

On the day that Sen lost Kamen's money, Asa Simpson sat alone at his desk mesmerized by the steady noise of the ticker. It was clicking out the market record that had become a record of only one stock: Northern Pacific. Hands folded in front of him, his desk clear of any distractions, Asa persuaded himself to remain perfectly still and clear his mind so he could decide what to do. There was a ghastly yet exhilarating event gripping the Street, and the market constituency was caught up in it. For several months, he had been carrying five thousand shares of Northern Pacific, a paltry position for him. His average price was fifty dollars per share for an investment of a quarter of a million. By 11:00 a.m., the stock had hit $840, and Asa was certain that the ticker had broken down and was printing nonsense. He called his man on the floor, and by the time he reached the phone, the price had been bid to $875. It didn't take a genius to know this was lunacy. The rest of the market had collapsed while everyone tried to raise cash to buy in.

Asa knew that the public's appetite for buying into fantastic stock run-ups seldom ended well. "Sell it all, Kenny," he said into the phone. "Sell it at the market." He replaced the phone and felt more at ease. Asa's shares were snapped up instantaneously at a price of $895 per share, netting him $4.5 million. The extraordinary gain reminded him of another windfall on the day his daughter had been born. Without hesitation, he took the money and added it to Faith's trust.

Sen and the other short sellers were seized with hysteria as they realized the stock had been cornered. The price climbed to $900 and then, in a frightening further leap, it hit $1,000. Sen knew a panic that was so complete, it blocked any rational thought. He couldn't allow himself to even consider the consequences of having lost Kamen's $50,000, let alone having incurred a debt of at least $60,000. It was a truth so frightening, he couldn't let it enter his mind. He knew immediately there was only one course open to him.

Without saying a word to his wife, Sen boarded a train for California, where he would catch a boat to China. He had $5,600 in the metal box and he took it, leaving Agatha with only enough for one month's rent and the money she had earned that day.

Agatha came home that afternoon and found Hope alone in the middle of their crowded room, reading her comic books. The place was a mess, and Agatha was sure they'd been robbed and perhaps something worse.

"Where's your papa?" she asked.

"Papa's gone. He was in a hurry and took all his things."

"Gone where?" Agatha looked startled.

"He didn't tell me. He just said I couldn't go. I had to stay here."

Agatha was indignant. "He didn't take you?" She walked around the room picking things up, putting things in their place, arranging and fixing objects to use up a burst of nervous energy that was making her limbs go haywire. Every few minutes, she'd turn and ask Hope a question. "Did he say where he was going?"

"Going home," said Hope.

"Home?" screamed Agatha. "You've got it wrong. How could he leave the house and say he was going home?" She gave Hope two hard shakes as if she were purposely being contradictory. "You're not making sense."

"He said he was going to his real home. Across the sific."

"The *sific*?"

"Uh-huh. On a boat to see his mama and papa." Hope had held herself together watching her father's strange behavior, but now she began to cry.

Finally Agatha saw the whole thing. She lunged across the room to lift the floorboard where Sen kept the metal box and opened the lid. There were two ten-dollar bills. She crumpled and sat without moving. The energy had evaporated. She sat for the better part of the evening, rocking back and forth and going over in her mind what was in store for her. In her despair, she forgot Hope and spoke aloud of her worst fears. *A woman alone with a half-caste child. Holy Mary. Blessed Mother, I will be alone. How will we manage? I don't make enough. I know why this happened. I missed Mass on two Holy Days. Haven't said my confession in ages. I'll have to take the cart out earlier. I'll have to cook all night and start out in time for breakfast.* As it happened, Agatha couldn't take the cart out for many weeks.

Kamen had expected $60,000 profit from his transaction. He had hardly slept with the excitement of it. When he discovered that instead, he was thousands in debt and facing ruin, he wanted to hunt down the tormentor who had caused it. The Five Points section had dozens of street gangs for hire to dispense retribution. Kamen rounded up two of the notorious Plug Uglies goons to recover his $50,000 plus the calculated profit of $60,000.

When they burst into the apartment, Agatha pleaded ignorance about the money and Sen's whereabouts, but they didn't believe her. It was said that Monk Eastman, commander of all the gangs, instructed his men to never hit a woman with a club. At most, they hit with their fists. They gave Agatha three chances to come up with the right answer. "She doesn't know. She doesn't know," Hope screamed, but they ignored her. When the first punch landed on Agatha's ear and blood spurted out, Hope screamed and threw herself at the man who had done it, pulling him back by his hair. He yelped and forced Hope into a closet, pressing a chair against the door, but she continued to scream and beg them to stop. The two men punched Agatha repeatedly, breaking her jaw, four ribs, the bone around one eye socket, and her right leg.

After the men left, Hope pushed through the closet door and threw herself over her mother, begging her to respond. "Mama, say something. Don't stay asleep. Don't, Mama. Don't." She caught sight of her mother's mangled eye, the white completely red. This sent her out into the street screaming for help until a neighbor took pity on her and went to see what had gone wrong.

Twenty-four hours later, pressure was put on Morgan and Harriman to settle with the short sellers at a reasonable price, which turned out to be $150. Kaman actually wound up with a profit of $28,000, but it was too late. Sen was gone, and Agatha lay struggling for life on the third floor of Charity Hospital, next to the penitentiary on Blackwell's Island.

Chapter Four

Alice Simpson had only selective memories of her life in Brooklyn. There was a dark spot having to do with her mother. Her father, Joe Bradley, had an impeccable lineage among the FIFs, the First Irish Families. He had so much pull with the archdiocese that he was allowed to keep the Holy Eucharist in the house. Financially, he had doubled the family fortune and had the largest house on St. Mark's Place, the best residential street in Brooklyn.

Joe Bradley had committed the needlessly stupid sin of marrying his secretary; needless because secretaries could easily be persuaded to be mistresses. Joe was far too valuable as a money manager to be criticized, but the family was cruel to his wife and his daughter. Alice once came upon a cousin, a boy of sixteen, shoving her mother against a breakfront in the parlor because she would not admit to indiscretions when she had been a secretary.

"Come on, Tess. Did you lend your bottom to the boss?" His voice was arrogant and accusing.

Her mother always answered with dignity. "There's no shame in earning a living, but there's plenty of shame in being a bully, Timothy."

If you had asked Alice to detail her childhood, she would not have alluded to any of this. She would have told you of her part in the Sodality of the Church of the Assumption and of accompanying her mother in acts of Corporal Works of Mercy, caring for the hungry and needy. Even though she never acknowledged the darker parts of her childhood, as a young woman, she was timid and unsure.

Alice knew that her escape was to marry early and marry rich, which she did. Alice and Asa's wedding was so socially important, the *Brooklyn Daily Eagle* had a full-page spread, and the bishop of Brooklyn officiated. The details of Asa's background were excluded, except to mention that he was a financier and entrepreneur who had control of most of the electric power produced in Quebec and southern Italy. It was only a slight exaggeration. Actually, by the time he married Alice, Asa had sold off his European and Canadian holdings and was concentrating on his newfound calling on Wall Street.

When she became Mrs. Simpson, Alice had obliterated the early abuse and painted a false happy childhood framed by merry family gatherings that contradicted and denied the constant bullying that had plagued her and lay in store for her daughter, Faith.

◆ ◆ ◆

When Faith was six, Alice got it into her head that the answer to her social discontent was to spend more time with her family in Brooklyn. Her sisters had strong social connections, and among her own, she wouldn't have to guard against snide assumptions that she was "too Catholic" and "too Brooklyn." She told Asa that she wanted Faith to get to know her Cavanaugh and Butler cousins and perhaps even attend Miss Fanny Darling's Dancing Academy. After all, that was where Alice had learned how to dance, hold a conversation with the opposite sex, and eat daintily in public. Faith was a reticent child, and Asa agreed that exposure to her lively Brooklyn cousins might bring his daughter out of her shell.

Faith had six cousins, all several years older than her. Of the six, just two were girls, and the boys were cruel and snobbish. Uncle Asa, they had decided, came from poor hardworking origins, whereas their own grandfather had been the Earl of Kilkenny, a centuries-old title. Faith became an easy target. The worst of them, Steven Butler, ran after Faith with a rifle and threatened to blow her head off. He made fun of her father, her clothes, the car that transported her. He especially made fun of Faith's looks and even created a poem about her eyes.

Eyes close together, just won't do.

Instead of a set, it's one split in two.

For a long time, Faith didn't understand what that couplet meant, but eventually, in the darkness of her flower-papered room at Seawatch, lying in her sleigh bed under an embroidered eiderdown quilt, she had to acknowledge the truth. She was only a little girl and she didn't understand everything that happened to her, but she knew this: she was ugly.

When she was alone with Steven, she was terrified that he would take a rifle from the gun cabinet and kill her. She had heard the grown-ups talking about how Harry Thaw had pulled the trigger and shot the architect Stanford White while he was having dinner on the roof deck of Madison Square Garden. *Click. Bang. You're dead.* Her aunt had read the headline. If it was that easy, Steven Butler could do it, too, especially since he was never reprimanded. The adults, including Faith's mother, thought he was precocious and a cutup.

Another cousin, William Cavanaugh, took Faith into one of Grampa Bradley's seven bathrooms and ordered her to unbutton his trousers. The buttonholes were small and her fingers inexperienced, so it took some doing. The fumbling caused William to get a mild erection. When she was finished, she pushed at the locked door.

"I want to find Mama."

"Why? We're not through here. I want you to touch it."

31

Faith was horrified. "I want Mama."

"Mama can't help you, little jerk," said William.

Faith began to cry loudly, and the housekeeper passing by pounded on the locked door. William let her out. Faith could hear his laughter all the way down the stairs. Whenever their paths crossed, he greeted her with the same invitation, "Want to help me undo my trousers again?"

Faith decided that to tell what had happened would seal her fate. How could she tell Mama that a boy in her own family—who was already registered at Portsmouth Priory and who might even become a priest—took a sausage thing out of his trousers and told her to kiss it? Or that Stevie Butler took one of Grampa's guns and threatened to blow her head off? If her father heard any of this, he would cease to love her. He might even send her away. The loneliness of painful secrets began with those hateful visits to Brooklyn.

As despicable to Faith as the taunts and bullying was the idea that she wasn't liked. Something about her made her cousins angry enough to punish her. She could barely admit this to herself, much less discuss it with anyone. Worse, she had not one idea of what she could do to change. If your own family couldn't stand you, what chance was there for the world to accept you?

From the first spring of her fourth year—and perhaps even before— from the subtle but unmistakable body language of Mama and Papa, Faith got the message that she was not the apple of anyone's eye. Her parents and the staff were in Billy's thrall. At first, she hid behind quietness, but as she grew, she began to act up. She whined and complained. On outings, she was too cold or too hot, or she felt sick to her stomach, or she had left her gloves or her doll in the park or at a playmate's house, and they had to be retrieved immediately. Her stomach hurt much of the time, and nothing anyone did for her seemed to help. Everyone had to tiptoe around her and hope she wasn't in a "mood."

The visits to Brooklyn nagged at her but weren't frequent enough to cause her constant worry. It was only in the summer of 1906, when the entire Bradley-Cavanaugh-Butler-McGuire clan built estates in Southampton, and Alice took Faith for long periods, that Faith's life became almost unbearable.

Faith didn't want to go to Southampton and began to cry and hold on to her bed. "I hate it there."

"But, precious." Alice was puzzled. "Why on earth not? Cousin Nancy is there."

"She has her own friends. I'm just a tagalong."

"This is a chance to become her friend, too. She's your cousin. A cousin is always your friend."

"That's not true. They are definitely not my friends."

"Now that is downright silly. Of course they are."

Faith stopped talking. Her mother spoke as if they were all in a storybook and everything had a happy ending.

At eight years old, Faith was expected to tag along with her cousins and be supervised by nannies. Southampton was worse than Brooklyn because the stays were long, and she was always separated from her mother by the unfamiliar sprawl of buildings and grounds. When she asked for her mother, she was told that Mama was shopping in town, or playing tennis at the club, or having lunch away from the compound. Her room in the children's cottage was not even in the same building as Alice, and she was ashamed to admit missing her mother because her girl cousins were thrilled to be rid of theirs.

On a hot August day when the temperature hit one hundred, and the only refuge was to seek the cool currents of the Atlantic, something happened that finally made Faith speak out about her troubles.

All morning, the children built sand castles and let the occasional wave cool their feet and bottoms. Steven Butler steadily built a replica of his grandfather's compound out of sand. When they came back from lunch, however, half of Steven's building had been walked on and destroyed. He was furious and vowed to kill whoever had done it. Faith's stomach churned. She knew she would be the prime suspect. After a while, to everyone's relief, the ocean waves were high and foamy, and Steven began bodysurfing. He rode a wave into shore and came up alongside Faith. "Come in," he said sweetly. "I'll teach you how to ride the waves."

"I don't know how to swim." Faith was momentarily thrilled to be included.

"You don't need to swim. Just hold my hand and ride the wave in to shore. I'll show you."

Faith followed Steven into the water until only her head was visible. A large wave was gaining on them, and she started to scramble back to shore, but Steven held her firm. "Keep your head down and go under it for now," he said calmly, but Faith was trying to break free and run. Steven pushed her down in front of the wave, and she felt herself tossed and thrust to the bottom by a powerful drag but still tethered to her cousin. She pumped with her legs wildly and was moving up when Steven Butler's hand clamped down over her head and bore down. Her mouth and nostrils filled with water. She couldn't breathe. She struggled to get out from his grip, but his hand stayed firm. At the moment when she felt she would explode, the wave receded and the water was shallow once more. She stood sputtering and choking. Her legs wouldn't hold her, and she had to crawl back to shore. She refused to speak to anyone for the rest of the visit, which mercifully ended two days later. Steven Butler had tried to drown her, and she was going to tell one person. Until then, she would not say one word to these hateful grown-ups or their hateful children.

◆　◆　◆

Faith entered the room, hesitated just inside the door, and waited to be noticed. "Hello," said Asa. "Look who's here."

"Hello," said Faith. She envied the way Billy could just go up to their father and grab his hand without thinking twice about it. Billy could interrupt Asa with only the hastiest "excuse me" and be welcomed with a smile. Not Faith. Her tongue became thick and her limbs heavy. Asa had never done anything unkind. He treated her with as much affection as could be expected with a child who became awkward and uncomfortable when she was hugged. He liked to communicate with little simple notes pointing out items in the newspaper that he thought she would understand and would amuse her. He was always reading her articles about President Roosevelt and the way he treated his own children. The president was learning jiujitsu from a Japanese gentleman who came to the White House. Asa admired Roosevelt, whose ebullient style had energized the country. No one had counted on McKinley being assassinated nine months after being sworn into office, and Asa relished telling his children of the moment when Vice President Roosevelt had learned he was president. "He had just climbed Mount Tahawus in the Adirondacks," Asa would begin. "The party had reached the summit, and Roosevelt saw a guide coming from the trail below."

"Wait." Billy had memorized every tidbit and made sure the story was complete. "They were resting before going down again."

"Correct. The guide had a telegram." Asa purposely left out details to give his son the pleasure of correcting him. "The nearest horse was ten miles away. The new president had to climb down to the clubhouse and get a horse and wagon to take him the thirty-five miles to the railway station."

"It was dark and foggy, and they had to change horses along the way, and the driver didn't even know he had a president," added Billy.

"Exactly. It was dawn when Roosevelt reached the station and caught the train to Buffalo."

Now, alone in his study, Asa smiled at his daughter, who still hadn't entered. "Come in. How long have you been there? I should think you'd be out of doors having a riding lesson along with Billy." Polo matches were the new favored sport, and Asa had invested in a stable of ponies, hoping to have Billy join in.

"I stayed in so I could talk to you."

"Really? This sounds important. What can I do for you?" Asa was pretending to be businesslike to put Faith at ease, but it had the opposite effect and made her feel that she had to be both quick and very interesting.

"I don't want to visit my cousins in Southampton anymore. I don't want to go to Brooklyn, either. I've told Mama, but she says there's no reason for me to feel that way. She thinks my cousins are good for me."

"I see. And why don't you want to go?"

"The boys are very mean."

"How so?"

"They make fun of me." She wanted to tell him they made fun of her looks, but suppose he agreed with them?

"How do they make fun of you?"

"They think the Daimler is vulgar. They say our house is decorated by the pound because we have no taste, and they say Mama is barely able to read. None of us speaks French or Italian. All we have is money."

"Is that so?" Asa smiled, but then put on a serious face. "It never does good to run away. My advice is to prove them wrong. We could have a French tutor. After all, Billy should speak another language, and you could learn, too. I don't know if your mother would join you. As for the Daimler, I had already decided to get a Packard. They're going to send two or three models, and Trevor and I will choose the fastest one. You can tell your cousins to 'eat my dust' as you whiz past them."

She wasn't getting through. He was agreeing with the boys. She would have to tell him the worst thing, and then he'd see who was right. "They did something worse. Steven Butler tried to drown me."

Asa stood up and brought Faith all the way into the room and took her to a small settee. "When did Steven try to drown you?"

"In Southampton. He said he'd teach me to ride the waves, but then he held my head underwater and wouldn't let me up. It was awful." She waited for her father to be outraged and horrified, but he listened calmly. Her heart fluttered. Her cheeks felt very hot. She was overcome with disappointment and began to cry. "I couldn't breathe. The wave had already pushed me under, and I had swallowed water, but then he pushed me down again." The tension of telling the story to deaf ears was too much. Faith became hysterical.

Asa let her have her catharsis without interfering. When her tears abated, he dabbed at her eyes and blew her nose.

"Faith, I can see you are very upset. And, I'm doubly sure that you felt as if Steven was trying to drown you. Very possibly you felt the same panic and fright as if you were really drowning, but one thing I can tell you for certain, Steven Butler did not try to drown you." Asa rose, went to his desk, and picked up his briefcase. "Along with the French, it's important to begin swimming instruction. When you become an expert swimmer and speak French like a *mademoiselle*, you can counter any teasing with real ammunition. That's the way to do it, Faith. Become better than your tormentors, and they will wither away." He walked to the door. "I've got to be off."

Faith remained on the settee, stunned and furious. Not to be believed was the worst humiliation of all. She had gathered her courage to expose all the ghastly behavior, and her father hadn't believed her. Her mother was weak and fearful, but Faith had been certain her father would take her side and avenge her. He had done neither. There was no one to turn to.

A few days later, a young graduate student from Columbia University began coming to Seawatch each week to drill Faith, Billy, and Trask in the French language. A swimming coach from the nearby Piping Rock Club appeared as well.

Chapter Five

After her mother had been taken to the hospital, Hope was alone in the ransacked room. Soon after, a social worker dressed in black came from the Children's Aid Society and told her to pack her things. Hope took only her comic books and a capelet her mother had bought for her the previous week. She liked it so much, she wore it over everything, even in hot weather. Hope and the social worker walked the twenty blocks to an apartment in a large building. A woman opened the door.

"This is where you'll stay until your mama's better," said the social worker. "Mind your manners and make yourself useful."

A boy came rushing through the room and tried to grab Hope's comic books. She held tight, and he began to scream loudly.

"Mine, you stinking orphan," said the boy, trying to punch her while the woman held him back.

"Mine," said Hope, and held them closer.

The woman took her to a room with a bed. "Take off all of your clothes," she said. "I've got to boil them. You've probably got sickness or lice."

Hope didn't take off her clothes. When she was alone, she gathered her things and slipped out of the apartment. She went back the way she had come to her old neighborhood. She was afraid of the boy. She knew the moment she was asleep he would take her books and maybe do something worse.

◆　◆　◆

The landlady at the rooming house saw her and asked who was going to pay her for the room. Hope invoked the name of Agatha's one relative, her old aunt from Willet Street. She didn't even know her name and called her Aunt Willet.

"So when's she going to come?"

"She's coming tomorrow. She'll pay you."

In 1906, despite the best efforts of the Children's Aid Society and the various settlement houses and missions, there were thousands of homeless children in Manhattan. Childhood had only recently been recognized as a particular state, and an eight-year-old in the streets alone was not an unusual sight, nor were sweatshops filled with working children.

Hope's parents were obsessed with making money, so she wanted to make money, too. Sen had laughed at the idea, but Agatha took her seriously. Sometimes, when she had waited with Agatha at the cart, the newsboy would ask her to watch his stack and gave her a few pennies. Her mother had told her stories of children who didn't have a place to go at night and had to live in the streets.

"See that boy?" she would say. "He catches rats for eight cents apiece for the animal fights. That job is only for boys." There was always a market for rats for the betting parlors. A good rat dog could kill a hundred rats in half an hour.

Hope decided she would find a way to make money and surprise her mother. She was not afraid of the streets. She knew every loose brick, every stain. She was used to being out of doors. She took off down Broadway, and when she passed Trinity Church, she ducked in to get warm. There were two Trinity Churches. One uptown, for the rich, and this one. Her father sometimes parked her at Trinity as a safe place to wait when he had a short errand to run. She was used to sitting in the pews and reading her rags-to-riches Bowery Billy stories, thinking she might do all the things that Billy did. She went into the church through the north entrance, stopping briefly to stare at the entombed effigy of Bishop Onderdonk, which made her shudder. Then she went to sit in the front pew. Sun was coming in through the stained-glass rose window over the altar, replaying the colors on the floor.

A large stand of votive candles sat directly in front of her pew. She watched people light candles and stuff money into the collection box, which looked to be full. The last coin put in had the tip peeking out. Hope looked at the stained window, at the image of God, and back at the coin. She decided it was meant for her. With her small fingers, she plucked out a fifty-cent piece and returned to the pew to wait for more. She made two dollars in barely three hours just sitting quietly, waiting for customers to light the candles and put their coins in the overstuffed box. She heard people begging God under their breath for love, to cure an illness, for money . . . and then lighting row after row of candles.

When the traffic died down, Hope walked out in search of food. She could always count on one of the food peddlers to give her the leftover broken pieces of pastries or sandwiches. As she neared the Astor, she saw another girl about her size, who wasn't wearing shoes. Hope watched her hopping around, and then got a glimpse of her filthy soles.

"Where's your shoes?"

"Ain't got none," said the girl.

"You've got to be lying," said Hope.

"They're buried till tonight," confessed the girl.

"Why don't you put them on?"

"Do better without," said the girl.

"Do what better?" asked Hope.

"Beg alms, you dummy. You think I'm going barefoot for my health?"

"You ask for money? How much do you make?"

"Depends on if I work for myself or for the woman that hires me to play her sick child. By myself, I can make two bucks if I stay out all day and catch the dinner crowd at the hotels. What about you?"

Hope was happy to have her own story. "Best money I ever made was from the candle box at the church."

"Holy Mother of God," said the girl. "You stole from the church?"

"God showed me how."

"God didn't show you how. More like the devil," said the girl, but Hope could see she was impressed.

"Yes, he did. God's proud of me."

"You're a real loony. And don't be hanging around me and stealing my customers."

Hope had already made up her mind to stick to the girl. She was relieved to find someone in the same situation. "What's your name? I'm Hope."

"Well, I *hope* you get lost," said the girl and laughed wildly. "Get it?" Hope waited for an answer. "The name's Grace. I hate it. I call myself Gloria."

For the rest of the day, Hope watched while Gloria worked the crowd coming out of the Astor.

There was a doorman there, Rory, over six feet, who chased her with a sweep of his hand. "You know you're not supposed to be here. Go home."

"Ain't got none," Gloria would answer.

"Go to the Mission House."

"Won't take me."

"Then go to the police."

"Ain't done nothing."

Hope was mesmerized by Gloria, whose courage appeared limitless. For the next few days, she followed slavishly, and Gloria tolerated her. At night, Rory looked the other way while they crept into the luggage room for the night. Hope preferred to stay with Gloria rather than go back to her empty room and the angry landlady.

Each morning, they walked to Rector and Moyers, bought a scone and an ice, and sat on one of the benches in a spit of grass to eat. Afterward they went to see what they could get from the votive candle donations. The metal box had a generous slot, and Gloria was able to put sticky caramel to one of the tapers and coax coins to the surface. It was a laborious task, and the chances of getting caught were high. They would quit after a few nickels and move on.

At midday, they hung around the window at the Crook, Fox & Nash restaurant, watching the steaming dishes brought to the tables. Gloria said you had to catch the diners coming out when they were tipsy and full if you wanted to get money. Hope remembered the hot lunches when her mother left her at the Mission House and urged Gloria to go there, but she could not be tempted. "They'll put me with a family that will make me their little slave. No, thank you. I don't want to be nobody's little slave in trade for a lousy lunch."

One day, Gloria said she had to go see someone by herself. Hope hung around the hotel waiting for her. She asked Rory about her. "Sometimes she doesn't come around for a few weeks, and then she shows up again," he said.

It took Hope a long time to figure out that Gloria was not coming back anytime soon. She kept going to their old haunts, looking around, and asking peddlers if they'd seen her. After a couple of days, she became angry with Gloria for not saying good-bye. She could not accept that the girl had vanished without telling her. It made her so furious, tears spilled out against her will. "I'm going to kill that girl. I will hit her in the head with a stick and knock her against the sidewalk. I'm going to kill that crazy girl," she muttered over and over as she walked the streets looking for her friend.

With Gloria gone, Hope had the first inklings of fear that she would be alone forever. Her mother must have died at the hospital.

She could not figure out where to go. She was dirty. Debris was embedded in the tangles of her hair. Dirt was embedded in her hands and feet. Her legs had scrapes, and her clothes were torn. She was always hungry and thirsty. She sat on her old stoop and began to sob, and she couldn't stop. She didn't want to stop. She couldn't articulate it, but sobbing kept her life in motion. If she stopped, she had to face a reality that was too frightening. There was no one who knew her. No one to even call her name. The loneliness was overwhelming. She felt the cold creeping up her legs and thighs. She was cold and hungry, but more than anything, she was filled with a horrendous sadness that threatened to drown her.

She raised her head and looked anxiously down the street. She was hoping to see Gloria, but she saw something else. A female figure limped toward her. The woman was so unsteady she looked as if she might topple over any second. Her hair was a swirl of tangles held down by a gauze bandage that covered one eye and wound around her head, barely leaving the other eye room to open. Hope stared at the woman for several minutes, hardly believing that the limping battered creature coming toward her resembled her mother. Agatha reached out her arm and Hope walked to meet it.

She could hardly breathe. Her mama, whom she was sure she would never see again, was right here, coming toward her. She knew that skirt. She had stared at the fabric many hours. They walked toward each other with the crushing relief of those who have barely escaped death. Agatha folded her daughter into her arms and held her with as much strength as her battered limbs would allow. They stood there, blocking the street, unwilling to move away from each other even for a second, not yet daring to hope that the moment was real. The full weight of weeks of fear and anxiety, sadness and dread exploded within Hope. She choked on her sobs and could not stop them.

◆ ◆ ◆

That winter was a bad one, but they were able to create some comfort in their room. The streets were paved with wooden blocks, and when they ripped them up to replace them with asphalt, Hope and Agatha went out with sacks so they could have firewood to keep the stove going. Agatha asked the landlady to let her reclaim her old room, promising to pay as soon as she got some work. She was a sober and clean tenant, and the landlady agreed.

Kamen, who had since recouped all of his lost money and a few thousand on top, felt some remorse and gave them enough for two months' rent and a few pieces of furniture from his shop.

The priest from the Mission House gave them a few dollars for food and urged them to come for the free lunch, but Agatha was a snob about food, and she didn't like the offerings. Everything was overcooked and soft.

There was a lot going on in the streets. Radical political parties, intent on bringing what they perceived as emancipation to the working class, made use of "street corner meetings." Political speeches pushing one agenda or another were a form of entertainment. Union men would recruit on the periphery.

Agatha would sometimes join the crowd and listen for a while, trying to understand how the government could actually make a difference in her life. One afternoon, she recognized a well-dressed man from the old days with the food cart. He had been a frequent customer, although he could have afforded a restaurant. He recognized her and after inspecting her bruised face, he asked why she had abandoned her cart. When she related her story, he said something remarkable. "I'm looking for a business to invest in, and I'd like to set up a little restaurant. I was in Chicago, and I saw a place where the food was laid out in a line and people selected what they wanted and carried it to a table. It's called a cafeteria. Would that interest you? You could be the cook and general manager, and I'll give you part of the profit."

It took her a few minutes to understand what he was saying, but she agreed to go to his office the next day. He took out his wallet and told her to buy a new outfit for her new position and then smiled at Hope. "And you should have a new outfit, too."

When the idea fully played out in her mind that night, Agatha felt a resurgence of her old energy. For all intents, she was a penniless twenty-seven-year-old widow with a half-caste child. Her broken leg was continuing to heal, and she limped. The skin around her eye and jawline was still bruised and discolored, yet in the space of a few hours she was renewed with optimism and ambition. This is what she had prayed for all along, and now it would be hers.

Chapter Six

Until Faith was old enough to be tutored, she didn't see much of her brother Billy. But as she grew, he let her know in little ways that they were a unit separate from their parents. Often, at the dinner table, when his mother related some astonishing social tidbit ("They had mounds of sand right on the dinner table, and we were encouraged to dig through like scavengers—Imogene found an emerald"), Billy would roll his eyes so that only Faith caught it. She would nod and smile, but they seldom shared private grievances until Faith was ten.

It was during the last few days of the year that Faith discovered she could count on her brother to be a sympathetic confidant. The two were sifting through the pile of Christmas presents still under the tree. Faith picked out a big doll with a delicate china face and movable arms and legs. "Look at this. I've never played with dolls in my life, and Mama gave me another doll."

"This one is very lifelike. Look, her eyes open and close." Billy took the doll, cradled it in his arms, and began to sing a lullaby.

Faith laughed. "Maybe you can hire out as a nanny if Papa loses all our money."

"Not a bad idea." Billy continued to rock the doll in his arms, singing softly.

This show of gentleness and caring prompted Faith to confess to Billy what had been going on with her Brooklyn cousins. Billy not only believed her but had a few stories of his own.

"Steven almost wrung the cat's neck when it jumped on him. The cat scratched him hard, and he finally let go, but he was ready to kill it. He's very strong."

"Mama'd never side against her sisters. She'd let Steven wring our necks first."

Billy liked having his sister talk candidly. "Tell me if that boy touches you. I'll make Papa believe you."

It was not by accident or for humor that Billy had picked up Faith's doll with such tenderness. He wasn't a boy who liked roughhousing. Asa had asked Tommy Rowland, the groundskeeper's son, to include Billy in boyish pastimes like climbing trees and playing ice hockey on Beaver Dam. Billy went along, but his heart wasn't in it. He didn't know why he resisted acting "like a man," but he kept it to himself and did his best. While Faith wanted more than anything to gain her father's attention, he felt the opposite. He often wished his father didn't put so much emphasis on being tough and militaristic. Billy hated being part of the Knickerbocker Greys. He hated the guns and swords and, particularly, the awful uniform.

Whenever Faith complained about learning to embroider, he would complain about the Greys. "At least you don't have to wear that horrid stiff uniform and carry a bayonet as if you were going to stab the enemy. I don't even know who the enemy is. Once, I had to make-believe stab Bobby Crowfoot. I barely touched him, but he started howling like a hyena."

The Greys met for weekly practice in the ancient Seventh Regiment Armory of the New York National Guard. Being accepted to the Greys was as difficult as gaining entry into an exclusive country club, and both his mother and his father had been thrilled to see Billy get in. Mr. Lucker liked to comment on his boys' physiques as he measured chests and waists for new uniforms. "Billy, I commend you. Most boys have gotten a little mushy about the waist, but you're as lithe as a . . ." He was about to say, "lithe as a dancer," but decided it was inappropriate. "Lithe as a young boxer," he said instead.

Asa had walked in as his son was being dismissed. "Well, Billy, this year, you have a chance to carry the flag, right?" Asa had looked so pleased.

Billy put down Faith's doll and hunched his shoulders. "You know what I say when Papa says things I don't agree with? I say, 'Whatever you say, Papa.'"

Faith was relieved to hear that he, too, had grievances and was willing to be honest about them.

"At least Papa expects you to do a good job," said Faith. "When I do well in something, he's almost disappointed. He wants me to be clumsy, so he can show me how accepting he is of clumsy little Faith. Sometimes I want to fail miserably to make him happy. I'm really good in mathematics and French, but I never tell him. It would be too confusing."

"When I leave for Yale, he'll be all over you, and then let's see how you like it."

"I would like it," said Faith.

"If I lived far, far away, without Papa, I would be a completely different person."

"What kind of a person?"

"Free. Never afraid. Just getting up every day and being whatever I turned out to be."

"But that's exactly how you already are."

"No. Every day, I wake up with the feeling that I can't let Papa down."

"That's awful."

Although Billy was candid with Faith about almost everything, there was one area of his life that he couldn't confide. How could he tell his sister that he might have a crush on one of the stable groomers? He wasn't even sure what he would do about it if nothing stood in the way. What tormented Billy was not the idea that he might be one of those men who preferred men over women. What tormented him most was disappointing his father. Within the walls of Seawatch, he had to be William Horatio Simpson, heir and only son of George Asa Simpson, one of the wealthiest men in the United States of America. Eventually he would be off to Yale and perhaps freedom.

Chapter Seven

When Peter Laughlin offered Agatha the opportunity to make food again and satisfy hungry diners, it was the miracle she needed to believe that life still had some good for her. The nightmares of being grabbed and pummeled subsided. She didn't jump at every loud noise or walk rapidly when she saw a street boy. As she watched the progress on the restaurant, the old energy and enthusiasm returned.

The space Laughlin rented was two blocks from her rooming house, in a sliver of a building just fourteen feet wide. They used six feet for a steam table and an aisle, and squeezed three long refectory tables against the opposite wall, leaving barely four feet for diners to pass with their trays.

The novel idea of a cafeteria was catching on. It was an upgrade on the old "grab joints," where diners hugged several dishes to their chest while hunting for a seat. Laughlin named the restaurant Your Mother's Table, capitalizing on the popularity of self-serve and the novelty of a woman chef.

Agatha took to her job with wholehearted dedication. She wanted first and foremost to make the best food possible, even though the idea was to create a simple, inexpensive dining alternative. The most important cooking lesson she had learned from Sen was to begin with the best ingredients. Two mornings a week, she and Hope walked with a cart to

Gansevoort and West Washington streets, where Manhattan's open-air markets had operated for more than a hundred years. The freshest goods were loaded off the docks at the Hudson River and trundled over the cobblestoned streets to all the wholesalers with stands to display their specialties. Farmers from New Jersey and Long Island would bring their fresh produce. There was an underground refrigeration system to keep the meat and poultry fresh. The purveyors for the restaurants and the pushcart vendors would be there at dawn, sticking their arms into sacks and barrels to get the best produce.

Agatha's efforts were rewarded because people loved eating her food. Her cooking style and welcoming personality made hungry people happy and trusting. Many of her old customers discovered and patronized the cramped space. She placed a chalkboard outside, itemizing the day's three main entrées to lessen the anxiety many felt over having to make a fast decision while on the steam-table line. There were always two meats and a fish. They served chicken and dumplings, roast pork with dried-currant dressing, ham and roasted pineapple with potatoes au gratin. If the meal was a ragout, it contained potatoes and carrots and mushrooms, and only needed a crusty baguette. For the fish, she would add spiced Chinese rice and tangy coleslaw. Besides the three main dishes, she offered some of her old specialties: apple-spice muffins; a savory lamb stew made with charred potatoes, vegetables, and a hint of fermented soy sauce from the Chinese grocer; and dumplings filled with pork or fish paste with a brown dipping sauce. Often diners took the entrée but also an order of dumplings. Soups, a fruit compote, salads, pies, and cakes completed the menu. The bread station came after the pies and cakes and included corn bread, baking powder biscuits, and dinner rolls. At a station beyond the line were carafes of coffee and tea.

The trick was to make each dish appear neat and the same size as others of its kind. Pie slices had to be identical, and fruit salad had to contain the same proportion of the different fruits. Diners had to be satisfied that their portion was not less than that of the person in front of them. Agatha also kept a good rotation of dishes, so that patrons could eat there every day without having to choose the same entrée twice. The big challenge was to make diners vacate their tables immediately upon finishing their meal, so Agatha hired a young woman who hovered nearby, ready to scoop up a tray with empty plates. They had to make room for new diners and keep the line moving.

Laughlin hired a baker, who made fresh pies and bread during the night, and a janitor, who cleaned the space for the next day. Everything else was Agatha's doing. She was there at six to begin her preparations. She made everything fresh each day and never deviated to save money. Leftovers, which were few, were sent to the Mission House at the end of the day. Laughlin knew Agatha's cooking and pleasant manner were the draw, and he was smart enough to let her run the kitchen in her own way.

From the opening day, Your Mother's Table had a line that extended to the end of the block. The cafeteria opened for business at 10:45 a.m., and there were always at least ten people waiting to enter. These early birds usually had a piece of pie or cake and tea. The deluge of luncheon diners began at noon, and there was a steady stream that kept every table filled until they closed at three. They did their best to have five seatings. The people who came in alone took half an hour from entry to exit. If two or more came together, they tended to linger. The average full meal cost about one dollar and fifteen cents. They sold 160 to 175 meals a day. Agatha had a salary of eighteen dollars a day, plus 5 percent of the day's net receipts, which, after expenses of rent, salaries, and provisions, netted her another six dollars. They closed on Saturday and Sunday. It was a demanding and exhausting job, and she spent most of Saturday experimenting with new dishes. What Agatha loved more than anything was the interaction with her customers. She loved catering to their whims, and they loved her back for treating them with special care. She kept certain plates with less gravy or more spices or without nuts or with nuts for regulars, and when they showed up, to their great delight, she brought out the customized dish.

Peter Laughlin was thrilled with the response to the cafeteria idea and thrilled with the way Agatha ran the place. Sometimes they would get written up in the newspaper, and an avalanche of new diners would fill the lunch tables and create a longer line in the street. Most days, they sold everything they had cooked, and often items ran out.

"We have to look for a larger space," Peter Laughlin would say. "We're losing money with this operation. We turn away half again as many as we feed."

"If we make it bigger, I can't run it by myself. If I lose control, the food is not as good. I can't take special care of the customers. Can't we leave it like this?"

Agatha was exhausted but happy. Hope was happy, too. Her life had settled into a pleasant routine, and she thrived in the safety of enough food, enough money, and enough warmth. Most days, Hope attended the Mission schools and learned quickly when she wasn't restless. The classroom was tame compared to the hubbub of street life or the cafeteria, but Agatha insisted that she go to classes. On the way home, Hope looked closely at the beggar girls, wishing she might catch sight of Gloria and tell her all that had happened. During any free time, she helped her mother in small ways at the restaurant, but also listened to the lively conversation of the young businesswomen who came daily. They wore shirtwaists and slim skirts and cloche hats, the uniform of the newly emancipated workingwoman. Their chatter was filled with the slang of the day. They described objects as being *darling*, and they said this or that occurrence had made them think they *would die*, or something they had seen was *hilarious*. Hope had never seen people laugh so readily and use conversation as entertainment. What impressed her most and sank deep into her psyche was the freedom the women had to blurt out whatever was in their head in a bold way. She decided that was the way she was going to converse for the rest of her life. She would say what she was thinking and say it with all the daring phrases at her command. *I thought I would die. She wore the most darling little hat. I adore this or that. This is the most hilarious thing I have ever seen. I'm going stir-crazy. Hey, kiddo, eat your heart out. You are getting on my nerves.*

Hope and Agatha still lived in one room, where Agatha draped paisley fabric over the walls and what she called *divans*, even though they were just dressed-up mattresses. The whole place looked like a paisley palace. Agatha said their room was right out of Cathay. She was besotted with design and color. There wasn't one inch of that room that was plain, but it worked in its favor.

During the second year of operating the cafeteria, Agatha began to get letters from Sen. He had abandoned them in the most heartless way, yet the letters were contrite and uplifting. Agatha asked Hope if she wanted to write back to her father, but Hope said no. The memory of seeing her mother pummeled by the goons was still vivid. Agatha had closed off her mind to Sen, but he often expressed sorrow and regret for leaving her. She softened and began to hang Sen's letters over the swaths of paisley. He was still her husband. And the calligraphy was beautiful. Hope loved that room. She loved being overwhelmed by design. Her mother was bold, not ordinary, and that's all that mattered to her. She knew, without a doubt, that she would be extraordinary, too.

In the third year of the cafeteria's operation, the downtown political machine began to interfere in many of the small businesses in the area. The Tammany Machine had originally served immigrants by helping them become citizens and helping them get to know the ways of the country. In turn, the newcomers became loyal voters.

When Laughlin was operating the cafeteria, Tammany had gone through several corruption/reform cycles. In the first decade of the century, it was back in full control and groups who were against the corrupt tactics went through the streets chanting, "Well, well, well, reform has gone to hell." The police also liked to hit up restaurants and bars, where they received free meals and demanded protection money. They hit

Laughlin in early spring of 1910, asking for small sums, twenty dollars a week, but quickly accelerating to one hundred dollars a week. They said it was for increased protection from the known downtown gangs. Within weeks, the Democratic ward captain came in and asked for a "get out the vote" contribution of several hundred dollars, which also became a monthly occurrence.

Laughlin told Agatha they had to economize on the food and cut down on the more expensive dishes, but he knew it was just a matter of time before the money demands would exceed his ability to pay. It was a miracle they had been left alone for so long. The cafeteria limped along for a couple of months, but by September, there was no more money and they had to close.

The closing hit Agatha harder than all of her other setbacks. She didn't think she could recover yet again.

Chapter Eight

Asa Simpson was a man who had never told a joke. He'd laugh at the slapstick of Oliver Hardy, but it was a laugh of short duration. It was as if he only had so much time, and there were other things that needed his attention. Unlike most of the other gold coast barons, he related to the lives of the people he employed. He understood their struggles because they had been his struggles, too.

He felt deep affection for a few—the groundskeeper, Chester Rowland, and his wife, Emma; and the dairyman, Joe Stokes, and his wife.

Chester Rowland's cottage sat on the grounds of Seawatch, and Asa dropped in some nights to play pinochle with Chester and his brothers. He loved Emma Rowland's apple crumble and her homemade wine. They got used to him visiting, and after a while it didn't seem like an odd thing. For Asa, there was a deep comfort to be had in that kitchen, and he didn't question it beyond that.

Emma wasn't shy about telling Asa to go home when they played cards late into the night. If the men were too tipsy to get behind the wheel, she'd send her son, fourteen-year-old Tommy, to drive Asa the mile to the mansion.

Even though Asa regularly visited the Rowlands and even kissed Emma on the cheek when he left after drinking her wine and eating her apple crumble, the Rowlands didn't receive any special favors, nor did they expect them. Generally, the staff loved working at Seawatch, and the children who grew up there had the run of the estate. Tommy, Emily—who was Joe Stokes's daughter—and Emily's little brother, Eddie, would swing on the ornate entrance gates every time they passed. In summer, they swam at the beach and went home up the back roads so they could pet the polo ponies. Sometimes they would hitch a ride with the man who delivered milk to the village.

The dayworkers all brought their lunch in a pail, and if it was cold outside, they ate around the stove in the cow barn. Most of the help had arrived at Seawatch with nothing. During the mansion-building boom, the Long Island Railroad offered one-time reduced transportation and free baggage hauling to any newly arrived immigrants who would settle out on the island. The ones who took advantage soon found work building the estates and stayed on as servants.

If they didn't have relatives already in service, new arrivals would go straight to the Hutchinson Employment Agency to be placed in one of the many mansions that sprang up on the North Coast in the first quarter of the new century. If you didn't speak English, the Muttonville Neighborhood House held classes to teach you how.

Sports were a big source of diversion. Occasionally one of the young men would fill out a polo team, but mostly they played soccer. Harry Guggenheim had built a soccer field in his cow pasture, and teams from surrounding estates played each other on Sundays while Guggenheim and, sometimes, his mother, watched.

Asa had asked Chester and Joe to let Tommy and Emily attend the tutored class with Faith and Billy. Yet the privilege didn't give Tommy a sense of entitlement. What he wanted more than anything else was to live in the outside world, away from the estate. When he and Faith talked of their futures, he said he wanted a job in an office, possibly as an accountant. He also wanted an automobile and a house of his own.

Faith was surprised. She had never thought of Tommy leaving Seawatch. "What kind of a house?"

"One of those little tract houses in Hewlett. By the railroad."

"That's a neat dream," said Faith, "but there's only one problem. The guy behind those houses showed Papa all the booklets with dreamy pictures. The whole idea is to make you a regular commuter and make the railroad owners happy."

"So what?" said Tommy. "It can still be a good idea."

"I guess."

He couldn't help but feel close to Faith; they'd grown up together. He'd given her rides on his bicycle to the beach and taught her to ice skate on Beaver Dam. But there were limits, and it fell to him to know where they were so he wouldn't cross them. If he told her he wanted to get away from the estate and have a different life, it would sound ungrateful. It annoyed him that it was always up to him to decide how far he could go, whereas she could say and do anything.

It would have mollified Tommy to know that Faith would receive a jolt that would alter her life and blur all status lines in the most invasive way.

Chapter Nine

Agatha had always felt best out of doors, moving with purpose, chattering to herself. After the cafeteria closed, she spent many days inside, in total silence, sitting by the one window, sipping tea often laced with whiskey. When the liquor made her groggy, she would go to her bed and remain there until the next day. Every day, Hope, now a teenager, would bring the newspaper home and read from the jobs advertised. Most of them were for hard labor that was only suitable for men. One job appeared every day, and Hope read it aloud every day. It was for the Triangle Shirtwaist Factory. Each time she heard it, Agatha would say, "I don't know how to run a sewing machine."

Hope would answer, "It says 'No experience required. We will train.' It's where they make those shirtwaists that the office girls wear."

Finally Agatha went to the factory to investigate. She was certain her poor eyesight and lack of sewing experience would shut her out, but that wasn't the case. They took her. It was an awful job for a person like Agatha. The shirtwaist—a fitted bodice garment worn with a tailored skirt—symbolized the American female's newfound freedom. Agatha wore the shirtwaists herself, but there was no freedom in the sweatshop. She sat at a machine in a cramped row with other girls for hours at a time. Her job was setting the sleeves for the garments, and when they were set wrong—as they often were—the foreman would berate her.

The only goodness was the chatter she heard from the more than one hundred girls around her. She had never had girlfriends, and it was entertaining to hear all kinds of love stories and hardship stories about pregnancies and weddings. It was a distraction and made the day go faster, but it was not enough to keep her at the job. She decided to work through Christmas and leave at the beginning of the year. January and February passed, and still she lingered. She marked a day on the March calendar when she would leave. It was March 30.

The factory was in the Asch Building on the corner of Greene Street and Washington Place. It was a true overpopulated sweatshop with too many people working in too little space. Two stairways led down to the street, but one remained locked from the outside to discourage pilfering. Of the four elevators, only one worked. The corruption pervasive in the garment industry and city government impacted the factory as well. The International Ladies Garment Workers Union had led a strike over the low pay and poor working conditions. But the factory owners had politicians in their pockets and had bribed police officers to arrest the women on strike. The effort dissolved. Agatha was disgusted with the corruption that had twice impacted her life, but when she tried to talk about it, her coworkers were frightened to discuss it. She was determined that she would become a soapbox crusader and talk about it, even if she lost her job and they put her in jail.

March 25 began like any other day. It was Saturday afternoon, and the machines were humming. The fire started when a rag bin caught a flame, and the manager couldn't put it out. The workers panicked. Some climbed on the machines. Others began the descent to the lobby by the stairs, only to find the door locked from the outside. The one working elevator could hold only twelve people, even though twice that number pushed in. The operator was able to make four trips before it broke down. Many grabbed on to the cables of the elevator and tried to ride them down, and many died in the attempt.

On the last trip, several girls grabbed the cables and thrust themselves out, landing on top of the elevator and crushing others. Some of the girls left waiting plunged down the shaft to their death. Those workers on floors above the fire escaped to the roof and then to adjoining buildings. As firefighters arrived, they saw many girls who had not made it to the stairwells or the elevator trapped and ready to jump from the windows. Three jumped together and tore the net that was meant to catch them. The rest simply jumped to the open air. In less than thirty minutes, it was over. One hundred forty-six men and women died, the youngest only fourteen years old.

Agatha Murphy, one month shy of her thirty-second birthday, was one of the jumpers. As she stood on the ledge, her last thought was how sweet the spring air felt in her lungs. She was certain she would be all right. She called out her daughter's name and died on impact. Pulp. That is how they described the remains. William Gunn Shepherd, a reporter at the tragedy, wrote, "I learned a new sound that day, a sound more horrible than description can picture—the thud of a speeding living body on a stone sidewalk."

The ambulances and police cars kept up a steady din throughout the afternoon. Word spread terror throughout the East Side. People ran to the factory to see the carnage. Hope heard the commotion and went outside. The landlady was out on the sidewalk and stopped her.

"Something terrible," she began. "A fire at the factory." She tried to hold on to Hope, but she was already running down the street, her mind frozen, her lungs constricting. A protective ring of police and ambulance workers tried to keep onlookers away, but she broke through.

Relatives of other victims thronged around the building. The bodies lying on the sidewalk were quickly removed to obliterate the ghoulish scene, but the stains and odd bits of personal belongings remained. When Hope saw her mother's purse sitting in a puddle of putrid water, realization took hold, and her body convulsed. She walked in slow motion to retrieve it. A few inches were still dry, and she could smell her mother's powder on it. She took the purse, pressed it to her lips, and lay on top of it on the sidewalk where she imagined her mother had landed. She began to tremble uncontrollably. Her face embedded in the filthy purse with Agatha's scent still lingering, the full horror of her mother's death, driven by flames into space, threw her into overwhelming fear. She began to scream and sob and call for her mother as if her will could summon her back. People walked past her and tried to comfort her, but she shook them off. There was no consoling. Accepting their touch, their sympathy, would mean that all was lost. That it was true. That violence and death were her mother's reward. That she was lost. Hope would scream out her mother's name until Agatha appeared. There was nothing else she could accept. A reporter snapped her picture, and it was on the front page of the morning paper. Hope Lee's beautiful face distorted in agony became the face of tragedy, the face of poor working conditions, the face of corrupt politicians, the face of poverty and despair. The ills of society voiced by the soapbox politicians around Union Square were made tangible. Eventually two women from the Children's Aid Society took her to a shelter, and a doctor gave her a sedative. Many people wanted to help the orphaned girl. It was finally decided that a group of girls affected by the fire should be taken out to the country to grieve in the fresh air and healthy atmosphere of the farmland.

Chapter Ten

Hope's face didn't fade from public memory. Within a few days of her mother's death, afraid of sleep, afraid of the images behind closed eyes, she traveled to Muttonville with three other girls and a chaperone. Two of the girls went to a farming family in Glen Cove. The other girl went to a schoolteacher in Roslyn. Hope was fortunate to land in the home of Emma Rowland and her husband, Chester. Emma knew how to treat a girl like Hope. She got Hope through all the long, agonizing days of acceptance.

"You've had some awful events, good Lord, but you can't give up, you hear," Emma told her. "Keep going. Put one foot in front of the other, and go where you need to go. I don't mind keeping you with me. I always wanted a girl. You don't have to worry about anything right now."

She could see Hope was still too raw to react. You couldn't hug her or touch her much. You couldn't hold her while she cried out her pain. Twice she tried to run away. Emma would find her huddled on a bench at the railway station late at night, waiting for the six o'clock train the next morning.

"I'm going to look for my mother," Hope would say. "Maybe there was some mistake and she's worried about me."

"Shhhh. Shhh. Shhhh." Emma would just use soothing nonsense sounds, wrap a shawl around Hope, and herd her back.

Emma sometimes tried to run her hand across the girl's brow and cheeks or to hold her hand. Hope would stiffen. But on the pretext of brushing Hope's hair, Emma could caress her face, touch those unbending shoulders, and give the poor creature some solace. Hope let her do that much in little increments.

Several months passed, and although she was not required to keep Hope longer, Emma couldn't send her back to New York. There was little for Hope to do during the day, other than help with the house chores. It wasn't enough for a young girl, and schooling her at home was inadequate. Hope should be tutored along with Tommy and the Simpson children. Maybe she could move to the mansion and be a companion to Faith. Emma brought up the Simpsons casually. "There's a girl there who could use a friend like you. And you could learn properly without having to go to a big new school. They bring in a tutor. Tommy goes."

"I already know how to read and write," said Hope. She had begun to feel some ease with Emma and had opened up about her former life, especially her mother's restaurant. Sometimes she'd talk without stopping while Emma listened. Hope was proud of her mother's accomplishments. With all that had worked against her, Agatha had made a big success of that cafeteria. "My mother was a good cook. Her dumplings were famous, and even the rich people ate her food."

"I could tell right away you came from a good woman," said Emma. "You're a beautiful girl, a smart girl." Emma approached what she wanted to say delicately. "But to make a good impression, you have to eat properly with utensils. You should know how to hold a fork and where to place the knife when you're not using it. Then we could send you to eat over at Mrs. Astor's." She smiled.

"My father used chopsticks. I can eat with chopsticks, but I can't ever find any."

"I don't know anything about chopsticks. You need practice holding a proper knife and fork and a napkin on your lap. Just a little practice and you'll be an expert, and I can send you over to the mansion."

"Where did Mr. Asa get all his money anyway?"

"Down on Wall Street."

"That's where my papa and me used to go every day. I know all about Wall Street."

"Good," said Emma, somewhat surprised by her statement. "You might like it over there. Think about it."

"I like it here," said Hope.

◆　◆　◆

In the beginning, Tommy kept his distance from their new guest and tried not to listen to the terrible crying. A few months in, his mother asked him to take Hope over to the Neighborhood House on the night they had bowling. Tommy thought she was a strange girl, but he had to admit she stood out in the looks department. The other thing he noted was the bold way she had of blurting out whatever was on her mind. He was a little afraid of Hope. No girl he knew spoke that way.

Tommy Rowland, barely fifteen, turned out to be Hope Lee's pathway back to the world. She hardly ever talked, but she let him drive her or walk with her to where she had to go. She would grab his arm sometimes to steady herself. She sat next to him, and when he said, "Get up. It's time to go," she would do as he said. Although he would never have admitted it, her trust in him made him feel capable and manly.

After six months of grief and mourning, she could be distracted and engaged for moments at a time. Tommy taught her how to bowl at the Neighborhood House, and she did it with such force, the ball would sometimes bounce before heading down the alley. The Neighborhood House also held dances and showed movies, and at his mother's urging, Tommy trudged back and forth in an awkward alliance with Hope.

Emily Stokes would sometimes come along, but she didn't like Hope. "She doesn't show one bit of gratefulness for all the things your mother has done for her, and, by the way, why does your mother coddle her? She's been here for a year now, and she's still being treated like a fragile little flower. Isn't she due to go back to wherever she came from?"

"My mother's trying to get her to live at Seawatch."

"I hate that idea. The last thing we need is another crazy girl over there. Faith won't put up with it anyway. Faith will let her know who's boss."

"Hope isn't going to let anyone show her who's boss," said Tommy, suddenly wanting to defend her.

Tommy continued to take Hope to the Neighborhood House and sit with her through showings of films, the one activity that she requested. She liked *The New York Hat* with Mary Pickford and Lillian Gish because it was about someone who overcomes a life of poverty. "That's what I'm going to do," she said when it was over. When he took her to see *Oliver Twist*, they had to leave in the middle because she became very agitated and got out of her seat.

Tommy, who never said much, asked her what was wrong.

"It reminded me of when I was on the streets with my friend Gloria," said Hope. "It was exactly the way it looked in the film. Gloria and me had to beg alms to get food, and then we slept in the luggage room of the old Astor Hotel. Gloria knew exactly what to do to get along. If I could find Gloria, I wouldn't need to be here at all. I could be on my own and do just fine."

Tommy had no response. He didn't know if his mother knew about Hope's background. He never told her, though, or anyone else. He never talked ill of Hope to his friends. He just said that she was kind of strange but OK overall. She would be Asa Simpson's problem soon, anyway. If she decided to steal him blind, let him find out on his own.

Chapter Eleven

The Neighborhood House had an educational arm that offered English classes for foreign-language speakers, and an occupational registry, where men who were out of work could learn a trade. In Hope's second summer in Muttonville, the association offered a class in English poetry. Emma made Hope attend, thinking she would find a friend or two her own age.

Robert Trent's Sunday afternoon class on the Romantic poets was so popular, there was seldom an empty seat in the large community room. Ninety percent of the participants were girls, and while they may or may not have appreciated the poetry of Lord Byron or Percy Bysshe Shelley, they all loved Robert Trent, the young Yale student who had become the image they took to bed each night. He was tall, lithe, and athletic, with a beautiful large head and thick light-brown hair that spilled across his forehead. He had an easy grin that was irresistible. If you listened closely and caught some of the emotions he culled from the poetry, it was plain to see that something hurtful had happened to him, and you wanted to comfort his hurts. When he entered a room, life picked up pace and the dullness evaporated. His impact seemed effortless because it was; he wasn't trying to do it.

During the third session of his class, the poem under discussion was John Keats's "Ode on a Grecian Urn." Robert read two stanzas and asked, "Can anyone decipher why the poet would have such an emotional reaction to staring at an old piece of pottery?" When no one spoke, he said, "In the poem, Keats is talking to the people depicted in the drawings decorating the urn. They are forever still. He calls the condition the 'foster-child of Silence and slow Time.' He's telling them they're better off frozen in the moment and not subject to the ravages of time."

"That isn't true," said Hope. "None of it is true. Even if something terrible happens that makes you want to die, it's better to be real and not some frozen person. Why do people think this is a good poem?"

She had sat mute for three sessions, never even touching the book he had handed out, never looking to the left or right. He had been watching her from the start. How could you not? He wanted to stare at her.

Throughout the series of classes, no one had ever disagreed. They asked mild questions and nodded at the answers. Hope had been forceful. She might as well have said that he was teaching something worthless. He was surprised and didn't know how to answer. "What's your name?" he asked.

"Hope. Hope Lee."

"Thank you for your comment, Hope Lee. I think it's an excellent comment for many reasons, but the most important one is that you have taken the poet to task for saying that being frozen and therefore not subject to the ravages of time, you are better off than if you just lived your life."

"Yes. That's it," said Hope, who had been reading the English poets with Emma at home. "I liked Shelley's poem 'Adonais.' 'I weep for Adonais—he is dead. Oh, weep for Adonais! though our tears thaw not the frost which binds so dear a head!' That's all I know. I like the words."

"That's one of my favorites, too," he said. Again, the burst of words surprised him.

When the class was over, he stopped by her seat. "Thank you for coming every week. I like it when students stick with me on these difficult poets. I'm always surprised to see you come back, though. You seem to be in your own thoughts."

"Oh, no," she said. "I like seeing you. It makes me happy when you walk in and I get to see you again."

"Thank you, Hope Lee. When I walk in, it makes me happy to see that you're here again." He wanted to say more. He wanted to tell her how beautiful she was, but she was just a young girl, and it might frighten her. He could see that behind those remarkable eyes lay a mountain of emotion and struggle. He could tell by the way her words burst out in one forceful shot that she found it hard to say much. He wished he could know more about her, but they'd warned him about fraternizing with the students. He knew that reaching out to comfort this girl was in the nonacceptable column. He packed up his briefcase and said good-bye. She never came back to the class, and he didn't see her again until three years later, when she was on the verge of womanhood.

Chapter Twelve

If anyone at Seawatch had extra influence, it was Mrs. Coombs. She came from a good family and could have been a nurse or a teacher outside of the estate. She'd come to Seawatch as a temporary nursemaid when Billy was born, and she had never left. The lifestyle suited her, and Asa let her know she was valued. She had a few close friends among the wives, like Emma Rowland and Ginny Stokes, but otherwise she didn't fraternize. Trask, as the butler, bought the wine and spirits and had the last word in hiring new help, but Mrs. Coombs could always add a maid if someone's cousin, newly arrived from overseas, needed a job and a place to live.

It was Julia Coombs that Emma approached about her plan to get Hope into the Simpson household. She knew it was the best thing for this girl. She had kept Hope far longer than the other families with grieving girls. She'd found that Hope had a quick mind and needed more than Emma could give her. Emma could have talked to Asa herself, but it might be awkward for him to refuse. Julia could approach him in privacy. Emma took the newspaper page with Hope's photograph and gave it to Julia. It was hard to look at that face and read the story without feeling compassion. Julia had to swallow back tears when she read the description of how Hope's mother had died and how Hope had lain in the street calling her mother's name. "Were you thinking of keeping her indefinitely?" Julia asked.

"Each time I think about sending her back, I can't do it," said Emma. "She has no one to go to. She'll end up in some settlement house or an orphanage until she's a couple of years older. I don't mind her being here, but I think she'd be a good companion for Faith, now that Billy's leaving for the university. She won't be intimidated by Faith. In a way, they're alike. It'll be good for both of them."

Emma continued talking about it with Hope. "What would you think of going to live at the mansion?"

"I'd prefer to stay here. I like it."

"I like you, too, but you could have a better life over there."

"How would it be better?"

"You would have a real education instead of just the two of us making do. And a real bedroom instead of that little closet where I stuck you. And you would learn how to eat at the table with all the proper manners. You're a beautiful girl, and that kind of life would give you a chance."

"A chance at what? I'm fine here. Maybe I could get a job and give you some money."

"That's not what I'm saying. There's a girl over there. You could help her and she could help you."

"I don't need any help."

"Yes. You do," said Emma sternly. "You need to come out of this sadness. I hear you crying and talking at night. Living with someone your own age would help. If they'll take you, you should try it for a few weeks."

Mrs. Coombs visited Emma to learn more about the girl. She tried several times to draw Hope out, without success. She wasn't as sold on her as Emma was, but maybe time would thaw her. She knew that Alice would go along with anything Asa decided. She approached Asa, stressing the benefit for Faith to have someone her age when Billy left for Yale, and Asa agreed to meet her.

When Asa went to the Rowland house to play cards, he asked Emma about Hope. Emma gave him the newspaper clipping as an introduction. Asa read it, and then looked at Hope's photograph for a long time in silence. Emma thought he was trying to find a nice way to refuse, but he just kept looking at the photograph and then folding the paper over and over, making creases all around until only Hope's face was visible. Without taking his eyes off the image, he said, "I'll take her." But not another word.

The photograph and story had shaken Asa Simpson. When he was a boy, his face had been in the papers, too. He had known the terrifying loneliness of being suddenly orphaned and not having one person who knew and wanted him. He remembered sitting on a dilapidated bed in an abandoned house without heat, shivering so hard his limbs danced uncontrollably. Then, the hot gulping sobs of relief when a kind stranger rescued him. All of it was many years in the past, but he could summon the pain in an instant.

Chapter Thirteen

Papa seldom called them to his office in such a formal way, so Faith knew something important had happened. She hoped they weren't going on another ocean voyage. She suffered from seasickness.

Asa didn't waste time with preliminaries. "I've invited a girl to come and live with us," he said. "Her name is Hope."

"What kind of a girl? You mean like Emily?" Faith asked.

"No. She's going to live here all the time, just like we do."

"How old is she?"

"She's just about your age, Faith."

"Is she a worker for the house?"

"No. She'll be part of the family. She'll eat with us and take lessons with you and Billy."

Faith looked at Billy. She wished he would ask Papa more questions, but Billy was quiet.

"Let's give her a chance," said Asa. "She's had a difficult life. Besides, you might find it enjoyable."

"What happened to her that's difficult?" Faith wondered what it took to have a difficult life. Sometimes her life was difficult.

"It's best if we don't talk about it. Maybe she'll talk to you about it when she's ready."

"How long will she be here?"

"I haven't set a time limit."

Faith could see that her father was already finished with the announcement, and she didn't have anything else to ask.

Later, Billy said, "Maybe Mama won't take you to Brooklyn if she has to take the new girl, too. This might be the answer to all your problems."

Faith wasn't ready to give in. "Papa should have asked us first."

"Why? I don't care, and you shouldn't, either. We're not going to be cooped up in a room with her. This is a big house. Unless she kills us in our sleep, it doesn't make much difference."

"Suppose she's a bully like Stephen Butler? I really don't want her here."

"It's all right, Fey. If she's a bully, we'll both jump on her and show her who's boss. We can even get Tommy if she's really strong."

"We can put her in the maze garden, and she won't find her way out." Faith knew Billy was right. It was easy to find a safe place in the house where no one could find you. She and Billy slept on the same floor, so she usually knew his whereabouts. But she often had to look for her mother and father when she wanted to see them. Maybe she would never even see the girl except during classes and meals.

Later in the afternoon, Faith stood by the window in the library looking down the long approach. She could see a figure walking slowly toward the house carrying a suitcase. The girl was taking her time and looking up at the sky. When she reached the entrance, she sat down on the lowest step.

Faith was surprised. No one had ever sat on the steps. The girl took out a magazine and began to read it. Was she ever going to come in? After fifteen minutes, Faith decided to go out and talk to her.

"I'm Faith," she said. Hope shaded her eyes to better see her. "I live here. Papa says you're going to live with us."

"I'm going to try it for a while."

"Would you like to come in?"

"All right." Hope stood up.

"I can help you with your suitcase," said Faith, picking it up and carrying it into the entry hall.

Faith took her into the library. Hope's clothes were all mismatched, but she was so pretty it didn't matter. She didn't seem nervous at all. She walked to the shelves and looked at the books. "Have you read all these books?"

"No, not at all. I don't think anyone reads these books."

Hope took out a volume. "*Vanity Fair*," she read. "Emma and I read this one together for school. It's about Becky Sharp, a poor girl that goes to live with a rich family."

"Becky Sharp was not a nice girl," said Faith. "She tried to steal the rich girl's beau."

Hope laughed. "I won't do that. That's the last thing I would do."

"I don't have a beau to steal," said Faith.

"Do you want one?"

"Not at all. I dislike boys. My mother takes me to visit my boy cousins. I hate them. One of them, Steven, tried to drown me in the ocean."

"Really? Did your mother shake the dickens out of him?"

"No one believed me. They thought I imagined it."

"Did you tell your mother the whole story? Maybe you left something out."

"My mother is too afraid that her hideous sisters and their hideous husbands and children won't like her. And you know what? They don't like her. They're snobs and don't like anyone. They finally sent that boy, Steven, to a sanitarium because he killed all the dogs in the house and told his brother and sister they were next. If you ask me, they should all go to an institution." A part of Faith wanted to shock Hope into a reaction, but Hope just listened. "Do your parents know you're here?"

"No," said Hope.

"Are you going to tell them?"

"My mother died in the shirtwaist-factory fire. Maybe you've heard of it," she said. Then she left the room and went into the front hall and sat on a bench by the door.

Faith could see she was agitated and left her alone. She thought of how she would feel without her father and mother. She would still have Billy, and Mrs. Coombs would see to it that she was safe and well fed.

She didn't know what to say to the girl. She didn't want to say anything false. After a few minutes, she went to where Hope sat. "You're going to be here with us now."

"Emma said I can still visit her."

"You can see Tommy every day. He takes lessons with us." Faith liked the direct way the girl talked. She didn't try to color anything to be polite.

Mrs. Coombs came into the hall.

"Hope, please come with me," she said. Hope looked inquiringly at Faith, who nodded, and Hope followed Mrs. Coombs to a bathroom. "This is Lillianne," Mrs. Coombs said, and indicated a young woman wearing an apron. "She is in charge of the laundry here, and she's going to give you a scrubbing and hair washing."

"I'm fifteen. I can bathe myself," said Hope.

"Lillianne is going to give you a washing and inspection to see if you need any special care."

She didn't say the word *lice*, but Hope knew that's what she was looking for. It reminded her of the woman with the violent boy, but this situation was different and she submitted to the ordeal. She had never been in such a luxurious tub. The room was almost as big as the room she had lived in with her mother. She sank into the warm water and closed her eyes. She thought about the conversation with Faith. This kind of frank talk was different from the way most people said things, and she liked the girl's honesty. The blunt words fell like little bullets and bounced all around the room. She had called the women *hideous*. What a wonderful word. What a wonderful way to speak. She might stay until her birthday, when she would turn sixteen. That was a good age to get a job and be out on her own. If she didn't like it, though, she'd leave right away and not say a word to anyone.

Lillianne was none too pleased to be demoted to nursemaid, and she scrubbed Hope as if she were a mangy dog. Once she saw how nicely her charge cleaned up, though, she took some interest. She brushed out her hair and trimmed and cleaned her fingernails.

"I'm going to put your hair in a French braid," she said. "Have you ever done it that way?"

"No. It's always been just loose."

"Do you have any objections?"

"No."

She put the wild curls into one braid, but little tendrils escaped and framed Hope's face. "You look like a different person," said Lillianne, surveying her work. "You look pretty."

She produced a new toothbrush and some toiletries that she gave to the girl.

Faith and Billy were surprised when they saw their new houseguest all cleaned up. Hope was too young to be ravishing, but she had all the components of a haunting beauty that was about to bloom.

◆ ◆ ◆

"You do your stock business here?" Hope asked, scanning the inside of the sumptuous paneled office and the massive desk, when Mrs. Coombs took her in to see Asa.

"Sometimes," said Asa. "Mostly in the summer."

"You should have a ticker machine," she said, looking around. "You could put it right next to your desk."

The minute she mentioned the ticker, he saw how obvious it was. He had never considered putting one in the house. "How do you know about the ticker?"

"My papa was a stock runner for a man who owned a furniture store. He used to trade on the curb. They wouldn't let him inside. They used telephones on the window ledges. A whole pack of runners worked at the curb using hand signals. I used to be able to do them. Buy, sell, how many lots, sell short. Baruch's runner was the one we watched. When he moved, Papa knew something was up."

It took a lot to get Asa's attention, but Hope had all of it. "I wanted to know what Baruch was up to, myself," said Asa.

"Harriman was another one. My papa always said, 'Watch out for Harriman.' But mostly people didn't watch out. They fell for it and lost their money but still hung around. They were stuck on the place and kept coming every day. I liked going there, too."

"Do you know how Harriman tricked people?"

"He ran a stock way up until all the suckers were in, and then he'd bring it back down. Or else he wouldn't let it move at all, and the suckers got bored and sold it. When it went low, he'd buy a lot of it. They fell for it every time, and he knew they would."

Asa was surprised at how simply she framed her experiences, but she had all the facts.

"And where is your father now?"

"He went back to China. A lot of Chinese men do that." She added this last detail to her story to make it respectable. She didn't want Sen to look like a bad person.

"I see." Asa didn't know what to make of Hope. He decided to give it time and keep an eye on her behavior. If he had miscalculated, it would be obvious soon enough.

"I think Faith is glad to have another girl in the household," he said, "and so am I." With that, it was clear Hope was dismissed, and Mrs. Coombs ushered her out.

For Billy and Faith, everything about the new girl was different. Though they'd known about a girl living with the Rowlands, they'd never seen her up close, and Tommy hadn't talked about her. Hope was beautiful, and it was hard not to look at her. She had a natural way of talking, yet most of the things she said were unexpected.

Faith found that she talked to the girl with a freedom that she had seldom felt. Now someone other than Billy knew Faith's hidden thoughts. The girl was as smart as anything, and Faith loved that nothing surprised her. Maybe this new arrangement wouldn't be so bad.

Chapter Fourteen

Hope stayed on the top floor of the house in an unoccupied wing. Her room's gabled roofline created slanted walls with a ridge in the middle. A bed with a white metal headboard, a small chest of drawers, a chair, and an enameled sink were in the room. A small window looked out onto the front lawn.

Hope had withstood many things, but she could not stand total silence in the night. Until her mother died, she had never slept alone in a room. Throughout childhood, she had been lulled by the sound of her parents' breathing a few feet away. She loved listening to their conversation as she sank into sleep. Agatha would be muttering over the next day's food offerings, and Sen would be half listening and also reading things aloud from the newspaper. Street noises drifted up from below. In Emma's house, she had slept in a cot in a room originally meant to be a pantry. The noises of the family could always be heard well into the night. Chester was up at dawn. Now at Seawatch, the large closed-off room on the top floor played into her nervousness and fears. It was without sound. It was far away from another soul. Her ears felt full, as if the silence were pushing against her.

She pulled out her old comic books, although she hadn't looked at them for a long time. She was too old for the simplistic tales, but she couldn't make herself lie down. Was this how it felt to be dead? Did her mother now live in a place without sound? She wondered what they had done with her mother's body. This was the first time she'd thought of it. They must have buried her somewhere. She would leave this place soon and look for her mother's grave.

She sat fully clothed on the bed until fatigue overtook her and she toppled onto the mattress. On the third night, she left the room and went to the floor where Faith slept. The door was partly open and she walked in. She could see Faith's face, soft and peaceful. Her hair was spread out on the pillow. She could hear her even breaths. She took a coverlet from a bench at the end of the bed and a small pillow. She lay down on the floor and fell asleep.

Faith woke early in the morning and saw her there. She was startled but not afraid. She didn't mind that the new girl had wanted to sleep next to her. She hadn't done any damage, and she was sleeping quietly. She, too, went back to sleep and when she woke again, Hope was gone.

Faith told Billy the story. "I woke up in the middle of the night, and she was sleeping on the floor next to my bed."

"What? No. Were you scared?"

"I wasn't scared. She was just lying there, asleep."

"Maybe she didn't like being up in the attic all by herself."

"I don't blame her. I wouldn't like being up there, either."

"Did you wake her up?"

"No. I went back to sleep and when I woke up, she was gone."

"What if she comes back tonight?"

"I'll let her. I won't say anything about it, and don't you say anything, either."

"That's a good idea, Fey. Let her keep her secret."

Faith had never been a source of comfort to anyone, and having Hope sneak into her room to sleep made her feel more grown up. It made her feel she had something to give. She knew that Hope would have hated talking about it, so she never raised it. She asked the chambermaid to put one of the feather-mattress toppers on the floor by her bed. Before she went to sleep, she placed a blanket and pillow on it, but in the morning it remained unused. The next night, she woke and saw Hope there, sleeping openly on her back, her arms bent above her head.

The arrangement continued for a week, and then Faith asked Mrs. Coombs to give Hope the empty nursemaid's room connected to hers. A door separated the rooms, but Faith made sure it was open every night. Nothing was ever said. It was better to let Hope keep her armor. She needed that armor to withstand all the things that had happened to her. What's more, Faith liked having her close by. Sometimes Faith would hear her talking in the middle of the night, but she got used to it and never interfered. For Faith, every quirk she tolerated and every accommodation she made for Hope enlarged her own personality. Hope gave her a new mirror to look into and she saw a more fully formed girl.

◆ ◆ ◆

Hope realized her life had taken a sharp turn. It wasn't the free life she was used to in the streets of lower New York, but it seemed safe. She still had terrible dreams. When she awoke in the middle of the night in a strange bed, in a strange room, so far from her former life, she felt afraid of forgetting her mother. She was afraid of that last day being so far in the past that she would no longer remember every minute of it. On these nights, she would get up and go to the window and talk aloud to Agatha. She would recite a sacred litany of all the things she didn't want to forget: "Mama, I want to remember your plaid skirt that buttoned all the way to the hem, the crimson fringed shawl, the black pumps that were run down on the outside of the heel, the little felt hat with a veil." She wanted to remember Agatha's face behind the veil, the vein at her temple, a scar on her arm where boiling water had splashed. "Mama, don't go too far. Don't go far." She tried to feel her mother's presence. She tried to remember her mother's scent. She listened for words. "Say something, Mama. I don't want to forget how you sounded." If she forgot her past, she would have nothing. She would disintegrate and turn to dust.

On nights like these, it wasn't enough to leave the door between the rooms open. She would take her blanket and pillow and lie on the floor near Faith. There she found the closeness that allowed her to feel safe enough to fall asleep.

Chapter Fifteen

Hope shifted the emotional content of Seawatch. She was a new focus and displaced some of the anxiety, especially for Faith, and even a little for Alice. Asa noticed. He was pleased that his experiment was working. The new girl hadn't stolen anything. She hadn't hurt anyone, and his daughter was suddenly laughing and saying, "Good morning, Papa," with a new lilt in her voice.

Billy had his own feelings about Hope. These were his last few months before Yale, and he was happy that his sister would have a friend in the house. Hope didn't talk a lot, but he could see she had understanding, and she had already assigned Faith the role of protector. She turned to Faith for solace in the most natural way because she knew it would be given. More important, it was an equal relationship—Hope offered Faith protection, too.

"She trusts you," he told Faith. "I think she would do anything you asked of her."

◆ ◆ ◆

At first, Alice was cautious with the new girl. Her behavior was unpredictable. Alice couldn't deny how well Hope got along with Faith, but she found her difficult to talk to. She had seen Hope in the upstairs hall one afternoon after she first arrived and called her into her bedroom. She saw a beautiful girl in ill-fitting clothes and wayward hair, and it bothered her.

"Are you happy here?" she asked.

"I'm fine," said Hope.

"You must miss your mother," said Alice.

"My mother is dead," said Hope.

"I'm sorry. Of course, Mr. Simpson told me." Alice opened one of her jewelry cases and chose a thin silver bracelet. "Would you like this?"

"No, thank you," said Hope. "I have no place to wear it."

Alice put the bracelet back. The girl had confidence and a certain poise. She wasn't impolite, but she did say what was on her mind.

Alice noticed that Hope had outgrown most of her dresses and skirts, and the hems were too short. Some of the shirtwaists were mended. Mrs. Coombs had bought underwear and nightclothes, but Alice, who took pleasure in reclaiming the needy, wanted to dress Hope in more stylish clothes. She would talk it over with Asa.

The five students had their lessons in the library at a long rectangular table. Hope and Faith sat on one side, and Emily and Tommy on the other. Billy was in his last year before Yale, and he worked on his lessons at the far end. Mr. Knudsen, a thin, bearded man with glasses, was at the other. He had a large easel with a chalkboard and a pull-down oilcloth showing a map of the world.

From the very first day, lessons were a problem for Hope. She did the work well enough and always answered correctly when asked, but she found it impossible to sit still for the lectures and would begin to circle the room as Knudsen spoke.

"Miss Lee, please take your seat," he would say.

She never disobeyed, but within a few minutes she stood up again.

It was distracting and everyone wondered how long it would take for Knudsen to tell her to sit down again.

Faith finally said something that stopped the cycle. "She has a condition," she said, pointing to Hope. "She has to get up and move around or else her legs will get cramps." She said it with such certainty, Hope looked at her as if it were the truth.

Billy seconded Faith's statement. "She'll cramp up and it takes hours to uncramp." He could hardly keep a straight face, and Tommy just looked from one to the other in confusion. Was it true? Her legs hadn't cramped when she lived at his house. Emily just shook her head.

The troubles with Hope in the classroom didn't stop with restless legs. Tommy's answers, particularly in American history, were long-winded. If they were discussing a Civil War battle, he got into the tactics as if he were playing soldiers and plotting out the battle himself.

Everyone would doodle on their notebooks and wait for Knudsen to jump in, when Tommy took a breath, and say, "Can you add anything to the narrative, Miss Lee?"

"The Missouri State Guard defeated the Union Cavalry. An upset victory at Lexington for the Confederacy. The end." Everyone knew that by saying "the end," she was shutting down anything more from Tommy.

The others would look up from their doodling, grateful to move on. Emily was the sole exception. She would glare at Hope and sometimes would say she wanted to hear Tommy's ending, but Tommy would say, "That was the extent of it."

◆ ◆ ◆

Emily Stokes was a beautiful girl. Her eyes were blue and her complexion as creamy as the milk her father collected from the prized cows in the dairy barn. She was used to being the prettiest girl in the room, but when Hope came to Seawatch, Emily and her beauty lost their prominence. Faith, who had always envied Emily's looks, although not her personality, was happy to see her taken down a notch.

Emily did not like the new girl at Seawatch and couldn't imagine why in the world Mr. Asa would want to bring someone like that into his house to live right alongside Billy and Faith. It didn't make sense. What she disliked even more was that Billy and Faith had fallen in love with the ruffian. Instead of being annoyed, Billy laughed at everything she said. Faith, who had sort of been Emily's friend, now stuck to Hope.

"I hate her," she would say to Tommy. "I hate, hate, hate her."

"Emily, stop saying that. She doesn't interfere with your life."

"That's where you're wrong, Tommy. She does interfere with my life. She's rude and annoys everybody during lessons. She might as well have told you to shut up when you gave that long answer about Lexington. You should hate her, too."

Tommy smiled. "I was going on a bit too much, and Knudsen did call on her."

"See? Now you're defending her. She has all of you in a trance. Your mother babied her for almost two years, and I bet she never even said thank you."

"My mother was attached to her and misses having her in our house."

"She should have an attachment to *me*. She's known me much longer."

"She has an attachment to you. She always says how pretty you are."

"Really? What does she say? Tell me exactly what she says."

"She says, 'Emily has the most beautiful eyes. Do you notice them, Tommy?' And then I say, 'Yes, I do.'"

"Tommy Rowland, you're just teasing me now."

Although he would never say it aloud, Tommy had a little crush on Hope. It was a complicated crush because sometimes, like Emily, he hated her, too.

◆ ◆ ◆

Up until he was thirteen years old, Tommy Rowland was an uncomplicated boy. He liked fishing off the bridge or digging for steamers at low tide at the spot where the creek emptied into the sound. He liked swimming in the late afternoon in the sparkling waters of the sound and then riding his bike home for dinner. Often, he'd bring back a bucket full of steamer clams or a couple of bluefish, and his mother would look at him and say, "Well, you certainly earned your swim, Tommy boy." His parents always felt you had to earn any small pleasure because they had been brought up hardscrabble poor. He didn't feel that way, but he liked work. When his mother sent him to drive Asa home because he'd had too much wine, it made him feel capable. He was one of the few boys who could drive, and it set him apart. He would park the Packard in the garage and either walk or ride one of the bicycles home. When he entered the house, his mother would call down, "Be sure the cat didn't sneak back in."

"He didn't," Tommy would answer. He knew that his mother stayed up to know that he was safely home and hadn't killed himself or Asa, but she didn't want to say it.

It was the background for an ideal childhood, if he could extricate himself from the unspoken suspicion that he, too, belonged to the Simpsons just like his parents, and he would need to escape to a different life.

Although Billy was more than a year older than Tommy, Asa suggested that Tommy should take him along on his escapades and teach him how to be a "boy's boy." Tommy balked at the suggestion because he had no idea what being a boy's boy meant, but he invited Billy to tag along when he did his chores and would let him hammer in a nail or help saw off a broken branch.

"You want to come along?" he would ask awkwardly when Billy came to the mansion door.

"Where are you going?"

"Fix some of the boards around the vegetable-patch fence. You can help me hammer in a few nails."

"Sure."

For Billy, it was easier to do it than explain to Asa that he had little interest in these things. The boys would also climb trees and fish occasionally, although Billy was not athletic and found it difficult to cast a line far enough to ever catch a fish. Tommy didn't know what to make of Billy, but it didn't matter if Billy ever caught a fish. His life was already a success because of his father.

On the day that Hope Lee had arrived at his house, Tommy Rowland lost some of the innocence of boyhood. It wasn't that she awakened sexual stirrings (although she did), but she elicited from him so many complex and sometimes contradictory emotions. She was not coy like most girls he knew. She was bold. She said what she was thinking and didn't worry over the consequences. In a way, she was like his mother, but unlike his mother, she had an unsettling face and eyes. You wanted those eyes to focus on you, and you wanted that face to grow soft because of you. None of that happened, but it didn't keep Tommy from wishing it did. While Hope made his mind churn and complicated his feelings, he knew he would never marry a girl from the streets. He wasn't snobbish or disapproving, but rather he worried about Hope's temperament. He was frightened for her, frightened she would get in trouble and be sent away.

Chapter Sixteen

Faith had no intention of changing anything about her new roommate, even though everything about her stood out like a big spotlight. All the hems of her clothes showed marks where they had been repeatedly let out. The waists no longer fell in the appropriate spot.

"What in the world is she wearing today?" Faith had heard Emily ask Tommy more than once. The servants stared and whispered. Faith would have offered clothes from her own closet, but she didn't want to risk offending Hope, who seemed perfectly comfortable in what she wore.

Almost every day, Faith saved her from criticism and ridicule. One afternoon, when on a break from lessons, the group discussed ways to make spending money. Hope talked about her days begging alms on the street.

"I had a friend, Gloria, who took off her shoes to get pity. She was an expert at it. We always made about two bucks a day."

That sentence stopped the conversation, until Faith asked calmly, "Who gave you more money? Men or women?"

"Definitely men. They were more sympathetic."

"There, you see," Tommy said. "Men are good."

The moment passed.

If her oddness was all right with Faith, it was all right with everyone. Hope admired the way Faith could so easily dispel an awkward moment.

One problem, though, involved modesty, and it couldn't be ignored. Hope needed a brassiere. Faith had begun to wear one a few months earlier and was acutely aware that Hope's breasts were more developed than hers. Emily had been the first in the group to wear a brassiere because she'd had C-cup breasts since she was fourteen years old. Faith had been next. Her Brooklyn cousin, Nancy, had taken Faith into her bedroom and shown her a lacy contraption that she wore under her clothes; it fit over your bosom and fastened at the back.

"Why?" Faith had asked.

"So my breasts don't wobble all over the place and boys get the wrong idea."

Faith didn't have a clue what she was talking about. Her breasts didn't wobble. "Should I wear one?"

"All women have to wear them eventually. You'd better ask Aunt Alice. She'll tell you."

When Faith told her mother what Nancy had said, Alice immediately took her to be fitted. "We should have done this already," she said.

Faith hardly ever wore the brassieres in the beginning because she didn't want to be bothered, but when she got a glimpse of Emily at the beach without support and saw how big and jiggly her breasts looked under the stretchy bathing top, she began wearing her brassiere every day. She didn't want the boys staring at her the way they stared at Emily. It was in this spirit—to keep Hope from being ogled—that she brought up the subject.

"We have to ask Mama to take you brassiere shopping. Your bosom is growing, and your undershirts aren't enough."

Hope looked confused. "I don't know what you're talking about."

Faith showed her a brassiere from her bureau. "This is what they look like, and all girls wear them eventually."

"Why?" Hope was sure she didn't need the item Faith was dangling before her.

"For lots of reasons. It keeps your bosom from wobbling around, and it makes your clothes fit better. It's time you wore one."

"If you think I need it," said Hope, who decidedly didn't agree.

"You know how boys are," said Faith. "They're always looking at things and having their imaginations go haywire."

"You think they're looking at me?"

"They look at all the girls. I hate the way they stare at Emily. She can't help that she has those big breasts."

Hope finally got the picture. "I stare at Emily, too. Can't help it."

The following week, Alice took both girls to a corset shop and out-fitted them in bras and lacy camisoles to wear over them.

"Mama wants to hide our bosoms under a double armor," said Faith.

That night, as Hope put away her new undergarments, she held up a brassiere. "It's uncomfortable as the dickens, but it does hold every-thing together. If you hadn't told me, I would be wearing my old under-shirt until I was a hundred."

"If your mother was alive, she would have told you," said Faith.

"Maybe. I never saw her wear one, though. She was small on top."

Faith could see that thoughts of her mother still made Hope sad, but she could absorb it without falling apart. "Do you ever hear from your father?" she asked.

Hope was startled. Sen didn't know that Agatha had died. Maybe he was still sending letters to the rooming house. "He used to write us all the time," she said. "Before he went to China, he took me with him to Wall Street every day. It was just the two of us." She wanted to defend Sen.

"I've never been anywhere alone with my father," Faith confessed.

"Why don't you ask him to take you somewhere?"

"I couldn't do that. I don't even know where we would go."

"He'll probably take you anywhere you want to go. Tell him to take you to the zoo in Central Park. Go see the sea lions at lunchtime."

"I doubt Papa would think that was a good place to go," said Faith.

"This is about where you want to go. Don't you want to see the sea lions eat their lunch? People feed them fish with their bare hands, and then the seals make a racket to show they like it."

Hope made it sound so simple and natural. Why did she find it so hard?

After brassiere needs were met, it was Alice, with her urge toward works of mercy, who changed Hope in the most dramatic way. She brought in the dressmaker to create a new wardrobe. The results were satisfying all around. The well-made outfits in good fabrics and flattering colors turned a beautiful girl into a stunning girl. Hope couldn't help but feel and see the difference. She began to pay attention to her table manners, taking small manageable bites and placing her utensils at the top of her plate when she was done. She said good morning to everyone at the beginning of the day.

Faith noted all the incremental improvements with mixed feelings. Hope wasn't waking up at night and murmuring her soliloquies. Some mornings, she didn't run out at dawn and wander down to the beach. Faith sometimes wished for the old Hope, who had been so bowed by grief and sadness that she had grabbed at Faith to stay afloat.

Chapter Seventeen

The girl is not improving, Miss Jane Howell, the cooking coach, stated to herself as if dotting the *i* on a document. Miss Howell had a history with the family. She had taught Alice and Faith embroidery before the cooking lessons. She knew from Julia Coombs that Faith needed to build her confidence. "She has to compete with a brother that is charm itself," said Julia. Miss Howell got the picture. Faith was nobody's darling and didn't know how to use opportunity. Miss Howell had witnessed the boy greet his father when he arrived at the end of the day. "Hi, Papa, how did the market treat you today?"

"It treated me just fine, Billy boy."

Billy knew how to gauge his father's mood and either approach him jovially or keep out of his way. Faith didn't know how to read her father, and her greeting was often a stark "Hello, Papa." She couldn't pull off the kind of greeting that tripped off of Billy's tongue without effort.

To the outside world, however, her position as Asa Simpson's daughter made everything right. She didn't have to try. Someone would always befriend her and take care of her. Miss Howell knew Faith would marry well, and her looks would improve when the teenage years were over. She had all the ingredients she would need: good height; a lovely, even complexion; shapely legs; and a good full derriere. Her eyes were small and her nose had a slight bump, but these flaws could be easily fixed with a little contouring powder. With proper styling, her thick brown hair would be a great asset.

Miss Howell, like all of the tutors and coaches, was asked never to show by word or deed that Faith was an heiress or that her status had any special meaning. Asa Simpson wished to raise his children so they were oblivious to privilege. He wanted them to be self-reliant, industrious, and unafraid of making their way in the world.

Many society families made it a point to keep the children in the dark about their special status. It was the vogue to teach cooking to the girls to inspire humility. In many homes, the learning kitchen sat in or near the nursery, where the children made dishes such as meat loaf, mashed potatoes, or creamed corn. Every couple of weeks, the children would serve a simple dinner to their parents.

It was in cooking classes that Alice Simpson chose to put her stamp on her daughter. Alice's intention was that Faith learn to cook and offer her skills to the church sodality and help feed the poor of her Brooklyn parish. Once a week, Miss Jane appeared with provisions for the day's lesson. Faith hated the cooking lessons because they caused her to revert to the unsure girl she had fought to overcome. She was clumsy with the tools, and even the simplest dishes never tasted right.

"Put the masher square on the potatoes and press hard from above. Then you can turn it in the opposite direction and press again." Faith had helped peel a few potatoes, and Miss Jane had boiled them.

"I did that, but they're still lumpy. They're not only lumpy— they're hard."

"The potatoes don't have a will of their own," Miss Jane said kindly. "They will surrender to your masher if you persevere. I promise you. Try again. Like this." The coach, in her starched white chef's jacket, guided Faith's hand holding the potato masher. "Press down with all your might from the top and see how well it works."

Miss Jane took a step back and looked at Faith. "Here, dear, wipe your nose. It's running a bit. Where's your hanky, now?"

Faith pulled a lacy square from her pocket and slid it past her nose. She was the picture of discontent with her forehead narrowed, her shoulders hunched inward, her legs pressed together.

"I can't do it, Miss Jane. I can't." The potatoes sat at the bottom of the pot, lumpy and cold.

Hope didn't like seeing Faith sniveling over something so worthless as mashing potatoes. She had witnessed her mother mash potatoes many times and spoke up. "You're doing it all wrong. If you want to mash potatoes, you have to pick at them with a fork until they are apart. Soak them in some very hot milk and melted butter before you use the masher. The job will be ten times quicker, but I wouldn't mash the stupid potatoes at all. Why would you want to learn that, Faith?"

Both Faith and Miss Jane looked at Hope with alarm.

"Her parents want her to learn how to cook," said Miss Jane.

"She's sniffling over a pot of ugly boiled potatoes. I'll teach you anything you want to know about cooking," she said to Faith. "My mama owned a cafeteria, and before that she sold food from a cart. I know about cooking, and I wouldn't do it for anything, especially if my papa was a millionaire. We'll tell him your side of this."

Miss Jane regained her senses and had a sharp answer for Hope. "Mr. Asa does not intend for you to disrupt the household."

"I'm not disrupting the household. I'm showing Faith her rights as a person. She has rights, and she can object to things. Have you ever been downtown near Union Square? There are people objecting all over the place. They even object to the government. They call President Taft a jackass. Faith, you want to object, don't you?"

"Yes."

"See, she wants to object."

The cooking coach packed up her provisions and ended the lesson. The following evening at dinner, Asa brought up the incident.

Faith looked at Hope. "That was my fault, Mr. Asa," Hope said. "I didn't see any benefit in it, because the lesson was doomed. You can't mash big cold potatoes with no hot liquid and hot butter to help you. It was bad from the start, but Faith didn't know it. She thought it was her fault, but she was an unknowing victim."

"Is it true that you called the president a coarse name?"

"It wasn't me. Those speakers down in Union Square. They didn't like the things Taft was doing. They called him a fat jackass."

Alice stopped eating and looked at her husband for direction. Aside from the colorful language, who was this strange girl to talk like an equal to Asa? The ease with which Hope laid out her argument had silenced everyone. Asa remained attentive. He had a similar opinion of Taft, who had lost the support of Asa's hero, Teddy Roosevelt. On the other hand, the girl's boldness could turn into something worse. He would have a chat with Hope and see what she was really about. "Thank you for bringing this to my attention," he said and began to eat his dinner.

The next day when he arrived home from Wall Street, he asked Mrs. Coombs to bring Hope to his office. He purposely faced away from her as she entered. He knew this was an off-putting practice to gain the advantage. The guest didn't know whether to wait or make her presence known. Hope wasn't put off.

"Mrs. Coombs says you want to have a talk with me, so here I am."

Asa turned around and for the first time had a good look at the girl from top to bottom. She was tall for her age and thin, but she wasn't willowy. Her coloring was unusual. Rounded pale cheeks and dark-green eyes that hinted at the oriental, surrounded by a robust cloud of copper curls so plentiful and unruly that it created a backdrop for her face. She was a presence. He was glad he had agreed to shelter her, because life on the streets of New York would have ravaged her. On the other hand, he had a calm, orderly house and he didn't want a trouble-maker or a wiseacre that needed constant reining in.

"I wanted to know a little more about you," said Asa. "How do you know so much about cooking?"

"My papa cooked for the gold miners, and when that dried up, he cooked on the Atchison, Topeka and Santa Fe. He was Chinese, and he didn't like cooking French food. It made him sick. My mother had a food cart near the Astor Hotel, and people loved her food so much that one man opened a cafeteria for her. Then she ran into bad luck."

"You have no relatives? Grandparents?"

Hope shook her head. "My mother said the men in her family didn't grow old. They were killed young or went to prison over the stupid mistakes of the poor."

"And what were the stupid mistakes of the poor?"

"They took bad jobs."

"And what jobs were those?"

"My grandfather was a gravedigger, and no Jew, not even an Italian, would have taken that job."

"Why not?"

"Those jobs drove the men to drink too much. My grandfather was a gravedigger who fell into an open sewer hole and drowned because he was drunk. He didn't even drown in an ocean or a lake." She said all this without any shading of emotion, although Asa knew it must be affecting her.

"So you have no one?" She shook her head. "I'm going to share something with you that I seldom speak about," said Asa. "I was very, very poor when I was a boy."

"I can't believe it," said Hope. "You had no food or a place to live? What about your mother and father?"

"Now here's where you and me share something," said Asa. "I, too, was an orphan. I lost both parents when I was eleven. A hobo, who had just eaten a plate of my mother's rabbit stew, shot them both. My mother wouldn't turn away anyone who was hungry, but the man repaid her with a bullet so he could steal money that wasn't there. No one wanted to take me in because of the lingering depression. There was little money and few jobs, especially in upstate New York. The orphanages were overflowing. I was so frightened, and I had lost my loving mother and father."

When he said that, her eyes filled. She walked out of the office. It was at moments like this that her will betrayed her and the terror won.

She sat on a chair in the hallway, and after a moment, Asa came out and sat next to her.

"So there was nobody who knew you?" she asked.

"I had an uncle, but he couldn't provide for his own family and moved away."

There were so many ideas going through Hope's head, she couldn't speak. The idea that this powerful, rich man—who lived in a house that was bigger than the Astor House Hotel, and nicer, too—was at one time as poor as herself and also without parents, was astonishing.

"How long did it take you to get rich?"

"The first job I had was lighting the lamps of Troy in the evening. That let me stay in school for one more year. One day, I passed a soda shop and the manager was mixing a drink. I thought how the mixing would go ten times faster if there was a machine to do the work. It would need paddles of some sort that could be electrically driven and twirl in opposite directions. Only three homes in Troy were electric at the time, but there was a small electric plant. I made a contraption, took it to the soda store, and asked the owner if he wanted something mixed."

"I bet he said yes," said Hope.

"No. He wasn't interested, but something better happened. There was another man at the counter having lunch, and he offered me a job. A little later on, he took me to live with him. When he died, he left me a working mill that was very valuable. I knew the need for electricity would explode, and with my mill as collateral, I bought up small power companies. That good man left me a business, and after that, it was my brain figuring out how to make that windfall grow."

"That's the way I'm going to do it, too," said Hope. "That's a very good way to do it."

Asa smiled. "First you have to get someone to leave you something valuable in his will."

They walked back into his office. "Look," he said, pulling a cloth off a brand-new ticker machine. "I took your advice." Asa had found out all he needed to know. "You've proved that you know a lot about cooking, and you know a lot about the financial markets. I can teach you more if you're interested."

"Oh, you bet. I'm more interested in the stock market than almost anything else. You can teach me anything you want." Normally, Hope spoke sparingly, but Asa had opened the floodgates of memory and longing for the happy days with Sen. "I bet you keep your money in old Mr. Baker's bank near Trinity Church. We used to see him all the time going in and out of the building on the corner. My papa would point to the doorway and say, 'Look. That big tall man owns the richest bank in the whole country. He and Morgan are thick as thieves.' Only millionaires and their companies were allowed to put their money in that bank."

"I did keep my money in that bank and still do. Mr. Baker was from Troy, New York, where I once lived."

Hope was inspecting the ticker machine. "It needs paper," she said. "You need to put the paper in."

"Well, see? I need you already," said Asa. "That can be one of your jobs when you become my assistant."

Neither Asa nor Hope thought of asking Faith how she would feel about the arrangement.

Chapter Eighteen

Alice insisted that Trevor drive Billy to Yale, but Billy asked Asa to intervene.

"I don't want to be chauffeured to Yale. Can't we ship all my stuff, and I'll take the train? I can take the Greenport ferry over to New London and catch a train to New Haven."

Asa, who had begun wearing reading glasses, took them off and turned from the papers on his desk. Billy knew this meant that he had his father's full attention.

"If that's how you want to do it, I'm sure your mother will agree."

"Thanks, Papa. I'm a little nervous as it is, without looking like the spoiled rich boy being chauffeured in."

"That couldn't happen even if you arrived on a pasha throne atop an elephant."

Billy smiled. "Now that sounds like something I'd like. I wouldn't have to do anything else to prove myself."

Asa stood and walked over to his son. "Let's take a walk, just the two of us. I'm going to miss you, Billy boy."

"I'll miss you, too, but I'm eager to go. I already know some of the boys who'll be in my class. Jimmy Coe and Randall Firestone. We'll have each other until we fit in somewhere."

It was a crisp late-August day, a relief from the usual muggy Long Island weather. Asa and Billy could smell the salt air rising from the bay, and they naturally walked toward the water. Asa was in a contemplative mood. He took Billy's hand as if he were still a toddler. "The happiest day of my life was when you were born," Asa said. "I had no close blood relatives until you came. It was a comfort to have a son, and I slept on a cot in the nursery, worried you might disappear."

"I'm not going to disappear. I'll be back home for Christmas. And don't forget you still have Faith to keep you company."

"Faith marches to her own tune. Hope has been a good match for her. She's brought Faith around."

"I think it's the other way. Faith has brought Hope around. She's much calmer and easier to relate to. That's all Faith's doing."

"You think so?" said Asa. "I never found her difficult to relate to. She doesn't prattle. Is that what you mean? That's one of the things I like about her."

"When she first came, she was up half the night talking to herself. Faith helped her through it."

"Really? I wouldn't have thought that."

"I know, Papa," said Billy, but stopped there. He was not about to lay out all of the cues that Asa missed. He was on his way out, and he needed to leave the household in a calm way without stirring any pots. He was sure Faith would find her own way to survive their father's blindness. She had already used the summer to get better at swimming, an activity that used to terrify her. He or Tommy had swum beside her in the beginning, but now they waited on the shore and watched when she went out alone. If she could conquer swimming, she would find a way to open Asa's eyes.

Billy and his father turned to go back. Again, Asa took his hand, and Billy let him.

Later, Faith sat on Billy's bed and watched as he packed the last suitcase.

"You think you're going to need a shoe horn?" she asked. "That's the last thing I would pack."

"Your shoes are soft leather. You don't have to struggle to put them on."

"Are you all happy or a little sad?"

"All happy."

"What about me?"

"I can't think about you, because then I would be all sad, and I want to be happy."

"Really? You are all sad about leaving me?"

"Of course, you little nitwit."

"Me, too," she said, then was quiet a moment. "Now that you won't be here, I wonder what Papa will do with me."

"What do you mean?"

"He's all done with you and he must have plans for me."

"I would do it the other way around. Figure out what you want and present it to Papa."

"Maybe. But I'd really like to know what sort of future Papa sees for me."

◆ ◆ ◆

Once Billy left, it was Hope—not Faith—who seamlessly filled the vacancy for Asa. Though bonding between Asa Simpson and Hope Lee was unusual, anyone who had known Asa's early life would have at least understood it.

A couple of months after he promised to teach her about stocks, Asa began to do something he had never done before. When he did business from home, which he did more frequently since installing the ticker, Hope would sit at the machine, and Asa opened his thought process and strategies to her. He asked her to analyze what he had done to see how adept she was. If she saw something that caught her eye on the tape, she would tell him. "United States Gypsum is up again today. It's been up all week."

"You have the railroads to thank for that. They keep urging people to move to the country and buy one of those little box houses. All those houses need gypsum board to cover the walls."

"That must be it. Why don't you get in and buy some, too? Or buy the railroads. If the houses sell, the railroad has more commuters."

"I might. But how do you know it isn't some manipulator baiting us?"

In the early days, Asa had invested in railroad stocks. On the day he was born, the tracks of the Central and Union Pacific lines were joined, making the opposite shores of the continent only seven days apart. His father named him Asa after the chief engineer on the maiden voyage from Oakland to New York. But the recent history of the railroad was fraught with terror and murder. Morgan and his cohorts would destroy a line and blow up innocent people because they were in competition with the lines they owned. What's more, the railroads had erratic periods of solvency and bankruptcy. They were at the mercy of the seasons, the ridership, the farmers' bumper crops that needed transport, and the economy.

"I know people are buying those country houses," said Hope. "Tommy can't wait to sign up. He talks about it as if he's a grown man with ten children following him like ducks. Faith keeps telling him that the railroad has sold him a bill of goods and he's swallowed it hook, line, and sinker."

"Really? Faith tells him that?" Asa said, surprised and also proud.

"If Tommy's any indication, gypsum will probably go through the roof."

Asa found that Hope made quick assessments. Her mind could jump from the fact to the probable cause with good accuracy. She was a raw thinker. She shrugged off greed, pretense, or cunning as ordinary parts of life. She understood that the market was sometimes run by economic forces, but mostly it was run by flawed, avaricious men. He found it both amusing and alarming that she knew all of the strange anecdotes of the market and the big players. Some of the things she told him had been talked about secretly at board meetings. He had no idea when or how the girl could have learned so much. She was not shy about questioning everything he did. She would question his strategy and point out flaws in his thinking that he had not considered.

With Billy gone, he liked having her at his heels, always ready to be engaged. She was good company. When she had something to say, she said it and then kept quiet. She was interested in what he did, and her interest didn't waver. It was ridiculous, but life was often ridiculous. After all, look at him, an impoverished orphan boy with no resources and now the ninth-richest man in the entire country.

If Alice Simpson had possessed even a smidgeon of maternal instinct, she would have pointed out to her husband that as he filled Hope up, Asa siphoned comfort and love from his daughter. In the beginning, Faith saw the alliance as a novelty that would run its course. When almost two years had passed, she realized that Hope engaged her father in a way that she had never done. It would have been natural for Faith to feel bitterness but something else distracted her. Robert Emory Trent came to Seawatch, and minds and hearts had no room for anything but him.

Chapter Nineteen

Asa Simpson brought Robert Emory Trent to Seawatch for the summer of 1915 to fill out his polo team and to be a readily available tennis partner. Asa had expected a modestly athletic, serious student who would make little difference in the household. That was not the case. Robert Trent was a young man so stellar in looks, persona, and charisma, he blinded everyone. He blinded Faith, who, from the very first day, had a stream of new emotions. Billy, two years behind Robert at Yale, felt admiration. Tommy and Emily were mildly awed.

As he became visible in the village and on the estate, Robert generated a lot of chatter. Many quibbled that life had been overly generous to the new summer resident. They didn't know he'd seen tragedy. Hope had noticed it immediately, from the way he'd taught the poetry class. She was surprised to see him again but quickly shut down the attraction and wasn't spellbound like the others.

◆ ◆ ◆

Six years before he set foot on the Seawatch estate, Robert Trent was on a path of privilege. He attended Saint Paul's School, located at 325 Pleasant Street in Concord, New Hampshire. That was the street address, but for Robert Trent, Saint Paul's was a state of mind meant to enfold him into a noble tradition.

Saint Paul's would catapult him into Princeton or Yale (he hoped Yale), and it would further catapult him into Yale Law and a good Yale firm. Saint Paul's was the school of governors and presidents and captains of industry. The curriculum was serious and sprinkled with religion and ethics, the big sport was ice hockey, the climate was harsh, and the winter air seared the lungs. He went home for holiday breaks but was relieved to return to his dormitory, with its low gabled ceiling and the beautiful light of the New Hampshire hills playing softly over all his belongings.

One morning, three months before graduation and with his acceptance to Yale firmly in hand, one of the deans came to his mathematics class and asked him to step out. "We've had a call from your mother," he said. "There's a situation with your father that is very public, and she wants you to go home for a few days. Your teachers can give you lessons to do while you are away."

"Can you tell me what's wrong?"

"I could, but I believe it's better if you hear it from your mother. It's delicate in nature."

"Is my father dead?"

"No. Your father is not dead."

He caught the next train that connected with the Boston line, which he then took into Pennsylvania Station in New York City. His mother was waiting for him when the train pulled in, and she appeared disheveled and drawn. Her eyes were red and had deep circles around them.

"Is Dad ill? What's wrong?"

"Your father is in legal trouble. The newspapers have the story on the front page, and I didn't want you to see it that way. I wanted to tell you what happened in private."

"What happened with what?"

"Your father has been accused of mishandling a large amount of money from clients in his firm."

"But it isn't true."

"He has pleaded guilty."

What they accused Simon Trent of doing was no worse than the insider stuff that went on every day on Wall Street, but Trent was set up to take the blame by thugs who threatened his family. He had no choice but to accept the blame to insure safety for his wife and son. Trent became the embodiment of the disgruntlement many felt with Wall Street. Here was proof that it was rigged against the little guy; finally someone was going to pay for that rigging.

Within two days, his father was taken away right in front of him, and as they shoved him roughly into the back of a black car, Robert saw one of the policemen twist his arm behind him. He heard the snap and knew that they had broken his father's arm.

Robert did not return to Saint Paul's, even though they offered him the opportunity. He felt tainted. He came from a thief and a liar, that was his heritage, although he never believed it. There was something worse. His mother had been an heiress to the Latham Woolen Mills fortune, but her father disowned her when she married Simon Trent. Now that hateful family would feel vindicated. His mother went to work, and he went to work, too. He worked in the Manhattan diamond district for Herschel, a Hasidic Jew who tended to speak in philosophical terms. "Hey, kid, you want someone to be nice to you, don't look here. There is no niceness in life. Just work."

One day, he was held up. A gun was put to his head, and the thieves demanded his sack. That day, he had nothing more than some silver rings and bracelets, and the thieves, expecting diamonds, were furious. They took him to an alley and punched and kicked him until blood came from his ears, and his nose was pressed into the cobblestones.

After that awful day, the bleakness began to lift. Yale did not rescind its acceptance letter to Robert. He was allowed to attend summer classes on the campus to make up the necessary credits and entered as a freshman in the fall of 1911. Among the four thousand students on campus, he didn't stand out as the son of Simon Trent, the thief of Wall Street. In May of 1912, as he wrapped up his freshman year, one of the operatives who had set up his father cooperated with the FBI in a plea bargain deal on a murder charge. He told them what they needed to know, and in a dismissive aside, also divulged that they had set up Simon Trent. Trent was freed and his name cleared. His old firm offered to take him back, but he declined. He had had enough of Wall Street and took a teaching post at New York University.

Yale gave Robert a special scholarship and recommended him for a coveted summer internship with the firm of Wentworth, Blanchard and Grunwald, one of the most prestigious law offices in New York. They had on their books Bethlehem Steel, E. R. Squibb & Sons, Columbia Gas & Electric, and Studebaker. Paul Wentworth happened to be on the board of the Muttonville Neighborhood Association. In addition to Robert's regular work that summer, Mr. Wentworth, the firm founder, asked him to travel to Muttonville every Sunday and teach a poetry class at the association.

It was Wentworth who evaluated Robert Trent before he returned to Yale. "We have three categories of achievement for our interns," he said and handed him a sheet of paper that itemized the categories.

1. Those who did a decent job and showed average interest in doing the work and interacted well with the rest of the staff.
2. Those who did an exceptional job, more than was expected and were an important resource for the rest of the staff.
3. Those who had an excellent work ethic and also a stellar lineage with social connections.

"You fit none of these categories, but you most closely resemble the third group," said Wentworth. "While you don't have the lineage or the connections, there is an intelligence and compassion. I've seen the way you interact with even the least educated clients and how you adjust to reach them in the right way. I see the look of relief on their faces. You communicate compassion without false sentimentality or irrational promises. That can be gold to the practice of law, and we want you for our firm. Finish up at Yale. We want to pay for law school, but it has to be at Columbia so you can keep one foot at the firm while you attend."

It was here that Robert realized he had to make Wentworth aware that his father had gone to jail. "There's something you should be aware of, sir," he said. "My father is Simon Trent and—"

Wentworth stopped him. "I know all about your father. Let's put all of that away. All you have to worry about is keeping yourself aboveboard."

By the fourth summer, before Robert entered law school, the senior man asked him for a favor. "I have an estate in Muttonville, and one of my neighbors, Asa Simpson, has a fine stable of polo ponies, but he never wins anything because his players are always second-rate. I want you to spend the summer there instead of interning here and ride for him."

Robert was familiar with Muttonville, having taught the poetry class. Teaching poetry and playing polo were two vastly different things. Robert didn't ride, but that wasn't an answer in this man's world. You were meant to accomplish the task by whatever means. That was part of the training at this level of success. "It sounds like a very good way to spend the summer," he said.

Now all that remained was to learn how to ride a horse and, after that, how to play polo.

Chapter Twenty

The forty-eight thousand subscribers to *Town & Country* magazine looked at the Thanksgiving-issue cover and saw Alice Simpson in a lace-fringed pale-pink *peau de soie* dress, a light-gray shawl loosely covering her shoulders. At her side stood her son, Billy, in a dark-blue suit, his blond hair neatly parted; and her daughter, Faith, who had her hair in loose curls and wore a drop-waisted pale-yellow sheath with a wide pleated hem. The subscribers approved. This was what they wanted of their aristocracy. They gazed approvingly at the manicured gardens and the ornate entrance gate of Seawatch and were satisfied that although London had their royals, America was catching up.

Woodrow Wilson, who resumed the progressive agenda of Teddy Roosevelt that had been briefly interrupted by William Howard Taft, was in the middle of his first term in the White House. One of Wilson's more controversial positions was that he supported tariffs that favored Europe.

"We'd better sell more milk, Joe," Asa told his dairyman. "President Wilson is trying to put us out of business. That's what we get when a sentimental schoolteacher is elected president. I never thought I would miss Taft."

"Yes, sir," was all Joe said.

Still, the country was in a good mood and successfully keeping out of the hellish war going on across the Atlantic. The battles were far away and not yet interfering with America's summer pastime, baseball. Walter Johnson pitched fifty-four consecutive scoreless innings, feeding the optimism that all was on an even keel.

What was changing dramatically was the county. Since the East River Tunnel had been completed and allowed a continuous commute right into Pennsylvania Station, the population of Nassau had almost doubled. The railroad's agent, Fullerton, had done a good marketing job selling the Sunrise Homeland as the new paradise for families. The commuter class was now a distinct classification. Suburbanization was in full swing and the word *mortgage* slipped into normal conversation.

What was changing at Seawatch had nothing to do with the government or with sports or suburbanization. Billy had crossed over to adulthood. He had finished a second year at Yale and a more confident man had come home for the summer. Faith, at seventeen, was on the edge of womanhood. Tommy had graduated and was enrolled at City College in Manhattan. Emma and Chester had a hard time imagining their boy would leave the house, but they were happy that he was too young to be called up should there be a war.

The person who had changed most of all was Hope Lee, and both Asa and Alice were sure they had had a hand in it. Asa's tutelage easily spilled over into fatherly attention. Alice had become used to having Hope in the house and, driven by her charitable impulses, continued to dress the girl well.

"The dressmaker is coming to measure Faith for summer dresses. She'll measure you, too. And we'll all get a hair trim for the hot weather. I've talked it over with Asa," Alice added, in case Hope refused her, "and he agrees."

"I'm growing out of all my clothes," said Hope.

Alice took that as agreement and breathed a sigh. The girl was a beauty, and she wore clothes well. Both Hope and Faith had grown a few inches and filled out. Hope still needed some practice with her table manners, but in every other way she was a beneficial addition to the household. By the time the warm weather rolled in, Hope and Faith had new wardrobes of skirts, shirtwaists, and colorful summer dresses. The girls and Alice had their hair trimmed and styled, but Hope's curls quickly reverted to their unruly state, a look that suited her.

◆　◆　◆

When Billy returned to Seawatch, Faith could see he was not the same. He was calm and assured. He looked different. He parted his hair in the middle and slicked it back. It was a man's haircut, and he wore it with confidence.

"How is everything here, Fey?" he asked. He was sitting on his bed changing shoes when she walked in.

"The same," she said quickly, but then changed her mind. "Maybe not quite the same. Hope has replaced you as Papa's favorite." Billy had gone on a ski trip with friends for the Christmas break, and Faith had not seen much of her brother since Thanksgiving.

"Good," he said without thinking.

"I thought when you left, it would be my turn, but it's not." She sat next to him on the bed.

Billy put his arm around Faith's shoulder. "Does it bother you?"

"What bothers me more is that Hope doesn't depend on me the way she used to. She doesn't get up and talk in the middle of the night. The more normal she gets, the more I miss the old Hope. I know I should be happy, but I liked it when she would crawl out of her bed and sleep on the floor next to me."

"Do you want her to leave?"

"I'm glad she's here, even if Papa really likes her. I like her, too."

"What about Mama?"

"Mama has the dressmaker come and make her clothes. You know that's what she likes to do. Hope's given her a chance to attend to the needy without leaving home."

The next morning, Billy saw the dynamics in the family first-hand. Hope was out early on the front lawn, setting up a croquet set. She took great care, measuring the distance between the wickets with a tape measure and laying out the course. She wore a light-green cotton dress with a square neckline and short bell sleeves. Her hair was loose, and her skin had a light tan, making her eyes more prominent. The haunted girl with mismatched mended clothes was gone. In that moment, he understood what his sister was up against. Without doing anything, Hope commanded the stage, and she wasn't even aware of it.

"Who's going to play?" he asked.

"The whole family."

"How are you going to get Papa to play?"

"He plays. Your mother likes it, too. If you want to play, we have to get Tommy here so it will be even."

"I'll be a spectator today," said Billy, not quite believing his father and mother would appear.

By eleven o'clock, they were all there. It was a scene worthy of a magazine. The lawn was perfectly groomed. The sun arced overhead. Even the geese that congregated on the lawns many mornings had left this portion clean and clear of their droppings. Asa was in shirtsleeves and had on sport shoes. Billy had seen his father dressed like this only when they had gone to Europe on the *Queen Mary*. His mother appeared in a sporty skirt, short-sleeved blouse, and a graceful straw hat to keep her face out of the sun. Faith appeared last, but eager to start.

Hope blew a whistle. They took their mallets and proceeded to push their balls through the wickets, hit the stake, and continue back. It was competitive and boisterous, and there was a great deal of good-natured groaning. To Billy's surprise, Asa had a good swing and quickly took the lead. Even more surprising, he was laughing. Just as Asa was about to finish a round, one of the dogs came running onto the field, took the ball in his mouth, and ran away with it. Everyone began to laugh. Billy had never heard his father laugh so heartily. Hope, who was also good at the game, hit her last stake and won the round. Everybody clapped, including Billy.

Hope shaded her eyes and looked at everyone. She was confused. Were these strangers suddenly hers? Did she have a family?

After he'd been home for a couple of weeks and Billy saw just how much time Hope spent with Asa, Faith asked her brother if it bothered him.

"It doesn't. I'm glad, in a way, in case I want to do something other than Wall Street. I know I do, but I wouldn't dare tell Papa. It would crush his plans."

"What do you want to do?"

"Now don't laugh because it sounds flimsy, but it really isn't. It's theater management."

"What do you mean?"

"It's the business side of putting on plays and musicals. Making sure the space is right for the production and that the expenses are met by the money that comes in. Yale happens to have one of the best drama departments. They even have a summer-stock theater, where they try out Broadway plays. I wanted to volunteer for part of August."

"That sounds very good to me. Why do you think Papa wouldn't approve?"

"He has his own plans."

"Why doesn't he put some of those plans on me?" said Faith.

"He doesn't see you as the type, Fey. I'm sure it's a female thing."

"Hope's a female, last time I saw."

"Hope has a hunger for it. I've seen her in there. She's glued to the tape and not only to recite the numbers. She's looking for clues and momentum and everything that Papa is looking for, and he didn't have to teach it to her. She just knows it."

"I think you're wrong about one thing. Papa doesn't want to see me as capable. He's already decided that I'm weak, and there's very little I can do to change his mind."

"I could talk to him."

"I think he likes it this way. He likes the idea that he's protecting me. It would be a disappointment to find out I'm as capable as his protégé."

The conversation was lighthearted, but Billy knew it was true. Faith was the smartest one in the tutoring class and could have leaped above the others, but that wasn't her style. She seldom was the first to answer. She was neither fragile nor nervous as she had always been painted. The marvel was that she'd stopped trying to convince anyone otherwise.

Billy worried that Faith took her lot so calmly. He wondered if one day his sister would realize what had happened and pick Hope up by the scruff of the neck and throw her out. He knew that was a silly image, but it came to mind from time to time.

"There are two people who know how smart and capable you are," Billy said. "One of them is me, and the other one is Hope."

Faith was thoughtful a moment. "Do you think Papa likes her more than he likes us?"

"Don't think that. We're his real children. Papa has no hobbies, and he doesn't like social gatherings. Hope's his diversion."

◆ ◆ ◆

Faith was certain Asa found it easier being with Hope than being with her. Hope could make her father laugh, and not over something funny. He laughed with delight when Hope made comments that surprised him. The thought that Hope delighted her father while Faith was seen as a burden made her squirm.

That was the last conversation Billy and Faith had on the subject of Hope that summer. The following Sunday, Robert Trent arrived at Seawatch, and Faith's attention and emotions were completely diverted.

Chapter Twenty-One

In preparation for his summer, Robert Trent researched the known facts of Asa Simpson. He had a wife and two children, a boy named William, who was two years below Robert at Yale, and a daughter named Faith, who was almost seventeen. Robert was excited at the prospect of spending the summer at the home of a man many considered a financial genius.

He started out at the Claremont Stables, which had horses you could rent to ride on the trail in Central Park. Once he got the hang of mounting and trotting at a mild speed, he went back to his alma mater. Yale had one of the oldest polo clubs in the country and a regulation-size indoor arena.

Polo, he learned, was an uncomplicated game played by gentlemen with skill and courage. It was also incredibly dangerous, although it was bad manners to say so. A player rode a horse at forty miles an hour while hitting a ball toward a goal. Meanwhile another gentleman rider would try his best to keep the first rider from continuing by using violent shoulder bumps and mallet checking. The only protected entity in the game was the "pony"—the deceptively cozy name given to adult horses that could trample you to death—whose legs were wrapped.

Knowing the dangers, and apprehensive at the prospect of being not only nudged but unseated by a seasoned defenseman and ending up under the horses' hooves, Robert soldiered on.

"You have to be strong," said the trainer. The trainer had looked him over.

"I'm strong," said Robert.

"You have to be polo strong."

Polo strong meant you had to control a horse, galloping along at forty miles or more an hour, while holding the reins in your left hand and a mallet in your right. Of course, holding the mallet meant nothing if you didn't use it to hit a small wooden ball along the unmarked path called the *right-of-way*.

The most humiliating aspect of the game was the handicap that began at minus two. If by some miracle you managed your horse so you could stop and whack the ball, another player with a better handicap could hook your mallet with his mallet and seriously interfere with your elation. Worse, he could physically connect with you and ruin not only your shot but potentially your life.

"What happens if someone shoulders you so hard you fall off the horse?" Robert asked the trainer.

"Don't call it a horse. It's a pony."

"I think they call it a pony because it sounds small and benign. In reality it's a one-thousand-pound horse, and if it fell on you it would probably kill you."

The trainer looked at him. "I don't know what you're asking. All you have to know is that they're called *ponies*."

"Good enough," said Robert. Apparently any attempt at humor was a violation. "What happens if you fall off the pony?"

"The other team gets a penalty. Don't worry about it."

"The penalty is small reward if you're trampled under the pony's hooves."

"That seldom happens. The horses play better polo than the people," the trainer said.

After a month of weekend lessons, Robert experienced an exhilarating moment when everything aligned in his favor. Galloping at top speed, he felt the head of his mallet whack the dickens out of the little wooden ball. That happened only once. The rest of the time, other players shouldered him viciously, hit his mallet so hard it flew out of his hand, or consistently stole the ball from him. Twice he fell off his pony, but luckily the animal had the good manners to ride away without touching him. In the end, he had to go to Seawatch with the little knowledge he had garnered because it was time to go and play the game. He would do his best. *Finesse* and *interference* were the words to live by, the trainer had said. "Ride with finesse and rebuff interference, and you will do fine."

Chapter Twenty-Two

Alice and Asa threw Seawatch open for Robert Trent, and although he was there to play polo, he also replaced Miss Hortense from the Piping Rock Club as a partner for tennis and all else that took place out of doors.

He arrived on a Tuesday. Faith, Billy, and Hope were at the bay, swimming and sunbathing with Tommy, Emily, and a crowd of students from the local high school who were celebrating their last day of class. In the middle of the boisterous afternoon, Robert Trent emerged from the bathhouse, walked straight toward the water, and proceeded to swim far into the sound. All movement on the shore was suspended. They watched his every stroke and waited until he walked back into the bathhouse before they continued their celebrations.

As they walked home, the three who belonged in the house still had no idea the swimmer was a guest at the mansion. They changed for dinner and went to their places at the table as always. Asa came in with Robert when they were all seated and introduced the newcomer. Faith's attraction was immediate, and she began to engage in complicated calculations. Billy tried to recall any meetings with Robert at Yale. Hope recognized him from the poetry class years before but said nothing. This was not the time or place. She was quiet, but inside she was churning. The girls didn't eat much of the excellent lobster au gratin served for dinner.

The next morning, Faith was at the tennis court, hitting balls against a practice wall, when she saw Robert walking toward her. She continued her strokes, but blood began to collect all around her ears, making a humming sound.

"Good morning." He looked at her with a pleasant smile and raised eyebrows, awaiting her response.

"I might be hopeless at this game," she said, in case he'd seen all the balls she had missed.

"That would make two of us. I'm going to confess. I'm here under false pretenses. I'm pretty average at tennis, and I had to take a crash course in polo before arriving."

"I don't mind," Faith said, "but why did you agree to come?"

"Besides the great opportunity of spending time with your father," he said, "Paul Wentworth told me to come here, and interns don't refuse the head of the firm, especially if the firm is about to pay for law school. Interns say 'yes, sir' and learn what they need. Did you know that polo is a hellish game?"

"Our team's not very good. Two stablehands play, and we borrow a couple of players from the Guggenheims. The stables are behind the house if you want to practice."

"I'll do that. Thank you. As long as we're here, let's do some volleying?"

"All right," said Faith and took her place at one end. She liked that he had confessed his inexperience to her. It was charming. He was charming. She felt light and happy and played better than usual.

She might have felt different if Robert Trent had confessed his other dilemma. He remembered Hope Lee right away. He remembered their conversation in the poetry class. Her quirky beauty had matured. He had wanted the luxury of examining her face at dinner without embarrassment, but that was not possible. He kept looking away as if someone were going to catch him at it. He didn't know what connection Hope had with the Simpsons, but he was already troubled by the effect she had on him.

"We've met before," he said to Hope when they were alone out of doors. He had been surprised to see her but also happy to know that he had the whole summer to get to know her.

"Keats," she said.

"Do you live here?"

"I'm a take-in. Asa Simpson has taken me in."

The way she said it made it sound like a carefree accommodation. She was no longer the struggling, hurt creature he'd wanted to protect. Every morning, when the tennis games began after breakfast, he looked for her, but only Faith came regularly and Billy occasionally. When he asked about Hope, Faith said she spent the mornings working with Asa. That was surprising, but then everything about her was surprising.

All the females of Seawatch and even those in the village soon saw or heard of Robert Trent, the good-looking Yalie who was summering with the Simpsons. He was well into his twenties and considered a grown-up, and he was not only athletic but also too good-looking to be believed. The attendance at the polo matches grew, and it was obvious that all of the girls were there to cheer him on. He was not the best player, but he played with heart and daring, and he earned the respect of the other players. Tommy, wary at first, gave him some leeway. Emily talked about him too much. She was not ashamed to admit what everyone was thinking. "Robert Trent is the best-looking man I've ever seen," she said to Faith and Hope. The three girls always grouped together on the lower bleachers at the matches and chatted between chukkers, the timed periods of play.

"Are you crazy about him?" asked Hope.

"I didn't say that. I just said he was good-looking. Don't tell me you don't think so?"

"I think so," said Faith quietly. Faith did not usually like to talk about her feelings to Emily, whose opinions she considered too simplistic, but she was relieved to be able to say out loud some of what she had been feeling and thinking.

Faith had not fallen in love with Robert Trent. What she felt for him was much stronger. It was an attraction that filtered out all else. She was attracted by waves of longing. Where did all this longing come from? She hadn't been aware of it until he appeared. When she awoke in the morning, there was a jolt of purpose—he was there. She wanted to be near him.

She knew that a dreamy lassitude was not what was needed. He must not suspect the depth of her feelings. She showed up daily for tennis practice, and later in the afternoon when she knew he would be at the stables practicing strokes, she was at the stables, too. She joined him but didn't say much. She put real effort into improving her tennis and riding. There was never more than a casual greeting and good-bye. He got accustomed to seeing her daily, and they developed an easy camaraderie.

He would be gone from Seawatch by mid-August, but Faith could not accept that as the end. She would find a way to stay in his orbit. Faith was realistic. She knew that all men had an advantage. They made the choices. She had to lead him to the right choice. Hearing Emily prattle about him was comforting. It put him within reach.

"I like him, though," said Emily. She stood up and waved down the iced-tea vendor who was wending his way between the bleachers. "He isn't stuck on himself. His eyes are nice. They're kind."

"I see something else," said Faith. "His eyes are sometimes sad."

"That's what makes him so attractive," said Hope. "His sad blue eyes are saying, 'something hurtful happened,' and then you want to kill whoever hurt him."

"Really? You want to kill whoever hurt him?" asked Faith, who was surprised to hear all these thoughts being spoken aloud.

"Well, that's just a way of speaking. I personally don't want to kill anyone. I'm just saying that look of his really gets into you."

The next chukker began and the girls sat down, sipped their tea, and continued their thoughts in private.

Robert Trent, unaware of the turmoil he was causing, went about his day with two objectives. To be the best polo player that his limbs could accomplish, and to quell the intense desire he had to embrace and kiss Hope Lee.

Hope had stared at Robert more than once to try to interpret the emotion in his eyes.

"Why are you staring at me?" he had once asked.

"Trying to find out secrets," she said lightly.

"Did you find any?"

"Nope."

"I'm safe," he said. There was always the hint of sarcasm in her responses, and he wondered why he evoked that in her. Usually that was a defensive maneuver. Was she trying not to like him?

The instructions given to him when he was recommended as the "summer visitor" at Seawatch were printed in bold letters on a piece of Wentworth's stationery.

Be friendly but never too friendly. In case you don't know what "too friendly" means, let me spell it out for you because it is a fine line that must never be stepped over. Friendliness, pleasantries, cooperation, and politeness are all the emotions that should be displayed. Any interaction that doesn't fit into those categories must be cut at the stem. That includes intimacy of any sort. Secrets, confidences, talk of the parents' social or financial

situation, any acceptance of money from the children. If in doubt, err on the side of aloofness.

Robert Trent mentally reviewed those rules each time he was near Hope. It wasn't only her manner, that careless indifference, that drew him in. It was the unusual combinations that made up her face and body, and the vitality she exuded. When he saw her in swimwear, he was surprised. For a slim girl, she had muscular calves and thighs. Like everything else about her, they excited him.

His fourth week at Seawatch, Robert went back to the city for a few days, and when he returned, he upset everyone by bringing a girl with him. She was a beautiful girl, and he put her up in one of the local inns. She came to the polo match dressed in a silk flowered close-fitting dress and a big floppy hat. During the game, she sat with binoculars and watched everything Robert did. At halftime, he went over to her, and she moved his damp hair off his forehead with her hand.

"Oh nuts," said Emily. "He has a girlfriend. That has to be his girlfriend."

"Maybe it's his sister," said Hope.

"Uh-uh," said Emily. "She touched him. His sister would not touch him like that. It's his girlfriend. I wish he'd kiss her. I would love to see him kiss her."

Faith was actually startled to hear Emily say exactly what she had been thinking. Even though she was disappointed to see that he had a girlfriend, she, along with all the other girls, watched the two with anticipation. It was like watching a film. They would have all been satisfied if he had taken her in his arms and kissed her. That night, Robert did not eat with the family, nor could he be found on the grounds the next day. Everyone had the same thought: *he was out with the girl.* What a lucky, lucky woman. He was back on Monday, and there was no sign of the girl. He was theirs once again.

"Who was that girl at the polo match?" asked Hope when she saw him on Monday. It was the end of a scorching day, and they were on the beach standing at the water's edge, cooling their feet.

"Someone I know."

"Of course it's someone you know. Is she your girlfriend?"

"That's hard to say. She's a girl and she's a friend."

"Are you going to marry her?"

"No. I'm not going to marry her."

"Does she know that?"

"I don't know. Why do you want to know all of this?"

"I don't know."

She did know why she was asking all the questions. Even though she had shut down her own interest, she was asking for Faith, who needed to know his status. She could reassure Faith that the coast was clear.

Before dinner that evening, Hope made sure to corner Faith. "Don't worry. He's not going to marry that girl." Hope could sense Faith's intense feelings for Robert and wanted to bring her that news and alleviate any disappointment.

"How do you know?"

"I asked him if he was going to marry her, and he said, 'No. I'm not going to marry her.' Even though he lets her touch him, I heard it from his own mouth. He's not going to marry her. The poor dumb cluck, she doesn't know it. She's probably dreaming about going down the aisle, and it's not going to happen."

Faith looked at Hope. "I feel sorry for the girl. Maybe she really loves him."

"I know you like him," said Hope.

"I do. And it's not just the looks and that stuff. He notices things, and he's honest, and he makes fun of the things he's afraid of."

"What is he afraid of?" Hope was surprised to hear this.

"Before he came, he had never played polo, and he thought it was dangerous." Faith looked at Hope. "What about you? Don't you like him?"

"No." She was going to say more but decided that was enough. "I have an idea. Why don't you tell him how you feel?"

"That would be impossible. Suppose he doesn't like me back? It would be humiliating. I would be too afraid. Wouldn't you be?"

"No. But that's because I don't like him. I can tell him anything."

"I'm happy when I'm near him, and I think about him all the time."

"I know you do," said Hope. "That's why I asked him about that girl."

"You're a strange, crazy girl, Hope Lee. Very strange. Very crazy. But you do bring back good information."

"At least you know there's no one else in the picture," said Hope.

"Yes, I do. Thanks to you." Faith was speaking lightly, but inside she felt a wave of love for Hope, who had understood her emotional need and was trying her best to protect her.

"I still think you should tell him."

"Oh, sure," Faith said sarcastically, "why don't I just do that? That's not the way it's done. Normally, the man likes what the woman has to offer and pursues her. What do I have to offer him?"

"I can't believe you would say that. To begin with—and this is not the most important thing, because that would be insulting—you are probably the heiress of the decade. Why don't you tell your father? He could do something about it."

Faith was horrified. "I would never tell my father. Why would you say that?"

"When you're up that high, marriages are arranged by the parents, like the queen of England or something. That's the way they do it, so why wouldn't your parents arrange it for you?"

"Stop." Faith did not want to hear another word. "I would never ever tell my father or mother about Robert. Never."

"That's up to you, but it's done that way lots of times, Faith, and maybe that's not a bad way to do it."

For several days after that, Faith thought of that conversation and while she still held to never mentioning her feelings to Asa, she couldn't help but be impressed with the way Hope attacked life's problems. She didn't see the obstacles—only the solutions, and her solutions were plucked from the most available source. She proposed an arranged high-level marriage. Faith began to think of the logistics. Paul Wentworth was Robert's boss and her father's good friend. It was almost a family thing. *Ugh. No.* How could she ever submit to that? How could Robert, when he had his pick of any woman he wanted?

◆ ◆ ◆

Later that week, during a lull in the dinner chatter, Asa asked, "Are you going into corporate law?"

"I know that's the obvious specialty," said Robert. "Wentworth has mostly corporate clients, but we have our share of other clients, even pro bono cases, and I have my heart set on being a trial lawyer. I like that the best."

"Excellent," said Asa. "But don't waste your talents bailing out the thieves of Wall Street."

Robert flinched. "Sometimes the thieves of Wall Street are innocent, and they need a good lawyer. My father was wrongly accused."

"Of course. My apologies. I should have remembered."

Both Faith and Hope became alert at this information. Here was the dark spot in his life. As Faith listened to her father approve of Robert Trent, her ideas about the future solidified. She was going to marry this man. Whatever it took, he was going to be hers.

Hope tuned out of the conversation. She didn't want to know about Robert Trent's future plans or how he was going to live his life. She had created a mental space where she could lock out any feelings. She had learned to do that early in life, and now it served her well. She knew if she opened the floodgates, her attraction for this man would engulf her, and she could not withstand any more havoc in her life.

◆ ◆ ◆

It was the happiest summer Asa Simpson could remember. One day in early August, he actually said it to himself. *I'm happy.* Life had become lighter, and there was new energy in the household. Although he was not big on sports, he was happy that his polo team competed at the Piping Rock Club on Sunday afternoons. And he also liked the croquet matches on Saturday mornings on his front lawn. He liked spending weekdays doing business from home and having Hope for company. He was happy with the obvious changes in his own children as they grew into adulthood. Even Alice was participating and spending more time with the family instead of rushing off to Brooklyn.

In the back of his mind, Asa was aware that a serious world war was raging in Europe, but so far the war had been good for American business. US Steel was soaring. England, busy fighting the Central powers, depended on America for loans and goods. New York was fast becoming a more important financial center. The isolationists were holding their ground and keeping the country from the fight. A part of Asa (and he was not alone) was fascinated with the air war and the pilots who flew the missions. If Billy ever had to go to war, Asa would be sure he was trained as an airman. Teddy Roosevelt, whose estate was less than five miles from Seawatch, was itching to send his boys, even to go himself, because of the air war. Air warfare was an exciting development, and the flying aces were glamorous.

What Asa was unaware of that perfect summer was that his daughter, Faith Celeste Simpson, had fallen in love. She looked healthy and energetic and participated in athletics more than usual, but he didn't connect her behavior to the salutary head rush of a girl in love. He also failed to notice that Hope Lee, his astute protégé, characteristically calm and unperturbed, was wound up tighter than a spring.

Chapter Twenty-Three

Faith never missed a morning at the tennis court and was always the first one there. She practiced against the wall, concentrating on every shot, determined to improve. Robert didn't come every day, but when he did appear through a copse of laurel bushes flanking the approach, her heart—already beating hard—would pound. The sound pulsed against her ears. She thought he could hear it. Thud, thud, thud. She always said hello, but continued to focus on her technique until the pounding faded.

One morning, he stood at the edge of the court and watched her. "You've really come along," he said. "Your backhand is strong. You could beat me now."

She was surprised that he'd noticed her progress. Was it just kindness? "Slow and steady," she said.

"Not that slow," he said. "Just a few weeks." His comment sounded sincere, and his eyes lingered on her face as if he had missed something and needed a moment.

She could have acted coy and elicited more compliments, but she shrugged. She had a plan, and coyness was not in it. "Thank you. Let's have a volley."

For the next ten minutes, Faith held her own in an impressive show of energy and concentration, and when they stopped, they were both breathing heavily. "Let's walk down to the shore and cool off," he said.

"Sure." This was the first time he had initiated spending free time with her.

They started off without speaking, arms swinging at their sides, walking off the heat of their exertion. It was a pleasant moment. As she walked, Faith felt the solidity of the muscles she had developed over the weeks. She felt happy having Robert Trent willingly beside her. He had reappraised her ability that morning. Maybe he had reappraised her as a person. His eyes had lingered on her face as if he were recalibrating her appeal. She would not analyze it. It was enough that it had happened.

They walked all the way to the far jetty that separated the Seawatch beach from the Creek Club next door. This was the place Hope visited many mornings, and Faith was relieved that she wasn't there.

"This is a beautiful spot," he said. "It's going to be hard to leave and go back to the city."

"Columbia is not that far. Once you get your bearings, you can come out again," she said.

"My free time is committed to Wentworth, but that's to my benefit. It's a great firm."

"Did you always want to study law? If I didn't know better, I would have seen you as a writer."

"I chose law deliberately. A good lawyer can right many wrongs. Most influential men I know started out as lawyers."

"My father didn't."

"Your father is a special case, Faith."

"Where do you want to put your influence? Politics?"

"I don't know yet. What about you? You have so much open to you. Where is Faith Simpson going to use her legacy?"

"Papa has never encouraged me to think that I have any special privilege. I don't know that I have a legacy."

"That's all very modest, but you do have a legacy, and the brains to use it."

"What if I just get married?" She hadn't meant to say that. Until he came along, that was the last thing she wanted to do.

"You won't 'just get married.' You're a package."

"Doesn't sound very romantic," she said lightly. "It sounds as if I'm going to blow up in someone's face like those party favors that throw confetti all over everything. I'm going to go to college next fall." She hadn't applied to any college yet, but she had mentioned it to Asa, and he had said they should talk about it. "I definitely plan to go. Probably right in the city. Barnard is an obvious choice."

"Good. Columbia is just across the street. They let the Barnard women sit in on classes."

Faith cupped her hand on her forehead to shield her eyes from the sun so she could look at him. "That's nice of them," she said. She already knew everything he had said. She made no mention of the other obvious fact. She and Robert Trent would be able to continue their friendship and take it as far as it could go. She was playing it just right with him, and it was progressing.

There were more morning walks to cool off after tennis. Not every day, but several times a week. Faith's nervousness dissipated, and she felt a new freedom. Whatever else might happen, a man she liked wanted to spend time with her. She could talk to him easily and honestly about her life, and he did the same.

"My mother came from a family like yours," he told her. "They were Lathams."

"From the woolen clothes?"

"Yes. The clothes came later—first there were mills. My grandfather and his brother were the founders."

"So you know what it's like."

"I've never met my grandfather. He's still alive, but he disowned my mother when she married my father."

She was shocked but didn't react. Her father would never do that to her, no matter whom she married. "Does it bother you?"

"All the time. Not for the status. But I know it still bothers my mother. She misses her brothers and sister. Her mother died, and she never got to see her."

"I'm sorry," said Faith, really moved. "I'm sorry."

That day, they continued the walk in silence, and when they got to the rocks, they sat down and stared at the far horizon without any more words. When they climbed down, Robert took her hand to steady her and held on for a moment before letting go. Faith felt his sadness, but she also felt a new excitement. Something new had passed between them.

Chapter Twenty-Four

There was a lot of natural beauty at Seawatch, and it was never more evident than on summer evenings, just as the light was turning but darkness had not yet slipped in. The estate children loved to swim at that time of day. Everyone biked the mile down to the water and rode back through the trails in the woods. They would stand at the water's edge, awkward in their swimming outfits, trying not to look at one another. Emily had developed early, and it was hard not to stare at her large breasts clearly outlined by her suit. Everyone privately eyed and approved of Faith's good legs and derriere. Tommy was tall and strong, with a good broad chest. Everyone was used to Hope's lithe slim body and her face, but the summer sun added a special glow to her complexion and lightened her hair. The surprise was her strong legs.

When Robert Trent swam, everyone wanted to swim, too. He wasn't as tall as Tommy but had a broad chest and muscled legs with a multitude of scars from his hockey playing at Saint Paul's. He always swam way out in a straight line and then came back the same way.

Hope was a good swimmer, although she had to learn from Tommy because she had never been around water. He had taught her in the early days when she lived at his house. He still kept an eye on her when she swam far out.

After her experiences with her cousins in Southampton, Faith had become a competent swimmer, although she didn't like to put her face in the water, and it still made her anxious.

One afternoon close to the end of the season, they all biked back to the main house after swimming. It was almost dusk. Hope left the others for a shortcut, wanting to stop by the stables and visit the horses. She had gone a ways but was still visible when her bike hit a rock. The impact sent her tumbling over the handlebars and dumped her on the ground. Her knee caught a jagged rock. Blood began to form and spread down her leg. She was dazed from the fall and sat on the ground getting her bearings.

Robert, who had seen the fall, rode toward her. "Are you hurt?" He swung off his bike.

"It's nothing. Just a small cut." Still dazed, she continued to sit on the ground.

He took her leg in his hands and looked at her knee. "It looks deep. We should clean off the dirt and bind it, or it will bleed all the way to the house. Here." He took out his canteen and poured a little water over the wound. "I have a handkerchief in my knapsack."

"All right." The moment he touched her, Hope forgot about the wound. Her body reacted with explosive speed. She could almost feel her blood racing, and it frightened her. He still held her leg firmly by the calf as he poured the remains of his canteen over the wound. When he was satisfied that the dirt was off, he wound his handkerchief around, lifting her leg as he placed the cloth underneath. When he was through, he continued to hold the fleshy part of her calf.

"Does it hurt?" he asked. The moment had become electric. He might as well have said "I want to kiss you."

She locked eyes with him and spoke almost in a whisper. "I don't know if it hurts. I feel numb."

He pulled her upright, and while he still had his arm around her waist, they stood close to each other, and he placed his lips over hers.

It was over in a second, a touch so brief it was hard to believe it had happened.

She decided to make light of it. "Now I don't have to wonder anymore," she said.

"Wonder what?"

"How it would feel to kiss you." He was used to her blunt responses, but it was still a jolt and he was silent. "Well, thanks for the water and the bandage. I'll be sure you get back your handkerchief."

"Do you want me to ride you home? You could sit on my handlebars."

"Nope, nope. I can make it. I'll ride standing so I don't put pressure on the knee."

She was off before he could say anything else, but when she reached the house and went to the bathroom to clean up, she began to tremble. She touched the place where his lips had been. She looked at herself. Her face was flushed and smudged with dirt. Two pebbles were embedded in her cheek, and when she took them out, tiny wounds appeared. She knew that the kiss could have been longer if she hadn't pulled away, but she hadn't wanted it to be longer. She wasn't ready. The feeling that would spring forth for this person was too strong. She was afraid of it, and she didn't want him to know. As long as he didn't know, she held the upper hand. One thing was certain. He would have kissed her for a long time if she had let him, and that was very unusual for the self-contained Robert Trent. She felt elated about that. She had provoked his feelings. If she had shown her own, the magic would have gone. That was life in a nutshell. The wanting of the thing was everything. Fulfillment lessened the thing desired. There was nothing to gain by giving in. Love could ruin your life. She didn't see the kiss as a betrayal of Faith, but nevertheless knew it was important that no one should know.

When they gathered at the dinner table, Hope was limping and her face had two welts. Faith caught a look that passed between Hope and Robert, and she knew something had happened.

"How's the leg?" he asked.

"It's fine," she said. "Mrs. Coombs gave me some gauze and adhesive to keep it together. She poured iodine over the cut, and I nearly passed out."

Faith watched them throughout dinner. Twice she caught Robert glancing at Hope, but Hope didn't glance back. She was looking at her plate too intently. Faith reviewed the afternoon. There had been nothing that would point to a moment of intimacy between Robert and Hope, yet the looks that had passed between them had emotional content. She felt dejected. Her plan to capture Robert could withstand many things, but maybe not Hope. Maybe she was imagining things. And anyway, in a couple of weeks, he would be safely at Columbia.

Hope stayed away from Robert after that day but took every quiet moment to examine the tremendous pull of love. Was this love? It was as if you had a terrible illness and the only cure was to be with the person. It was almost impossible to ever again look at Robert Trent objectively because he became a force, an idea, a hole in her being that begged to be filled. It was as if she had been deprived of something, and then it was there. She had been waiting for someone, but she hadn't known whom until he arrived. For her own good, she learned how to close off those thoughts. She would not be another of that summer's lovesick girls.

Chapter Twenty-Five

From the moment they saw each other that first day at Seawatch in the overly decorated dining hall, and especially after the brief kiss on the riding trail, Robert Emory Trent and Hope Lee set up a wall to displace the intense and immediate attraction they had for each other. He had thought of her often in the years since the poetry class. Now she was older, but the rules were the same. She was a girl in a room outside his sensory field.

Hope went through the same thinking. He was a man from the city who had come to teach them some sport that only rich people thought they needed to play.

It was only at the end of their summer at Seawatch, on the last day of his stay, that their guard was down and they saw all they might be to each other. When he came to say good-bye, she was on the lawn playing with one of the terriers. The dog was jumping up, and she sat on the grass while he licked her face. Robert watched her for a few minutes and felt both longing and loss. What was he to do with these feelings? He was on his way to law school. She was someone's take-in, a charity case if he were to put it bluntly—even though she didn't behave like it. There was nothing here for him. He would say good-bye.

"Hope, I came to say good-bye. I'm not going to be coming here anymore."

"Did we learn everything you know?" Her voice was uncharacteristically soft, and there was no hint of her usual challenging tone.

"Not only that, but I learned something from you," he said.

"Oh? What was that?"

"Your honesty is startling, but I'll take it any day over polite small talk."

"Not sure I know what you're talking about, but that's OK. So I won't see you anymore, is that it?"

"I don't want to say that. If you're ever back in New York City, be sure to look me up."

"You'll be at the top of my list."

He couldn't leave it at that. At the very least he could shake her hand. She stood and smoothed her skirt. "Well, good-bye." She reached to take his hand, but the touch was so electric they both pulled back. Touching was not something they could endure. It was best to keep their hands at their sides and simply say good-bye.

Chapter Twenty-Six

Faith envied Tommy's relationship with his parents. Chester and Tommy often spent afternoons with their heads under the hood of a secondhand car Chester had bought. They tinkered amiably without a thought about their relationship. She had never spent an entire afternoon doing something with Asa.

That last summer before college, Tommy had wanted to make as much money as he could before leaving home. He worked behind the counter at the hardware store, and he also had his own side businesses. He would order a hundred newly hatched chicks, coddle them along for a while, then sell them for fifty cents apiece. Faith would often watch Tommy tend to the chicks. It seemed like an easy and foolproof way of making money, and she saw an opportunity to get Asa's attention.

"Can you order me some chicks?" she asked Tommy. "I want to go into the chicken business."

Tommy just shook his head. "What do you need a business for? You don't need the money."

"Don't ever say that, Tommy Rowland. Money is always good to have. I want to have an enterprise. Maybe I'll be good in the chicken business. You can tell me what to do."

"Huh. Your father's a better one to ask than me."

"I don't want my father to know anything about this. Order me one hundred chicks. How much are they?"

"A nickel apiece. Five dollars plus transportation. Six altogether. Where are you going to keep them? Joe Stokes won't let 'em in the cow barn."

"Can't I keep them with yours?"

"I guess. But you have to watch them carefully, especially the first week."

"Keep them with you, but I'll do the work. You just show me what to do."

The chickens came a week later. Tommy told her to take the chicks inside and keep them warm. She intended to do it, but there was a severe thunderstorm. When the rain let up, she went to look at her new charges. Tommy was waiting for her. "The chicks drowned in the storm. I told you to take them inside. They're all dead."

Faith was surprised at how quickly her enterprise had failed, but she wasn't daunted.

She asked Tommy to order a new batch. Losing the chicks was a lesson learned. When the new crop arrived, Faith found a warm spot in the garage and kept her eyes on them. Tommy warned that losing 10 percent was normal, but Faith didn't lose a single one. She bargained for the feed and got it for four dollars. When she sold the young hens a month later, she had a profit of forty dollars. She gave Tommy four dollars of her profit. "You're the middleman and should get ten percent of my profit."

Tommy was impressed. "You want me to order you another hundred?"

"No," said Faith. "I've done that. I want to do something else."

"You can go into the bait business. Sell worms."

"Get me the worms."

The success with the chicks inspired Faith to write a letter to Robert Trent. She didn't want him to forget about her, and a letter about her enterprise would be just right. He would be amused to learn that rain-drops could murder baby chicks.

> *Dear Robert,*
>
> *Without the diversion of your presence, I've turned to commerce for amusement. I asked Tommy to order me one hundred baby chicks that he assured me I could sell for ten times the price if I fed them for a couple of weeks. The first batch he ordered I left in the yard and a thunderstorm drowned them in the first hour. I have the image of a hundred little mouths open to the sky for a drink. And then, poof. Lights out.*
>
> *I stayed glued to the second batch and they were able to reach adolescence and bring me a good profit. Now, we are on to a new commodity. Bait. More reliable. Less work. Smaller profit.*
>
> *Greetings from Seawatch.*
>
> *Faith*

He wrote her back within two weeks.

> *Dear Faith,*
>
> *Thanks for the lesson in market diversification and cost control. For my manslaughter defense class, I put the accused in the baby chick business and, with the details you supplied, defended him successfully. I find it especially charming that Asa Simpson's daughter is not above find-ing new revenue streams. Please send more case studies.*
>
> *With admiration,*
>
> *Robert Trent*

She read the letter until she could recite it by heart. She parsed every sentence for additional meaning. *Charming* had been the only intimate word. He found her charming, and he admired her enterprise.

Faith sometimes daydreamed that her father would find out about her business success and come to her full of love and admiration. Perhaps Trevor, Asa's driver, who had seen the chicks in the garage, would mention her enterprises during the drive to New York. She imagined Asa would come into her bedroom before she went to sleep and tell her how proud he was of her. It didn't happen. October turned into November without a mention from either her father or her mother.

Robert and Billy were gone, and Faith, who was setting the stage for changes in her life, was taking stock of the climate at Seawatch. Hope still had her space in the inner sanctum of Asa's office. She sat in the leather armchair and read aloud to Asa. Faith often heard them evaluating business ideas as if they were partners.

"Huge volume in Duke Power."

"I would bet on anything headed by Buck Duke," Asa would say. "He's gone into the power business now that the court broke up his tobacco trust."

Asa would sit at his desk reading reports and the business news but also listening to Hope's comments. More than once, Faith had heard Asa say something like, "What you just said about broadcasting is absolutely right. Mass communication might be the next big thing if they can get it to work. RCA has been inching forward. I think it's time we got in."

Hope elicited a playfulness and delight that had never been a part of Asa's personality. Like a sorcerer, she had reinvented Asa. He often invited Faith to join them, but she declined. She didn't feel up to grappling for attention.

When Billy came home for breaks or holidays, Asa would invite him, too, but Billy would demur. "Papa, you have a living, breathing stock-market machine right here in Hope. This is the one you want to guide you. Maybe when I finish at Yale, I'll be able to compete with Miss Smarty-Pants." Billy said all this with admiration for Hope, not with resentment.

Despite not getting Asa's attention, Faith continued with her enterprises. She liked making money on her own. When she had amassed four hundred dollars, she began to study the business pages of the *New York Times* and the *Wall Street Journal*. This was probably a quicker way of making money. She asked her math tutor to invest her money in the stocks she picked and to do so in secrecy. Throughout the next few months, Faith bought and sold stocks with a simple formula of taking in their historical highs and lows, their recent trading range, and the stability of the dividend they sent to shareholders. It was a very good year for the markets, and with this straightforward approach, Faith easily doubled her money. She was playing with real money and it was growing, while Hope was merely playing. Faith had something else. She had three letters from Robert Trent and had, with her father's consent, applied to Barnard.

Asa talked of renting something in New York City for the winter months. Her mother had gained some stature in one of her Brooklyn charities and was back to spending much of her time with her relatives. Faith wondered at her father's patience with an absent wife. She knew men and women did things in the bedroom, and while women may have submitted out of duty, men were compelled and had to do them or become ill.

She had heard Tommy tell this to Hope and Emily. Emily said it wasn't true about the women doing it out of duty. Her mama and papa kissed each other every day and embraced when he came in from work.

"I'm not talking about kissing and embracing," said Tommy. "I'm talking about something they do in bed."

"I know," said Emily, holding her ground. "I'm talking about that, too."

They stared at Emily. Who would have thought that Miss Prim and Proud would talk about sex in such a carefree way? They all spoke more freely to each other, knowing it was the last year they would be together. Tommy's life had already changed. He was studying accounting at City College, bartending at night, and living with two other boys from the village in a cold-water apartment. Childhood was over, and they had to go out into the world.

◆ ◆ ◆

One day, as Hope and Asa stood together in his office, he noticed that Hope was already as tall as he. That particular day, he realized he was facing a young woman. He had not given much thought to what would happen when Hope reached adulthood.

She had to go out into the world, especially since Faith would be leaving for Barnard. When Robert Trent had lived with them, Asa had often caught him looking at her. At first, he saw it as negative. He knew that Trent had a big future in mind, and any interest he might have for Hope would be superficial. Robert might even think he could use her. Asa would make short work of that. Yet later in the summer, as he had a better assessment of Robert Trent, his thinking modified. Robert was ambitious, and any marriage would more than likely be evaluated as a fit for his career. Even so, he and Hope might be a good match. Asa didn't see Robert as a snob who would balk at her background; he had just enough kinks in his past to make him accept Hope. Besides, she was beautiful and smart. What more could you expect in a wife? Maybe Asa was prejudiced because he knew her so well. Nevertheless, it would make him feel better if Hope was settled and her future safe.

"Faith will be in college next year. Does that idea interest you?" he asked Hope. "I could send you, but there are many excellent free schools. Tommy's going to one. I could give you a stipend to help with rent and food. How does that sound? You've grown up, and soon you'll want to have a life outside of here."

"Are you going to kick me out?"

"Not tomorrow," said Asa, "but we have to think of what comes next. If not college, does marriage interest you at all? I was thinking I might try to find you a suitable beau?"

Hope jumped out of her chair and went to stand at the door. "What? If you had put a gun to my head, I would not have expected to hear that from you." She shook her head in disbelief. "You're looking to marry me off to some beau?"

"Eventually your life will change. Faith's and Billy's lives will change. People grow up, and things don't remain the same. That's the way life is."

Hope went to her chair and sat down. "I guess. I guess I'll have to make something of my life. I can't expect you to keep me forever."

"That's not the point. The point is I want you to have a full life, and that couldn't happen here. I thought if we could find a suitable young man, you could make a home together."

Almost out of the air, she plucked the name. "You mean a young man like Robert Trent?"

"Yes, as a matter of fact. He came to mind."

"No, no, no. He is not suitable at all."

Asa was not on solid footing. "Has he done anything you didn't like?"

"Oh no. Not at all. He's nice enough. He's more than nice."

"Let's give the idea time," said Asa. "At least I've introduced it. We don't have to do anything right away."

"Good," said Hope. "Good."

Asa decided to talk about it with Alice and see if she had any thoughts. Women had a good sense of these things.

"I was thinking that Robert would be a good match for Hope," he told his wife that evening. "She's growing up, and I would feel better if she had the prospect of marriage before she leaves."

"Really? Robert for Hope?" Alice was surprised. "What made you think of him?"

"She'll need someone strong. They're both smart. She has some rough edges, but he can smooth them out."

"Hope and Robert would make a dazzling couple. We could have the wedding here, don't you think? Maybe out of doors. Yes, out of doors."

Asa put his palm out to stop his wife. "I've only thought of this in the last few days. Hope could have totally different plans. And Robert, I think, wants to conquer the world. Let's not say anything just yet."

◆ ◆ ◆

It would have remained that way, just an idea floating in the air, if Alice hadn't shared it with her daughter.

"Your father wants to marry Hope off, and he's thinking of Robert Trent."

If her mother had shot an arrow through her head, Faith could not have been more startled and confused.

"What? Papa said this?"

"Yes. Hope's growing up, and she can't stay here forever. He wants to see her protected by marriage."

"To Robert Trent?"

"He mentioned that name. What do you think?"

Faith found it difficult to answer her mother's questions because a terrible anger was exploding in her head. "I don't think anything," she said. "I have no thoughts about that." She left her mother and walked out of the house. Why hadn't they thought of Robert for her? Why was Hope their priority? She felt too agitated to stay still and began to walk briskly toward the shore. At the turn where the creek emptied into the bay, she spotted Tommy digging clams and walked over.

She stood at the edge of the muck, watching until he looked up.

"Hey."

"What are you doing home?"

"I had a long weekend."

"I want to talk to you," she said.

"OK. Talk while I do this."

"No. This is important."

He looked up. "OK." He stuck the rake in the goo of the creek and came to where she was standing. "What's wrong?"

"I don't know where to start. Do you have any feelings about Hope, good or bad?"

Tommy thought. "Mmm. Not bad. Annoyed sometimes by her behavior."

"OK. What about how she's totally taken over Papa now that Billy's gone?"

"Well, that's more your problem. It doesn't affect me."

"You're right. It is my problem and it only gets worse, but I'd managed it because I had something better to distract me."

"What was that?"

Faith hesitated and looked at Tommy to see if she could risk baring her feelings about Robert Trent. "Tommy, you have to be my confidential friend now that Billy's gone."

"OK. What's going on? What's been distracting you?"

"I'm crazy about Robert Trent, and he seems to be warming up to me. Now Papa has told Mama that he's thinking of claiming him as a husband for Hope." Faith exploded into the sobs of anger she had held in since leaving the house.

Tommy wiped his hands on his trousers. He wanted to pat Faith's shoulder, but he was caked with muck. "That's a terrible thing to happen. Hope probably doesn't even want him, and here your father's just throwing him over to Hope like a piece of meat."

Faith stopped crying, surprised by Tommy's immediate understanding. "Yes. That's it exactly. It's the way Papa treats her that's the problem.

Since Billy left, it's become worse. I want her to go, Tommy. I want her to go before she decides to take Robert along with Papa."

"Wow." Tommy said it softly as if he was just getting the whole picture and was surprised at the crisis. "Emily saw it all from the start."

"What do you mean?"

"Emily always saw Hope as a taker without any conscience or gratitude. I don't think that's true, but people treat Hope as if she deserves things. It's not always her fault."

Faith had never thought much of Emily, but in this instance, she was grateful for the opinion. "It's time for Hope to go," she said again. "She's old enough."

"Are you sure? I thought you were thick as thieves."

"The way it is now, I can't feel good about her. I'm going to find a way to make her go, and I'm counting on you to help me."

"You won't need any help," said Tommy. "Just don't leave any holes for her to wiggle back in." Tommy had no idea why he added that, but it was the most important thing that Faith heard. Hope had to leave in a way that left no room to come back.

In his lessons about European history, Mr. Knudsen pointed out Great Britain's overbearing habit of planting the British flag in a territory and, with little to back it up, annexing it for England. It was called *imperialism*. Hope had planted her flag in Asa's office and declared the territory for herself. Now Faith's mesmerized father was going to gift Hope with Robert Trent. Faith felt infuriated and sad at the same time, that someone she had wanted so much could be taken away from her without a thought. Some days, she was afraid it had already happened, and they were keeping it a secret. Suppose her father had already arranged it.

During classes, Faith no longer made excuses for Hope's inability to sit still. Only the three girls were in the room, and Hope's behavior had more of an impact.

"Sit down," she said sharply one day. "I can't concentrate with you circling around like a caged animal."

Hope, surprised by the tone, sat down immediately and stayed in her chair.

Faith began to see Hope's indifference as selfishness, or worse, entitlement. Couldn't she see it bothered everyone and wasted time? The annoyance tore away at her affection for Hope. She could feel the resentment as a physical thing—ping, ping, ping—coursing through her body, sometimes in her head, sometimes in her heart, sometimes in her ears. When Tommy came home for Thanksgiving she went to him to talk about a solution.

Her successful streak of moneymaking had given Faith some confidence. She had to take control of her life. Hope had to leave, and not on good terms. Faith knew how to do it, too, and Tommy would help her.

Chapter Twenty-Seven

The pairing of the scion and the street girl unraveled in a classic denouement. Something went terribly wrong.

The old guard of tycoons with their string of estates dotting the North Coast had a band of secrecy that was unbreakable. Banks had begun to pool depositors' money and bought large blocks of stock with their insiders' edge and usually produced healthy profits. They took their cut and provided a good return to their investors. The success of this buying and selling depended on secrecy and the order in which the bankers conducted their business.

Each month, the tycoons would meet, discuss their holdings, and take turns selling off large lots so that each could unload a particular stock at a profit. They would decide who would sell first, second, third, and so on. Asa participated in this group and liked the safety and efficiency of the process. There was always the odd public event that thwarted their plan, a sudden tariff from Congress, a production mishap, a strike, war in some part of the world. For the most part, however, everyone in the circle could sell without any of the group getting hurt.

After each meeting, Asa jotted down what they would sell, who would sell, in what order, and the number of shares. They always sold off in pre-entered small lots so as not to call attention to the source of the sale. This month, Asa was first on the list, and he was going to sell his forty thousand shares of Bristol Machinery. They all knew that the dividend would be lowered at the next board meeting, and this was the time to take profits. Asa tucked the list into a corner of his desk blotter as he did after every meeting. Faith knew the list would be there. She had seen it many times. She knew she had what she needed to bring Hope down, and Tommy was going to help her.

"You need to do me a favor. It's complicated and important."

"What is it?

"Oh, and I'm paying money for it."

"How much?"

"As much as you want. I want you to get in touch with a certain man and give him information."

"What kind of information?"

"About a stock that's going to be sold."

"Is this going to make your father mad?"

"Yes, but not at us."

"At whom?" The minute he said it, he knew who it was. "Hope. Have you really thought about this?"

"Yes," she said tersely, as if it were an unnecessary question. They were outside, and the sun was in her eyes. She squinted and looked up at Tommy.

Tommy was jolted by Faith's depth of feeling, but he understood. He, of all people, knew how Hope had taken advantage of Faith. It angered him over and over how Hope never saw how her actions affected others. "I'm sorry," he said. "I get the picture and I would like to help you, but I can't go against your father. It would be like hurting my own mother and father." He was also aware of how Emma was attached to Hope, but he didn't mention that part. "Maybe we can think of a better way," he said.

"No. It has to be so bold that there's no forgiveness. It has to be unforgivable."

Tommy wouldn't bend, though, so Faith said, "Fine. I'll do it myself."

It was breathtaking how quickly and well it all worked. The receiver of the insider information was the market maker in the stock. Once he was assured of the validity of the information, he began selling all the shares he could accumulate on the overseas exchanges, and by the time Asa's submitted market orders were executed, one after the other the next morning, the stock opened twenty-five points lower. Once the sales were completed, bringing the stock down another ten points, it began to go up again as the market maker scooped up the depressed shares.

Asa, who seldom showed anger, was furious. He knew what had happened and immediately thought one of the men at the meeting had leaked the information. That was hard to believe because they were all poised to sell after him. He saw the notations from the meeting on his desk and noticed one of Hope's notebooks on the floor.

He sat at his desk for a long time, turning the facts over and over. It was a significant loss, but even if it had been a small one, it was the loss of confidence that was the point. He felt a physical heaviness over his back and shoulders. He had sheltered her, and more than that, he had connected to her and felt an inexplicable closeness that was new for him. She had brought lightness and laughter back into his life.

Sadly, he had not done the same for her. He knew it was her early life that was behind this stunt. Maybe she had done it for a payoff, maybe she had done it to prove her know-how. He had not been able to leach the street mentality out of her. He had banked heavily on her loyalty and discretion. Everything else was in place, but without trust, it didn't work. He had sheltered her for more than four years, and now she had to leave.

She walked into his office as always, but he didn't greet her with the usual warmth. He just looked at her.

She sat down next to the ticker machine without talking.

"You have to leave us," he said.

At first, she didn't understand. "No, I don't," she said. "I can stay as long as you want."

"I can't keep you anymore." He held up the pad with the notes on Bristol Machinery, but her expression didn't change.

Watching her puzzled and wide-eyed face was not easy. Asa had some paternal love for this girl. It pained him to think of her future out in the world alone, but trust was the one thing that was inviolable. She asked no questions and offered no resistance. That was her way and one of the things he admired about her. She took everything at face value and didn't buckle. Her face, at that moment, brought tears to his eyes. He would send her off with a bit of money to tide her over.

"Good-bye, Hope," he said and turned his chair to face away from her.

It was Mrs. Coombs who gathered her things and told her the details. "You shouldn't have done that to Mr. Asa."

"What? What did I do? I don't know what anyone is talking about." She thought about the notepad Asa had held up, with his notes on Bristol Machinery. Did this have something to do with that? Had information leaked somehow?

"You'll have a nice long train ride to figure it out," said Mrs. Coombs, and Hope knew she didn't believe her.

There was an envelope with fifty dollars, and Mrs. Coombs found an old suitcase of Billy's. She gave them both to Hope. "Trevor will take you to the train station."

"I guess you're not too sad to see me go," Hope said.

"I don't like to see Mr. Asa going through a disappointment when he put his trust in you."

"I didn't do anything," Hope said calmly. "This was a good home for me, why would I do something like that? I loved being with him. I loved it every day."

"You learned ways in the street when you were young, and those ways stay with you."

"I didn't learn any ways. I learned to take care of myself because I had to. I don't know what ways you're talking about. You mean to betray Asa? I learned how to betray Asa? How do you figure that?"

"Don't tell me you didn't benefit from the information? You're more clever than that. There must have been some reward."

"There was no reward because there was no crime. I've done a lot of things because they were necessary to stay alive, but I did not tell anyone about Mr. Asa's plans with Bristol Machinery. I did not, and anyone who thinks I did has it wrong."

Mrs. Coombs was taken aback at this declaration because it sounded true. She wasn't sad to see Hope go, but maybe they had judged her too quickly. "Who else could have done it? Tell me, who?"

"I don't know," she said, although at that moment she thought of Faith.

"Then you are out of luck."

"Somebody didn't want me here anymore. Maybe Faith was done with me."

Mrs. Coombs recognized then that Hope was not the culprit. But unfair or not, perhaps this was the best way to end it. Mrs. Coombs had seen a lot of bad behavior at Seawatch. She had seen the lack of love for Faith from both her mother and father. She had seen the obsession with Billy, and she knew that sooner or later Billy would break his father's heart. She looked at the girl before her, and her feelings softened. "You'll be all right. You have the skills you need to survive. Be glad everything wasn't handed to you." She reached into the pocket of her smock and pulled out a ten-dollar bill. "Take this. You'll need it, and I know you'll make it go a long way. I wish you well."

Hope declined the bill. "I know you think I'm a taker. That I take whatever I can get, but you're wrong, and I won't take your money. Who knows what's going to happen next, but you won't have me to blame."

She knew there was no saying good-bye to Asa. He wanted to be rid of her without any emotional scene. She felt worse not seeing Faith.

How could it be that within a few hours, they would be completely separated? She could tolerate that Asa thought she was a thief and that Mrs. Coombs thought she was a taker, but she could not bear Faith's rebuff. The thought of it made her eyes fill up. There was only one person who would still like her. She could not leave without going to Emma Rowland.

When she came near the house, tears welled up again, and she stayed outside until she could control herself. Emma saw her through the window and came out. She said nothing, but took Hope in her arms and held her for a long time.

"You're like my daughter. I know you didn't do anything. You're a young woman now, and you'll make your way more easily in the city. Promise me you'll be careful, especially with strangers."

"But I'll only know strangers." Hope was smiling through her tears.

"Oh Lord. That's true. Please be extra careful."

"I'll try." She looked away for a moment to control herself. "Emma, you are the best person I have ever known besides my mama. I will remember you."

Emma pursed her lips and nodded. She handed Hope a paper bag. "There's some food for you to eat on the train. It isn't much, but you'll be happy to have it. Let me know how you're doing from time to time." She turned and went inside the house.

When she opened the bag on the train, Hope found a ham sandwich and a piece of apple pie. Tucked separately was an envelope with twenty dollars and a card. *From your friend, Emma Rowland.* Hope cried almost all the way to New York, but right before she went through the tunnel, she remembered to eat her ham sandwich.

Chapter Twenty-Eight

Flight was still in its infancy, but Asa could see how it would change the world, much like the railroads had changed the country a hundred years earlier.

New aeronautical feats and testing took place less than twenty miles from Seawatch. Asa, who didn't like small talk, enjoyed any discussion on the minutiae of aviation and would stand for hours at the fairgrounds every time a flying stunt was advertised. His colleagues, especially Guggenheim, were as besotted as he.

The rich men who were realists about all else had a romantic view of flying aces—Germany's Richthofen, the ace of aces, was legend. The flimsy planes they flew and the incredible skill needed to outmaneuver a daring enemy made their exploits all the more startling.

Asa had known it was only a matter of time before America entered the war. When Germany sank the British liner *Lusitania* in 1915, 128 Americans were lost. Then, starting in 1917, the attacks were no longer isolated events. Germany attacked every commercial ship en route to Britain. American ships were regularly damaged or sunk, and the hostilities could no longer be ignored. On April 2, 1917, the US Senate voted 82 to 6 to declare war on Germany.

Even before war was formally declared, the tycoons yanked their sons out of Yale and Harvard, trained them as an elite squadron of airmen, and sent them to France to fight with the Allied powers. It was odd that with all of his devotion to Billy, Asa would have been so eager to send him to war, but he and the others were blinded by the idea of airplanes dogfighting in the sky. They wanted their pilot boys to become flying aces and return from war glorious and triumphant.

Teddy Roosevelt sent four of his boys to fight for democracy, including his youngest, Quentin. Like his hero, Asa sent Billy with pride and excitement. This would surely make a man of Asa's son. The select crew trained on the Hempstead Plains, where the Jennies—JN-2 training planes—treacherous and unstable, lined up in perfect formation . . . if no wind was blowing. Floyd Gibbons' rapid-fire radio dispatches painted a romantic picture of heroics, without the deadly reality of hundreds of thousands of casualties.

"I'm afraid, Fey," Billy had said more than once to his sister. "I don't trust the planes. They gyrate wildly, and I'm not that good a pilot."

"Tell Papa. Tell him you don't want to go."

"He has his heart set on it. This one thing has caught his interest, and I'm the one that can make it happen. I'm his flying ace."

Billy did not like flying at all. It made him throw up every time. He told Faith all the boys threw up, but they didn't want to disappoint their fathers.

The night before he was deployed, Billy went to his sister's bedroom to say good-bye. Faith was already in her nightgown, and she made a place on the bed for her brother.

"I wish you had told him."

"He never asked me if I wanted to go. He's never asked how I feel about things. I hated the Knickerbocker Greys and I hate flying, but Papa never gave me the option of not doing either of those things."

Billy lay back on Faith's bed, and she lay next to him with her hand in his. "We could run away and come back when the war's over. I have money saved up. Seven hundred and forty-eight dollars. You can have it all."

He turned on his side, and their faces were only inches apart. "Do you wish Hope was still here? Do you miss her?"

"I did in the beginning," Faith said. "But at Barnard there'll be lots of girls to be friends with."

"Hmm." He looked into his sister's eyes. "I want you to promise something."

"Sure. What?"

"Be happy, Fey. Take what you need to be happy no matter what. Just take it. That's the only way to overcome all of this."

Faith didn't quite know what he meant by "all of this." Maybe he meant their parents or the fact that their father was so wealthy. She did know what he meant about taking what she needed, and that was an easy promise. She needed Robert Trent, and she would find a way to take him. Billy fell asleep in her bed and she did, too. When she woke up in the early morning, he was gone.

◆ ◆ ◆

Billy went down first. Barely two months in, but incredibly, he already had three confirmed kills of German aircraft. He was shot down during a dogfight over the Marne. At Seawatch, it was a beautiful Indian summer day and the family had a picnic supper at the beach pavilion.

Roosevelt's son, Quentin, just twenty, had one confirmed kill of a German aircraft before he would go down a few months later, shot out of the sky by a German Fokker near the village of Chamery, France.

Hazelhurst Field was renamed Roosevelt Field, but it wasn't enough consolation for Teddy, who died six months after his son. Asa would have been relieved to die, but it did not happen that way. The day the news came of Billy's death, no one believed it. There was surely a mistake in identification. It just couldn't be. When the military asked to return Billy's remains home to his father, an inescapable weight descended on Seawatch. It didn't matter that Billy had distinguished himself in the air. He had done what his father wanted. No one could bear to look at Asa, who tore at his clothes and choked out the most heartbreaking sobs. There was no solace to be had, and it was many days before he could or would speak to anyone. Alice was afraid to go near her husband and went to Brooklyn. Seawatch was tainted and alien. In a moment of clarity, Alice knew that Asa needed to be alone with his grief. Faith stayed and sat outside her father's office, keeping a vigil. She needed to hold on to someone, but there wasn't anyone available. Her father could not be touched. It would scorch his skin. He would disintegrate. She would have done anything to have Hope by her side.

Over and over, she heard Billy's words: *I'm afraid.*

She had gone to Tommy and wept unashamedly against his shoulder and asked if he had any word from Hope. He shook his head. Hope had been swallowed up by the outside world, just as Billy, her beloved brother, had been swallowed up by death. How could that be? *How could that be?* "Billy, it's me. Fey," she would say hoarsely, her throat raw from sobbing. "Please call me Fey just one more time."

She went to his room and saw that the bed still had an imprint from the last time he had sat there. She sat exactly on the spot and stayed still until she almost fainted with fatigue and thirst.

Chapter Twenty-Nine

Alice returned to Seawatch, no closer to unraveling her grief than when she left. Days after learning of Billy's death, having seen the narrow flag-draped casket, having touched the few personal items the military had returned to her (including his watch that had stopped at 3:18 p.m., possibly the moment he died), Alice could not mourn. Each time she tried to access the place in her chest where her grief must reside, she would freeze up. At least once each day she would sit on Billy's bed and play images of her son in her head. They were vivid and realistic. She could re-create Billy with no trouble, but her emotions did not respond.

She felt guilty and freakish, especially when she witnessed Asa's total breakdown. She kept to herself. There was very little activity in the house. Condolence calls were rejected. Faith and Asa did not appear for meals. Faith sat outside her father's office for hours at a time. The kitchen staff had little to do. The house had an unhealthy silence.

A doctor suggested a professional, who could counsel on the grieving process and perhaps help Asa. The doctor didn't use the word *psychiatrist*, but that was what he meant. The doctor feared Asa might try to take his own life. Asa refused to see anyone but suggested the man could counsel Alice.

So it happened that Whitley Adams, MD, one of the few doctors trained in the science of psychiatry, began to have sessions with Alice Simpson.

In their first session, Whitley's questions shook Alice. "Tell me how you feel about your son's death. What does it feel like in your head? What thoughts does it provoke? What does it feel like in your body? In your chest and in your heart?"

Alice had never been asked such direct questions about her feelings. "I don't feel anything," she said nervously and then regretted such a callous answer.

"That's normal," said the doctor. "When something so hurtful happens, it's normal to close off feeling altogether."

"Yes. That's what's happened," said Alice. "Asa is grieving enough for both of us."

"Did he especially love Billy?"

"Billy was the love of his life. The only one that mattered."

"Did that upset you?"

"Oh no. I felt that once I had given him Billy, I had done my duty toward him. It gave me a certain freedom. I spent a lot of time at my parents' home, away from here. Asa didn't seem to mind."

"What about your daughter? Is she the one you favor?"

"Faith is unto herself. Faith is not close to anyone."

"And what about Alice? Who loves Alice?"

Alice looked at Whitley Adams for a full minute before answering. She was searching conscientiously to find someone who really loved her. "No one. No one loves Alice." She burst into tears, and Whitley offered her his handkerchief and put his hand over hers.

The sessions continued for several weeks, and Alice found she looked forward to getting the first clear look into the dynamics of her relationships. She was discovering what motivated her behavior and what she had been willing to trade for authenticity. Whitley asked her about her relationships with her mother and her sisters, and finally, the intimacy she shared with her husband.

Alice was puzzled. She really didn't know what he meant by intimacy. It was an idea that she was unfamiliar with, and she couldn't attach it to any feeling. "What do you mean by intimacy?"

"Closeness. Physical closeness and mental closeness. Sharing of ideas, warmth, silent understanding, tenderness, touching without sexual overtones. Love. Who in your life are you intimate with?"

Alice again locked eyes with Whitley Adams and searched herself for a true answer. "I don't have any of that," she said, in one of the first serious declarative truths she had ever uttered to anyone. "Should I?" This was a unique moment of emotional growth for Alice. For the first time in her adult life, she wasn't grappling for approval or feeling insignificant. She was just being herself.

The room used for these sessions was beautiful. It was the most beautiful room in the mansion. It had long, narrow casement windows that let in a subdued light. The walls were covered in vermillion silk, and the furniture was a departure from the stiff horsehair construction of most sofas and chairs. The cushions were down, and the arms of the chairs were generously large and padded. The effect was of seductive comfort and security. It was the perfect room to unearth and accept all the secrets that had been ignored.

No one had ever directly or indirectly asked Alice what she was feeling or what she was thinking or what she wanted out of life or how she thought of herself. Whitley Adams not only asked all of those questions, but he also listened to her answers. He listened with his ears and his eyes, and it made Alice feel that she mattered. She felt that she mattered to another human being. She felt that she mattered without having to beg and hide her thoughts. Slowly, over the weeks as they discussed intimacy, self-worth, honesty, loyalty, and the love of self, Alice found out what she thought and how she felt. It was an astonishing revelation.

What happened to Alice Simpson after her son died was transformative, a unique gift that Billy had given to his mother in death.

Finally, on a rainy afternoon, she felt the ice begin to melt, and she experienced agony and grief over the death of her son. Faith's timid, self-effacing mother commandeered the entire house with her grief. For several days, the eerie single note, held for what seemed an eternity, would bounce from the walls of the red room and echo throughout the house. This was a different mother, but it was too late. This mother would have protected Billy and refused to let him go. This mother would have challenged Asa.

Even in grief, Alice blossomed. Her eyes glowing with despair over her beautiful boy and her hands tearing at her handkerchief, her true beauty came to the fore. She loosened her hair. There was a rosiness to her cheeks, her lips were always moist, and her eyes brilliant.

She became beautiful, and Whitley Adams fell in love with her and she with him. They decided to go away together.

For Asa, already wounded beyond repair, it was somewhat of a relief. He had not relied on solace from his wife, and now he turned more into himself. It was just Asa in the sixty-five rooms of Seawatch with twenty-five indoor servants, forty outdoor help, and his daughter.

After the initial despair, Faith had a pervasive sadness, survivor's guilt, and a hollow chamber in the middle of her chest. She missed her brother, who, above all, had been her confidant and friend. He knew who she was and had helped her navigate disappointment. She missed his humor, his pleasantness, his affection, and she went into his room at night and cried for him. In back of the grief, she saw a multitude of clear truths. She knew it was not the end of her life. She also had the ability to analyze the event clinically. They had fussed over Billy with his flying lessons and his uniform and all his impending glory. They had focused on their plan and never thought about the danger. Billy had known it was dangerous all along.

Faith also knew that her father probably wished she had died instead of Billy, but that's not the way it had happened. She was alive, and her father would get used to it. He might even come to depend on her.

When she heard that her mother was leaving them, Faith was not surprised. How could she stay? How could she ever forgive Asa or herself for that matter? Even so, Faith wanted to beg her mother to stay, but no words would come out. In her head, she was screaming, but as her mother packed the few things she took, no sound came out.

Faith saw it all with clarity, but the outcome that was the clearest—and chipped away at her sanity—was the truth that she now had her father to herself. No Billy. No Hope. No Mama. Just Faith. It was up to her now. She knew without a doubt that if Hope were still at Seawatch, she would have kept them from crumbling. She would have known how to bring them back.

One afternoon, she walked by her father's study and saw him slumped at his desk, staring out the window. She stood at the door, and a strong emotion took hold of her. She wanted to go in and touch her father. She wanted to embrace him and be held tight. She could feel his desolation across the room, and the sight of her strong, able father reduced to sadness and bewilderment blended with her own devastation and brought tears. Asa turned and reached out an arm. Faith walked toward it. "Papa," she said, "I'm sorry," and she fell into his arms. Father and daughter remained in this embrace for several minutes and Faith finally relaxed. She felt a warmth and connection that was new to her.

When it was over and Asa let her go, he touched her face and wiped her tears and kissed her tenderly. "Go," he said. "You're too young to be burdened like this. Go and play." Faith wanted to tell him that she was nineteen, and she hadn't played in a long time.

Chapter Thirty

In 1900, when Hope was just a toddler, there were only forty-five states. The average worker made twenty cents an hour. Fewer than 150 miles of paved highway existed in the entire United States, and the truck and bus were still not widely available. There had been no major wars for two generations, and the business of America was peace and prosperity.

When Hope returned to lower Manhattan an educated, confident young woman, a barbarous world war had been raging for three years but was winding down. On the home front, the average worker made sixty cents an hour. New York City's population had exploded to five and a half million people, most of them new immigrants. The Model T was being produced on an assembly line, and the subway system covered all the boroughs. In less than an hour, you could travel from one tip of Manhattan to the other. The Astor was gone, but some of the old restaurants were still around. Kamen's Furniture Store was in the same place and had expanded. Many buildings housed manufacturing plants. There were fabric buildings, an ink building, a paper building, and bookstores, whose wares spilled out into the street.

◆ ◆ ◆

On her arrival at Pennsylvania Station, Hope found a locker for her luggage and took the subway downtown. She emerged and began walking to her old neighborhood. She stood at the door of her old rooming house. She saw the window where she had looked out, waiting for her mother or her father to show up or just listening to the sounds from the street.

The feelings and images that she had put away came up and her chest tightened. The years at Seawatch collapsed, and it was the day of her mother's death. How could that have happened? She sat on the stoop. Thinking back, she should have stayed and mourned her mother properly. Life was here, in these streets, on this stoop, and even in the filth of the gutters. Yet she was not the same raw girl. Seawatch had smoothed the edges, and she had confidence in the new person. She thought of Faith, still stuck in that fortress with nowhere to go. Even Tommy had escaped. She could visit him. Robert Trent was in law school at Columbia University. She didn't know what to do about him.

While Hope sat on the stoop, her old landlady came out and embraced her. She kept looking at the well-dressed young woman with awe. "Your mother would be so proud." After a while, she said, "I still have some of her things."

"You mean her clothes?"

"A few clothes and some bed linens and her cooking pots. She loved her cooking pots."

"I don't have a place yet where I can store them."

"Why don't you stay here until you get settled? Your old room is empty. Let's set it up so you have a place. People came by to look for you after you left. Your mother had a lot of friends, and they wanted to make sure you were all right. Kamen came, and the man from the cafeteria, and a lot of your mother's old customers. They loved your mother. She was a fine woman."

The landlady aired out the room and dusted. She scoured the sink and made the bed. "I used your mother's linens on your bed. I had put

them away, thinking you might come looking for them. I'll bring the
rest of her things while you go get your luggage from the station."

The room looked larger than Hope had remembered. The little
cook stove was gone, but the sink was still there and a small empty
icebox. She walked over to each corner, touching the walls and looking
out the windows. A remnant of the paisley fabric still lined one of the
closets. Hope ran her hand over it and put her face against it.

When Hope returned with her luggage, the landlady had put all
of Agatha's clothes on the bed. The cooking pots were on the floor.
Hope unfolded the skirts and dresses, and a hint of Agatha's scent,
some ancient lady's dusting powder Sen had bought for her long ago,
rose up. Hope's legs felt weak, and sadness overtook her. She should
have stayed here and worn all of Agatha's clothes, lain in them, wept in
them, and sucked in every scent that still lingered. The pile of clothing
included a nightgown, some blouses and skirts, a dress, and two shawls.
She undressed, put on the nightgown, and lay across the quilt she knew
so well. She pressed her face against the clothes. She stayed that way
all night with the window opened wide to catch the street noises, her
face buried in the evanescent wisp of Agatha. This was all she had, and
she couldn't waste any of it. If she wanted to live through the hurt and
sadness, she had to transfer all of what remained of Agatha into herself.

Hope had not intended to live there again, but once she was settled
in, she decided it was a good place to start to put her life in order. She
walked over every block of the neighborhood, absorbing all the changes.
The familiar streets and places made her melancholy, but she continued
walking until exhaustion allowed her to return to her room and sleep.
Two months passed, and she knew it was time to look for a job.

◆ ◆ ◆

Three general categories were open to young women hoping to earn
a living in New York City. The most respect went to the nurses and

teachers, but Hope wasn't trained for either career. Next was the position of clerk. Clerk meant many things, but primarily it meant you sold merchandise at a counter or in a store. Selling was respectable, but the better stores preferred the blonde, blue-eyed girls with strictly Anglo looks. Hope's looks were too special. The third tier of employment was the domestic route. In her mind, with Agatha as a role model, being a domestic was not something to ever consider. She'd try for sales. Maybe there was a sales job where it wouldn't matter what she looked like. Every day, she read the want ads, looking for a match.

She spent most of her time out of doors and walked to every appointment. It was the only way she could dispel a restlessness that plagued her. She felt most at ease in the crowded streets filled with sounds, smells, food carts, and the political speeches that still attracted crowds.

By late summer, American boys had been drafted and sent overseas. The newsboys shouted the latest war news, "Pershing Arrives in Paris." One day, she saw a list in the newspaper of the recent war dead and was shocked to see William Simpson's name. *Oh no. Not Billy.* Alongside the list, there was a news story of the more prominent men who had died, and it verified that Billy's plane had been shot down. She could think of nothing else for the rest of the day. Asa must be shattered. She could imagine all of Seawatch covered in a black cloth, everyone bowed in grief. How would Faith manage? For the first time, she wished to be back. She knew she could comfort them. She went into Trinity Church and sat there for the rest of the afternoon. "I'm sorry, Billy," she repeated over and over. She didn't know how else to pray. "I'm so sorry." She wanted to send Asa and Faith and Alice a sympathy card, but the messages printed on them were awful. Most of them rhymed, and that was the worst sin of all.

For the next few days, she continued her walking. The street throngs threw off energy and lifted her spirits. One day, she went west to a new neighborhood they called Greenwich Village. This was where the really progressive women lived in a lifestyle they called *bohemian*—loose morals and no difference between men and women. She could see that the people on the streets dressed differently and painted their faces. These people wanted to overthrow the old establishment crowd and give the money to the poor people. That was nonsense. Why couldn't they work for it like everybody else? It didn't occur to Hope that she was one of the poor.

It was surprising that Robert Trent lived down here. Tommy, whom Hope had run into on the street one day, told her. If ever there was anyone who wanted to play by the rules, it was Robert. But maybe he'd changed. Maybe he'd fallen for one of those bohemian poets or one of those brainy Barnard communist girls. *Intellectuals.* That's what she'd heard them called, whatever that meant. She didn't even know what communism really meant. Faith would have a fit if Robert had fallen for a communist. Maybe Faith had already told him what they had accused her of at Seawatch, and he believed it. On her long walks, she made up bits of dialogue. *Hope sold my father's information and we had to make her leave.* It hurt to think that. No matter how she phrased it, it was impossible to believe that Faith had done that to her. But who else could it have been?

Whenever she felt wistful for companionship or thought of love, it was Robert's face that came to her. She chose him as a repository of her private emotions, even though she had shut down any thought of romance. She never allowed her thoughts of him to dissolve into longing. She couldn't afford any more heartbreaks. Robert Trent would march through her like Sherman had marched through Georgia. He would leave her with nothing. The certainty of that outcome gave her the strength she needed to keep away. She had never forgotten their conversation about the girl who had visited him at Seawatch. The poor thing had no idea he wasn't going to marry her. There was a lesson to be learned.

◆ ◆ ◆

While Hope adjusted to life on her own, changes took place at Seawatch. The right step, the next step, for Asa and Faith had been so simple: Get away from Seawatch immediately. Get out of Muttonville. They had all the resources they needed to live anywhere, and it wasn't healthy to stay in the mansion full time. They needed diversion and energy, more noise and more people. They would wither in the controlled beauty of Seawatch. It wasn't safe to stay.

One day, Hope crossed Broadway up where it split, in the twenties, and saw a familiar figure on the opposite sidewalk. *Holy Mother of God.* (Hope had begun using all of Agatha's expressions.) It was Faith. What was she doing here? Hope was so relieved to see Faith, it was unthinkable not to talk to her. She felt her constant longing had made her appear.

"What are you doing here?" asked Hope.

"I'm enrolled at Barnard." Faith tried to control the moment, but she felt both regret and sadness welling up in her. She had sustained two horrid blows without the solace of Hope close by. There were questions she wanted to ask. "Where are you living? How are you making the money you need to live?" But she knew there was no going back. Absolutely no going back.

"With Columbia across the street, you'll be able to keep an eye on Robert," Hope said. "That's a good move." She said it without thinking.

Faith didn't like that Hope had seen through her intentions to attend Barnard. It made her look weak and a little man crazy. Was it so obvious? "I'm coming here for an education."

"I know you are, but Robert's studying law at Columbia."

Faith shrugged. She didn't have the luxury of discussing Robert with Hope. "How are you doing?"

"I'm glad to be back in my old neighborhood." She looked at Faith intently. "I want you to know I was not responsible for your father losing all that money. You may not believe me, but it wasn't me."

"What does it matter? We're all in a different situation now. My father has rented an apartment on the West Side, at the Dakota. He's living in the city."

"Oh." Hope suddenly remembered. "I was very sad to read about Billy. It must have been dreadful for your father and mother. And you, too, of course."

"Thank you," said Faith. She was about to walk away but stayed. "Billy liked you very much. Right from the beginning, he told me how glad he was that you were in the house."

"Thank you for telling me. I didn't know what to do when I read about it. It was terrible, but I didn't have anyone to tell. I sat in that old church downtown and cried by myself."

"That was probably the best thing to do. Billy would have liked that, Hope." She wanted to reach out and touch her old friend, but she knew that was not possible. She would have to leave it like this.

◆ ◆ ◆

Faith would not have admitted it, but the whole exchange had upset her. The comforting familiarity had been right there for her to take, but she couldn't do it. She had her father back, and her emotions were still too raw to have Hope invade the family again. Hope was back with what she knew best, the streets of New York, and she would make her way.

When Hope left Seawatch, it had not been a clean break for Faith. She felt a whirlwind of contradicting emotions. She missed Hope. She could not forget the day Hope had come to tell her not to worry about the girl who had visited Robert at Seawatch. When she replayed that scene, a wave of affection and regret overtook her.

Billy's death had changed everything. It was a long time before Asa was able to take an interest in anything or even hold a conversation, but when he was ready, he reached out to his daughter.

Asa was surprised to see that Faith had the interest and ability to join in his business. She showed him what she had been doing on her own, and he was impressed, but also sad that she hadn't felt it was good enough to share with him.

"Your reasoning here is excellent," he said. "There are many strategies. Some are weak but risk-free. Some are bold but too risky. You've taken a good low-risk approach and had a good return. I'm proud of you. I had no idea you had been studying things so closely."

His words were a balm that healed past hurts.

"I'm glad we'll be living in New York," he added. "The apartment is large and pleasant. It overlooks Central Park. It will be good for both of us to leave Seawatch for a while."

"Papa, when all the New York hostesses find out, you'll be out to dinner every night. You have to think of yourself as a very desirable bachelor."

"Only if you begin to think of yourself as a very desirable heiress."

"That's so strange coming from you. I've never thought of myself that way."

"That may be, but others have. I'm sure there's a line of young men waiting to ask for your hand."

It was such a nice moment, she didn't want to ruin it by telling him that there was only one man she wanted to have ask for her hand and he wasn't showing interest.

She had had dinner with Robert once, and it had happened by chance. She was walking along Amsterdam, one of the avenues that bordered the campus. He was walking toward her and had seen her before she saw him. He was grinning as if they had decided to play a game and meet by chance, and it had happened. It was a victory grin. She began to smile, too, and by the time they were face-to-face, they just smiled.

"See how easy it was," he said. She knew what he meant. They had talked about meeting up, and now it had happened.

"Easy," she agreed. "What happens now?"

"I'm going to class, but how about if we meet up for an early dinner when I come out at six thirty? We can meet on the steps of the library and decide where to go."

"All right. See you at the steps of Low at six thirty."

She was happy to see him, but it wasn't the way it had been at Seawatch. She was a different Faith. Maybe it was Billy's death or her mother's leaving, but she was no longer the nervous girl. She had survived two tragic losses and had witnessed her father almost drowned by grief. Everything that happened now was weighed against that abyss.

As they sat across from each other at The Greek Chorus, a small restaurant four blocks from the main gate of the university, she was almost relaxed. What could he do to her that was worse than what had already happened?

"Before anything else," he said when they were settled, "I want to say how sorry I was to hear about Billy."

"Thank you. Papa got your condolence card, but it was a long time before he could look at anything. I'm not sure he ever read it, but I did."

"Of course. Three friends from Yale and one from here went and didn't come back."

She looked down and started picking at the tablecloth, so he changed the subject. "Are you living on campus?"

"Yes. And you?"

"I have an apartment way downtown. It belonged to my father when he was in school, and he passed it down."

She studied his face and suddenly she didn't want to make small talk. "I don't know exactly why I'm here," she said. "My father wants me to work with him, and I could get a better education right in his office, but he wants me to make friends and be around girls my own age. He never went to college, so he sees it as the Holy Grail. Did you make any friends here?" She didn't care if he had made any friends. What she wanted to say was *I'm here because of you. I want you, and I've gone to a lot of trouble to be near you.*

"When I'm not in class, I'm at the firm. The other lawyers and clerks are my friends, but we all work into the evening. It's rare for me to have a sit-down dinner like this. And I still have a semester to go."

"Oh. So how do I see you? Just roam the streets and hope for the best?"

He laughed. "It worked well this time."

"Yes, it did," she said and dropped the subject. He was not ready for anything yet. Or at least not with her.

When they finished their dinner, he walked her back to her dormitory, and they paused at the door. He took her hand in his. "This was nice, Faith. Thank you."

"You're welcome," she replied brightly and went inside. When she got to her room she mumbled to herself, *At least I didn't ask him when we would see each other again. Thank God I didn't do that.*

Chapter Thirty-One

Hope couldn't help but measure herself against Faith, who was moving her life along with all the advantages of wealth and connections. Faith was a Barnard student, while Hope was attached to nothing and had no prospects. She couldn't even do office work because, unlike Emily Stokes, she had refused to learn typing and shorthand. Emily knew her place in the world, but Hope was still searching for hers. Maybe she could go to college, too, but she still needed a job, and weeks of daily searches had yielded nothing.

Not long after meeting up with Faith, she had a breakthrough, and it came from an unlikely source. One morning, she passed Kamen's furniture shop, and Kamen called out. She ignored him, but he ran after her.

"You're Agatha's daughter."

"What do you want?"

"Stop a minute." Hope walked back. "Look at you, all grown up," he said. "I heard about your mother. I read her name in the paper. One of those poor girls. What happened to you?"

"I've been out in the country. That's where orphan girls were sent. But now I'm out, and I need to find some work."

"Come inside," said Kamen, and led her behind the counter.

"I'm not going to work for you, if that's what you're thinking."

"I hadn't thought of that." He picked up a jar of furniture wax from the counter. "There's a new company named Holden that makes pastes and liquids to clean and renew furniture. They sent me some samples because I own a furniture store. They're recruiting salespeople to go door to door and sell their line. They give you the products and containers. You fill orders and share the profits. They'll stake you to the first order, and once you're on your feet, you pay them and order more."

"Where would I sell furniture polish? The people around my neighborhood don't have the kind of furniture that needs polish."

"Go further up to the new apartment buildings. You'll be surprised. The lady of the house will let you in. You ask to demonstrate the wax and the dusting liquid on her table, and she'll order what she wants. You collect the money when you return with the products. The more you sell, the more you will earn. Don't tell the company you're a woman, though. They'll try to cheat you. Just use initials."

"What do I charge?"

"Charge whatever you want. The company will send you the products in bulk and the containers with their label. Double what the company charges you and keep the difference. That's how business is done. The bigger the markup, the bigger the profit."

Hope looked at Kamen. He had, in many ways, been the cause of a lot of grief, but he'd given them new mattresses and a table after Agatha got out of the hospital. The way he described the business, it seemed too simple. Her mother had never charged enough for all her hard work. Hope would not make that mistake.

"Besides finding customers and getting them to let me in, it sounds too simple. But I could give it a try."

"They'll let you in sooner than a man," said Kamen. "You're a beautiful girl and you'll have an advantage." She took one of the jars and the company flyer with a list of all their products. "Remember, just use initials," Kamen called out.

When she contacted the company and filled out the questionnaire they sent, she used the name H. A. Lee. She snuck in her mother's initial just to make it seem more serious. Hope didn't think twice about going into the polish business; she'd grown up with parents who were eager to take on work they knew little about and make a success of it. Within two weeks, she received the samples and was out on the street with polishing cloths and an order book tucked in a sack.

Manhattan had grown to the north, and large apartment buildings had cropped up on both the East and West Sides. The practice of door-to-door sales was a legitimate way to get goods to all the apartment dwellers. Past Fourteenth Street, each area had its own identity. There was Murray Hill in the thirties, Turtle Bay in the forties, Beekman in the fifties. The new, more luxurious apartments were referred to as French flats and usually had a liveried doorman guarding the entrance. But you could walk in and knock on doors in the less fancy buildings.

She started out at two new buildings not too far from the rooming house, the Stuyvesant on Eighteenth Street and the Villanova on Twenty-Eighth. She was barred from entering at both places. "No peddlers allowed," said the first doorman and pointed to a sign. At the second building, she struck up a conversation with the doorman. "I'm not really a peddler," she said. "I'm taking orders for a good product that will help in the house. I only need about five minutes of their time."

"These people have servants to do their cleaning," he said. "You'd do better on the West Side."

In the west teens, she found the brownstones were mostly brothels or gentlemen's clubs, where men were entertained by young attractive women in the employ of a madam. At the end of a week of fruitless attempts, she arrived at Franklin Terrace, a group of rental brownstones on West Twenty-Sixth Street, and finally, her knock was answered and she was allowed into a pleasant, bright apartment. A young woman with a baby on her hip seemed eager to look at her samples. While Hope rubbed at the dining table, the woman asked a lot of questions but not about the product. "Are you married?"

Hope was surprised that the woman thought she might be married. "What makes you ask that?"

"You're so pretty, I would think you'd be married."

Hope stopped rubbing the table and looked at the young mother. Her eyes had dark circles under them, and she appeared tired. "How old is your baby?"

"He's four months, and I haven't had a good night's sleep since he was born. It's not so easy as people think."

"I'm sure it's very hard. You have to keep it safe and feed it, I guess," said Hope.

"Oh, by all means, but you worry, too. I keep thinking he's going to stop breathing or something. Sometimes he sucks so hard for the milk, he starts choking and snuffling. Scares me to death."

For the next half hour, Hope listened to the young woman lay out all the anxieties and frustrations of motherhood. "You don't love them all the time," she confessed. She searched Hope's face for shock.

"I'm sure. You can't love anyone all the time. Sometimes you hate them."

The woman looked relieved and began to relax. "The table looks lovely," she said. "I'll take some of the cleaner and the wax."

Hope wrote up the order. The woman's name was Lynette Greene, and she was good luck for Hope. She sold to three more customers along the block, and two of them sent her to friends nearby.

Her presentation was friendly and confident. The lady of the house, worn out and bored from her chores, was usually happy to let this exotic girl show her a way to preserve her furniture. Between the demonstrations, they would chat about homemaking or cooking, and Hope was always ready with some of Agatha's tips. They were lonely and liked having an interruption to their day. Many were reluctant to see her leave, and sometimes she had to be firm after the order was signed or she would have lost the day.

Within a month, she had thirty-seven sales, each for more than one of the products. She sent an order sheet to the company for the wax, cleaner, and the scratch repair. The products arrived in bulk with instructions on how they should be stored and how much the containers should weigh when filled. She packed the orders that night to deliver the next day.

She had accomplished her goal, and she nearly ran down the street with her makeshift cart, darting through the crowds. By day's end, she would have more than two hundred dollars; 40 percent of which would be hers to keep. As she approached Fourteenth Street, a scruffy young man called out something lewd. When she thrust out her chin and ignored him, he came after her, knocked her down, and took the cart with all her orders. She ran after him, but it was too late. He had thrown all of it into an open sewer hole. The assault happened so quickly, it was hard to believe and accept. She had lost all her stock and had no money to pay the company, nor enough of the product to fill the orders. She was out of breath from running after the boy.

She couldn't go back to her lonely room without the merchandise or any money. She went into Trinity Church and sat in her old pew waiting for the panic to die down.

In the quiet serenity of the old church, it occurred to her that if she could find out what was in the polish and cleansers, she could buy the ingredients, replace the products, and recoup the money. She knew a chemist on the second floor of a building on Doyers. Agatha had often gone to him to mix up an efficient cleanser for the cafeteria pots.

Tico Sheraz, the chemist, remembered her and expressed sympathy over the death of her mother. Everyone in the neighborhood still remembered the shirtwaist-factory fire. She told Tico of her predicament. He smelled each one of the containers. "This is not so difficult. Come tomorrow," he said. "I'll analyze each one. We will find a good solution."

By morning, Tico had not only analyzed the ingredients but had already made small batches for her to evaluate. They tested everything on a piece of wood and decided it was acceptable. The wax or polish consisted of olive oil, white vinegar, jojoba, and boiled linseed oil, plus an essential oil, lemon or lavender, to leave a pleasant scent. The cleanser was mostly vinegar with some borax, lemon oil, and a sprig of rosemary. The scratch eraser was similar to the cleanser, with added tints for dark and light wood.

"Each portion should cost no more than five or six cents to produce," said Tico.

He let her mix the formulas in the back of the shop in vats, and she filled her containers and started out again.

This time, delivery went smoothly. No one complained, and some of the customers put in new orders for friends and family members. She returned to pay Tico and thank him.

"Why do you have to buy anything from the company?" he said. "Make it yourself and keep all the money. You've had a rough life. This is a way for you to make a few dollars. I can order the ingredients for you, and you can rent a cheap little space to produce everything."

It was that simple. She was happy to take Tico's advice. The formulas were easy to mix, and she mastered the sequence and the amounts and poured the concoctions into the jars and bottles.

Hope's formulas were something a housewife could concoct at home, but the women liked buying from her, and they liked to be shown how to use the products. It made them feel that they had left poverty behind and were going up in the world. The product itself was almost an afterthought.

Hope had kept and used the supply of empty containers from the Holden Company and ordered more. After a couple of months, when no requests for the product came in, but containers were being shipped out, the company became suspicious.

Consuelo Saah Baehr

One afternoon, Hope fulfilled an order for a customer who lived on the East Side, one block from the river. The woman, a return customer, was a motherly type who took an interest in Hope. "Why don't you have a beau?" she would ask. "Isn't your mother eager to see you settled down?"

"I don't have parents," said Hope. "So I don't have to get married. That's the last thing I want to do."

"I'm going to look for someone for you," said the woman. "I'll find someone you can't resist."

When she left the woman's apartment and began her walk home, she sensed someone following her. She crossed the avenue and walked on the opposite side, but a man also crossed and stayed behind her. When she was a block from her rooming house, she stopped in the middle of the street. If someone was really following her, she didn't want him to see where she lived. He might as well confront her in the street. A well-dressed man with brown hair and a strong, handsome face stood in front of her. She noticed he had several small scars above his left eye.

"Do you work for H. A. Lee?" he asked.

"Who wants to know?"

"Do you know H. A. Lee?"

"I'm H. A. Lee."

"You? That can't be."

"Why not? I'm H. A. Lee. Are you going to arrest me?"

"That's an odd thing to say. Why would I want to arrest you? Are you doing something illegal?"

"Not at all."

Hope was not afraid of the man, perhaps because of his look of surprise. If she could have seen the future, she would have been more surprised than he.

Chapter Thirty-Two

Martin Beck, a precocious boy with dark good looks and an easy nature, was the only son of Sidney Beck, a Jewish law clerk, and his wife, Magdalena, a beautiful Italian girl. The family lived near the Jewish quarter of downtown New York. Occasionally, Martin was harassed over his Jewish religion, but he was smart and good at sports, and after holding his own in a few fights, he was left alone.

Instead of sending their son to a yeshiva, a Jewish school, Sidney and Magdalena sent Martin to Collegiate, an upper-crust boys' school that was a pathway to Harvard and Princeton.

Martin was an ideal student. He had a superior intellect and also excelled at pitching a baseball. Early on, Ernest Lovelace, heir to a mining fortune, befriended him, and he often went home to the Lovelace mansion on Fifth Avenue instead of traveling to his own house. Upon graduation, both boys were admitted to Princeton, Martin on a scholarship.

In their senior year, Ernest was driving them home drunk after a party, and a milk truck hit the car head-on, killing him instantly. Martin suffered a concussion and cuts, but he didn't die. He felt responsible for his friend's death, and it didn't help that Ernest's father never spoke to him again.

Martin's mother came to his hospital bed with the news that he had been awarded a Rhodes Scholarship. It seemed a godsend to leave New York and spend a few years in London, despite the war. He remained in London and accepted a scholarship to the London School of Economics.

When he returned to New York in the spring of 1917, ready to tackle Wall Street, he was completely shut out of the top firms. One of his London friends, who considered Martin brilliant, laid it out bluntly. "My dear fellow, if you are in any way perceived Hebraic, you won't be hired by the big firms. If your surname ended in a vowel, it would be the same. Strike out on your own. I've got an inheritance to start you off. There's no one I would trust with my money more than you."

Martin's friend had it right. Wall Street was a tight club of privileged old boys, some of whom had anglicized their names along the way.

Martin took the seed money. It was the perfect time for a smart man to begin his rise. America had just entered the war, but there was optimism that Europe, exhausted by three years of fighting, would need goods from America, and the country would become a creditor nation.

Martin lived with his parents and often visited his father's office to exchange ideas. One day, he heard a client who owned a furniture-cleaning-and-care products company complaining of a rogue group mimicking their formulas and using the Holden labels and containers.

He wanted to bring a lawsuit against the perpetrators but needed to catch them in the act. The details of the story sounded familiar to Martin. Someone had sold his mother furniture polish two days before. He had heard the exchange and knew the salesperson was returning with the goods the following day. The order receipt was signed by H. A. Lee, the name Holden had mentioned. He offered to follow the perpetrator.

Martin said nothing to his mother. The doorbell rang and a young woman entered carrying a large case. Martin stayed out of sight, listening.

"I have the new product I told you about," Hope said to Magdalena. "I'll demonstrate it if you like." Magdalena cleared a small side table that had a round gray water stain.

"I can take care of this," said Hope. "I can rub out that ring and restore the color." She brought out a cloth and dabbed a few drops of a brown liquid paste onto it. She rubbed the entire top of the table with particular stress on the ring, and the stain was reduced. "Each time you use it, the stain will become less visible," she said.

Magdalena paid Hope, and she packed her case and left.

Martin followed her into the street. She had gone several blocks and crossed to the opposite side before he caught up and spoke to her. "Excuse me," he said, tapping her shoulder. She turned, and he was surprised by how young she was. After he established that she was H. A. Lee, he said, "You just sold my mother some furniture polish."

"Yes."

"I'm wondering who makes the polish. Is it a company? Where do you get it?"

"I make it. I'm the company."

"But the label says 'Holden Furniture Polish.' Are you one of their salesmen?"

She studied Martin before answering. She looked at his face and the small scars on his forehead that were still visible but didn't detract from his good looks. "Why are you interested?"

"Because the company knows a rogue group has mimicked their formula and is selling it with their label. Are you doing it?"

"So what if I am?"

"It's illegal. It's stealing."

"I'm not stealing anything. I make the stuff fair and square. I'm only using their labels. You want me to stop using their labels? I'll make some of my own."

"I want to know who's behind this. You're just an innocent girl. Who put you up to this? Who supplies you?"

"No one supplies me. I supply myself. I'm behind this by myself."

"Forgive me, I don't mean to insult you, but you're barely . . . what, twenty? I don't believe you're the mastermind of a swindle like this."

"It is not a swindle. It's a good living, so if you think you're going to ruin it for me, I'll open up in another neighborhood. I have a right to make a living."

"Should I speak to your parents?" he asked, feeling foolish. "Do they know you're doing this?"

"I don't have any parents. One is dead and the other lives in China. Are you going to go and speak to him in China?"

"Obviously not," said Martin, surprised at her boldness.

"Are you going to turn me in?"

"I'd like to help you, but I need to know more." He had no idea how he could help this girl continue to undermine the Holden Company.

"I don't need any help. I'm doing it just fine."

"I'd like to help you do it fair and square," he said.

Hope looked into his eyes. "Why should I trust you?" Her bravado was slipping away. She might be in real trouble. Maybe Kamen was behind this.

"You shouldn't. You just have to take your chances. Take me to see your operation."

"How do I know you won't turn me in or take it from me?"

"You don't. If you're telling the truth and you did this on your own, I'm impressed. But if you keep on the way you're doing it, eventually they'll find you and who knows what they'll do."

Hope didn't need any reminders of what happened to women who went against the big shots. She had only to remember her mother's battered body when Kamen sent his goons. She looked into Martin's eyes for reassurance and saw kindness. Maybe he was on her side.

"Let's go to Laight Street. That's where I have my factory."

What she blithely called her "factory" was nothing more than a damp basement with a single naked bulb. Martin said nothing. He saw the entire picture. He saw the vats of ingredients, the stacks of containers, the rats skittering over the floor, the flimsy lock on the door.

"Who helps you?"

"No one."

"You mix everything yourself? How do you know the formulas?"

"I hired a chemist to analyze everything. I had to. The batch that the company sent was grabbed by a street boy and thrown in the sewer."

"You hired a chemist?" Everything she said was a revelation.

"Yes. My mother used to go to him when she had her cafeteria. He mixed up something to clean the pots."

"What happened to your mother?"

"She worked at the shirtwaist factory. There was a fire."

"Were you in an orphanage?"

"No. They sent me to Muttonville, out in the country. I lived with Asa Simpson and his family. He's a very rich man."

"I know who he is. I'm in the same business."

She stared at him. "You're in the same business as Mr. Asa? You're in the stock business?"

"Yes. Do you know anything about that business?"

"I know all about it. I know everything about it."

Martin doubted that she knew everything, but he reserved judgment. Every answer she gave was compelling and almost tragic, but she didn't present it that way. She just answered in the simplest terms.

"Why are you selling these products?"

"It's a way to make money. I don't want to be a waitress, and I'm not Anglo enough to be a salesclerk in a good store."

"You should thank your lucky stars for that. You're too smart to be a clerk. What happens when it's cold? There's no heat in here."

"Everything freezes and separates. I have to throw it away and start fresh."

"That's too wasteful. You should find a better place. "

"I can't rent a better place. They want money up front, and I don't have it yet."

"Well, there. That's one way I can help. I can be your guarantor." He hadn't intended to offer help. He was here to identify a thief.

"What does that mean?"

"I sign a paper guaranteeing to pay the rent if you are unable, and I show them a bank notice that verifies I have the money to pay."

"What do you want in return?"

"Come and work for me. That's what I want in return. I need someone young and enterprising and smart. We can find someone else to sell the polish. That will come later. First we have to design a label for the company. You can't keep using Holden's labels. We'll do it fair and square."

"I have to think about it," she said.

He knew that was as far as he could push it that day. "For now, let's find you a new space that's dry and has a proper lock and you don't squash a rat every time you take a step."

In the next few days, Martin Beck did as he had promised. He made a list of what needed to be done and went about fulfilling each item. He hired a designer friend from Collegiate to create new labels and stationery with the name Hope had selected. She wanted to call her company Candelabra Furniture Care. She had even come up with a tagline: *shine new beauty on your old furniture.*

They went deep into the meatpacking district and found half of a floor for twenty-five dollars a month. It was clean and dry, and even had a sink with running water. It also had two long metal tables for production and shelves to store her containers. In a couple of weeks, Martin had taken the shoddiness out of her operation.

"Now we need a manager and a salesperson so you can come and work for me," Martin told Hope.

"I haven't said yes."

"Whatever you make from the polish business, I could match. How much do you make?"

"About a hundred a month after I pay for the materials."

"I can give you more than that. I can give you one hundred and fifty to start."

"How do I know your business is going to succeed?"

"You don't. You have to trust me. And I have to trust you. Why did you leave Asa Simpson?"

"He thought I gave out information that ruined a project."

"Did you?"

"No. It wasn't me."

"Good," he said. "I'm going to trust you with all my business secrets, and I need a solid character."

"Nobody on Wall Street has a solid character. But I wouldn't work against you."

"That's all I can ask."

"I haven't said I accept."

"True. Don't forget, though. I saved you from the Holden Company goons who would have hurt you."

"I'm not desperate."

"I didn't say you were. If you were desperate, you wouldn't be right for my purpose. You have to be un-desperate to be a good hire."

"I'll let you know in a couple of days."

He gave her his office address, and she promised to stop by.

She was waiting on the stoop when he came to open the office two days later. "I'll take the job," she said.

"Why are you here so early?"

"I wanted to look around before you got here. And also my boardinghouse is full of drunks who clump around all hours of the night. I couldn't sleep anyway."

He gave her a lengthy application to fill out. It asked her date of birth. It asked if she had any serious diseases or if she was hearing-impaired or needed glasses to see. It asked her marital status and if she had any children. It also asked how many grades she had completed in school. She put down that she had a private education with the children of Asa Simpson and some classes at the Muttonville High School and had passed all of her grades but left before attending graduation. In the margin, she wrote, "If it's important, I will ask them for my diploma."

In the space that asked where her mother was born, she put Ireland. In the space that asked where her father was born, she put China. She had never recounted her history like this, and it made her reflective. Her life seemed ragged and incomplete. Where it asked for her mother's full name, she wrote out Agatha Murphy Lee. Her hand trembled. She had never written out her mother's name. A tear rolled down her cheek. Where was Agatha Murphy Lee? How had she vanished so quickly? Could Hope have stopped it? She ran out to the street. It was too much. He watched her from the window until she came back.

What Martin Beck felt for Hope Lee wasn't lust. It was a desire to have her nearby. He never tired of looking at her. Her eyes appeared to have been dug out of her face, and the mass of copper hair presented her like a painting come to life. He wanted to stay close to her because that's where life was.

◆ ◆ ◆

Hope decided quickly that it was a good place for her. She had a stated daily goal that she shared with Martin. He was not Asa, the lord and master, not Mama with her insecurities and fears, not Faith who sometimes wanted to be a victim. He was a partner, perhaps not yet equal, but a partner still. What was even better, he was a brilliant teacher, and she was grateful that he had chosen her.

The very first day he sat her down and said, "Hope, I'm going to talk with you about money. It's important that you take it in because the way we regard money—emotionally and objectively—will determine the success of our business.

"My business is not what you witnessed with Asa Simpson. We are at the beginning and we have to make it work for us. Men like Asa Simpson arrived in Muttonville fully made. The men who built their places along the North Coast already had vast sums that are unimaginable to the ordinary man.

"It is not money as you normally think of it. It isn't bills and coins. It isn't what you pull out of your pocket to pay for food or rent. It isn't money you can put in a sock or under your mattress or even in a savings account in a bank. It is money that rises like dough in trust funds for children who can barely toddle and for carefree Yale boys with trim waists and straight hair. Some of the money is just a number on a bank statement. Some of it is in the form of beautifully engraved certificates that you could frame as art. They are stacked in private safes, or they're resting—musty and undisturbed—in the vaults of law firms. The money exists not for buying groceries or paying rent. It exists for the sole purpose of making more money. The sums grow silently through the night as interest compounds, doubles, and triples. The sum staggers the imagination and people grow quiet when thinking about it and it makes them want more.

"That is how we think of money in this firm. It exists for the sole purpose of making more money. Keep that always in mind, and we will do well."

Hope took it all in and understood. She felt important and grown-up. She liked the way he spoke to her and could see that he had an orderly mind. She saw also that he made decisions quickly and without second thoughts. Mostly they were the right ones. He spent the days visiting prospective clients, trying to draw their money into his firm. He told them the story of why his initial investor had handed him several million dollars as seed money for his firm. "Plain and simple, he trusted my instincts. To date, I have not let him down." He readily showed a date book of a year's worth of transactions and the rationale used for buying and selling. Many days, he took Hope with him so she could get a feel for the language and the expectations of the customers and the approach that inspired confidence. It wasn't easy to get clients. People tended to stay with what they knew, even if it wasn't working. You could show them how the current economic conditions no longer supported their strategy, but they were still reluctant to change. They always thought their luck would improve if they stuck with it. Martin would repeatedly tell them that luck was a poor way to grow their portfolios.

Hope thrived in the experience of normalcy. She had somewhere to go every day, where she was expected. If she didn't show up, Martin would probably come looking for her. She no longer felt so horribly isolated from the rest of society. The office now had a full staff and it was comforting to walk in every morning and see Elsie, the typist and receptionist, sitting in the front room hunched over her Remington, pecking at it with astonishing rapidity. Elsie had a photograph on her desk of herself and her beau at the beach in Coney Island. There was also Sam, who monitored the ticker and put in orders, and Beatrice, the bookkeeper, who sent out statements and managed the payroll. Each of them had a private life and someone who was waiting for them at the end of the day.

Hope liked the research work Martin gave her. He learned she had good instincts, as Asa had already told her. She could see patterns in a company's management that spelled trouble or good. She saw patterns that divulged secrets if anyone was interested in digging them out. Earnings reports, if you took away the pretty language, were candid mirrors of where a company was headed. Hope was becoming an adult. Emotionally, she was letting her guard down and becoming more self-aware. She was willing to offer an opinion and converse pleasantly. She dug into her work with energy and purpose. She felt comfortable with Martin and looked forward to seeing him every day, but her attraction was based on trust and respect, not romance. He, on the other hand, fell in love with her immediately, but he kept it to himself. It was too soon. He had to take his time with her, or she would bolt.

Chapter Thirty-Three

Billy's death had a profound effect on Faith's decisions for the future. She kept remembering how her brother had told her to choose happiness. The energy of the city and the purposeful routine of college were a good start.

She had chosen Barnard out of convenience but didn't feel invested in the leftist leanings that were prevalent. Juliet Poyntz, who had graduated a few years before, was a spy and a founding member of the Communist Party in America. Posters and leaflets on every lamppost and kiosk within the campus and along Broadway announced meetings, gatherings, protests, speakers, rallies, marches, and clothing drives to support what amounted to a communist way of life. Faith knew that most of the girls who were so enthusiastic about the movement knew nothing about it. If they had to share their allowance with all the communists, they would run the other way, but they were young girls and they liked rallying around a cause. They especially liked the boys from Columbia who came to the rallies. Rallies offered a chance to mingle without seeming boy crazy.

Barnard girls were allowed to attend classes at Columbia but were denied full admission. An unspoken feeling suggested that they were "less than" the boys across the street, even though most of the Columbia professors admitted that the women did better in Columbia classes than the men.

None of this interested Faith. She would never be a communist. And she knew that, although she hoped her father wouldn't die for a long, long time, when he did, she would be in command of an international financial firm that had rewarded its blue-chip clients with a 12–15 percent return on their money for twenty-five years. Now that the war was over, business boomed again, and the profits gushed in. She had no need of communism or a Barnard degree to distract her from her prime reason for being in New York. She was there to keep Robert Trent in her sights and launch a campaign that would end in marriage.

She filled her schedule with classes in political science and economics across the street. She sought permission from the Columbia professors, and it was always granted to Asa Simpson's daughter.

In addition to their dinner in the city, Robert had stayed overnight at Seawatch over Thanksgiving to discuss business between Asa and the Wentworth firm. Robert and Faith rode, played tennis, and even went to the Creek Club for a candlelit dinner.

"What do you think the median age is of the club members?" Robert had asked, looking around at the gray-haired diners eating their medallions of beef au jus.

"Probably midsixties. It takes a while to earn the money just for the initiation fee."

"Why is your father a member? I don't see this as his crowd."

"He allows the club the right to use part of our land for the seventh hole of their golf course," Faith said. "Papa hardly ever comes over, but Billy, Tommy, and I used to sled down that big slope near the creek when it snowed."

"I recognize a Wentworth board member two tables over," said Robert.

"This is the place to make connections. But if you need connections, you probably don't have the initiation fee, so it's a conundrum. Wait . . . is it a conundrum or just one big ironic mess?"

Robert laughed. "A bigger conundrum is how come you're always using irony? Irony is for starving poets. You're an heiress." He said it in a silly way, as if it were a station in life.

They were easy together and entertained each other, and Faith hoped there might be a moment in the future when the laughter would spill over into realization of desire. A singular look might take the relationship to a different level, but it wasn't there yet.

She knew Robert Trent would never fall head over heels in love with her. But that might not close the door to a marriage proposal. She now understood the brilliant advice Hope had given her about a marriage arranged by her father. Faith had seen the idea as humiliating, but she'd been wrong. She didn't need the sentimental template for marrying the man she wanted. Wasn't everything a business proposition? Her only concern was to keep Robert out of romantic entanglements until they spent more time together and she readied him for what was to come.

Her mother's experience had taught Faith a valuable lesson. At her lowest point, when Billy's death made pretense unbearable, Alice had an awakening that blocked out all lesser considerations. She recognized what she needed for herself and shut down a lifetime of doing "the right thing." In the same way, Faith needed Robert to begin her life and to complete it.

Chapter Thirty-Four

Barnard attracted brainy, forward-thinking girls, who tended to favor social causes, but a circle of young students dismissed the idea that they had to look like repressed librarians in order to be provocateurs. The leader of this group was Josie Klein, who knew every leading beauty and fashion establishment in New York City and patronized many of them. Josie shared a dormitory room with Faith, and she had frequently looked at the heiress and wondered why she did nothing to improve her appearance.

Josie was all about good haircuts and subtle lipstick and the latest fashion trend. She was also a brilliant premed student whose father had opened the first off-price women's store downtown. Josie did not shop at her father's store nor did she patronize Altman's or Lord & Taylor. She went straight to Mr. Henri Bendel, who had brought Coco Chanel to New York.

"Bendel," Josie's father told his daughter, "is just another Jewish milliner from Lafayette, Louisiana. He married well, a Lehman. But go waste my money uptown if it makes you happy. You have my blessing."

Faith thought she was above all the primping, but she liked to watch Josie apply makeup and style her hair.

"Why doesn't your mother take you to Arden's?" Josie asked. "They would tweeze those eyebrows down to size."

"My mother left my father and ran away with her psychiatrist, but even if she were still around, she wasn't the kind to take an interest in my looks. She was too timid and worried about herself. Although now, presumably, her new husband has changed all of that." Faith knew Josie liked that kind of sophisticated conversation. She didn't even know if her mother intended to marry her lover or whether they were just wandering around in Chicago cohabitating like the bohemians of Greenwich Village. Her mother hadn't communicated with her since the day she left, and it was a struggle to understand that indifference without feeling its sting. Alice had never been a nurturer, but Faith couldn't come to terms with being forgotten. Sometimes it made her angry, but most times she swallowed and absorbed it like something hard she'd eaten by mistake.

"Come with me to Arden's and get those eyebrows reshaped. If you don't like them, they'll grow out. What do you have to lose?"

"I could look like a lunatic," Faith answered, but she gave in.

If Alice had been a different kind of mother, Faith would have known what to do to make the best of what she had in looks and fashion. The Simpsons had the resources to get all the help they needed, but there had been no leadership or interest in enhancing the good traits Faith possessed. Josie was happy to oblige. One of Josie's "finds" was Elizabeth Arden's Red Door avant-garde spa on Fifth Avenue. She discovered it on a march with the suffragettes that included Arden. All the marchers wore Arden's signature red lipstick, as if to thumb their noses at those who would deny them the vote.

At the Red Door, Faith allowed the aesthetician to reshape her brows, tweezing aggressively to widen the space between them. The aesthetician smudged kohl on the outer corner of Faith's eyes and brushed a pale powder on the inner corner. The result was excellent. Faith's eyes appeared farther apart and larger. Josie shook her in excitement. "Look at you. Look at you. I'm going to take you to Bendel's. Henri will do for your figure what Arden did for your face."

In New York, the fashion capital of the world, posh department stores catering to the new wealthy class began moving from Ladies Mile, an area between Broadway and Sixth Avenue, to the residential blocks of wealthy Fifth Avenue. Samuel Lord and George Washington Taylor moved their Lord & Taylor Dry Goods Store, and B. Altman joined them. The stores' distinct European patina satisfied their clientele.

The cognoscenti knew that truly fine fashion—in clothing, hairstyling, and cosmetics—could only be found farther uptown on the Rue de la Paix of New York, on West Fifty-Seventh Street where Bergdorf Goodman and Henri Bendel had opened their shops in proximity to the posh Plaza Hotel. Goodman was the first couturier to introduce ready-to-wear couture. Madame did not have to wait for her frock to be made. She could take it off the rack, try it on, and wear it that night if she chose.

Even more exclusive than Bergdorf was the emporium of Henri Willis Bendel, a designer whose fashion line included fragrances, furs, hats, lingerie, and cosmetics. Bendel was so invested in perfection, he had 276 "masterwork" panes of glass commissioned from Rene Lalique to use in the windows. Bendel himself not only designed women's clothing but also could offer *mademoiselle* an entire in-store makeover. It was Mr. Bendel who took Faith Celeste Simpson and transformed her from an ordinary college student into an elegant and striking woman. He saw that she had what she needed for beauty, but no one had taken the effort to showcase it. As for Faith, Josie had awakened in her a new understanding of personal success. The first step was to make the absolute most of her physical attributes.

Henri made it his personal mission to remake Faith into a woman of allure and power. When she arrived at his store, she refused to deal with anyone but him, and when she was in his presence, she itemized what she wanted to accomplish.

"I might be lacking in native beauty, but I have many strong points and I need your help to use them," she said. He looked her over carefully. He twisted and turned her, measuring her legs, putting his hands around her waist, and even measuring her bosom. He didn't say a word and she didn't resist.

"You have an ideal frame for Coco Chanel and some other designers. We will put together a wardrobe and fit it to you precisely, and you will not be able to recognize yourself when I am finished. You will be stunning."

"Good," said Faith. "Let's begin."

Bendel put Faith on a raised platform and studied her from all angles. He kept rubbing his chin and muttering as he wrote down notes. "You have good legs, good proportions, and a slim waist. Cinch in your waist and show off the hips. Keep away from ruffles and peplums. You need good supple fabrics that drape well. Nothing too long with those legs. I know what to do with you. You don't need to camouflage any part of that figure. We will tailor everything to show off your curves and definitely cut the hair. The hair should be layered to touch the cheeks and end just above the shoulders. That will widen the face."

He personally escorted her to the hairstyling salon on an upper floor and presided over the cut. Faith had always worn her long hair loose or tied at the back with a ribbon. The stylist layered Faith's abundant chestnut hair so that it flipped outward just above her shoulders. Shorter wisps fell playfully against her cheeks. She cut long irregular bangs that grazed Faith's new eyebrows, further accenting her eyes. The haircut was transformative.

Faith became Bendel's prima makeover success. Every time she came in for a fitting or a trim, he would say, "Ah, there she is. My success girl. How many proposals did you have since I saw you?"

Bendel's had eight floors, and on each there was something necessary to create the Bendel woman. He knew Faith could afford the best, but more than that, she gave him the opportunity to transform a young woman of modest looks and demeanor into a woman of fashion with the charisma to command a room. He dressed her in his own designs as well as Chanel. She wore his signature perfume, an earthy, almost decadent scent, with no hint of sweetness. He styled her thick brown hair to look windblown and not fully combed. It gave her a racy look, while the rest of her attire was formfitting and buttoned-up. "You look like a love-crazy headmistress," he was fond of saying. For evening, he put her in bias-cut slinky slip dresses with the barest of cowl folds at the neckline. "Please, no brassiere with my clothes," said Henri. "I sew in the right support without losing the form." Henri was right. The way he presented her breasts was incredibly provocative, and both men and women always stared. The new Faith—the whole package—was magnetic.

Faith was happy with her new clothes and makeup, but even more satisfied with the way she felt. Who would have thought that a haircut and some tricks with eye makeup would make her feel so confident? Sometimes she behaved like a sappy, lovesick girl listening to love songs. When Josie turned on the radio and Ma Rainey or King Oliver's band played, Faith swayed to the music, certain that the lyrics of love could be hers.

Her first public appearance at a charity event for the Children's Aid Society held at the Waldorf Astoria certified her new allure. Several men hovered over her throughout the evening, and although she enjoyed the attention, she only wanted one person to approve, and she anticipated showing her new self to him. For the first time since her brother had died and her mother had left, Faith felt the healing balm of anticipation.

Chapter Thirty-Five

Tommy Rowland had accumulated a basket of nagging regrets, and one that stayed with him was the mischief Faith had perpetrated on Hope. No one understood Faith's final resentment better than Tommy. But Faith should have confronted Asa and told him how he was hurting her. Instead she made Hope pay the price.

One afternoon, he went to the office address Hope had given him the last time he ran into her on the street. She had looked good enough, although not as well dressed as she had been at Seawatch. She had hugged him warmly and both said good-bye with promises to get together. At the very least, he wanted to be sure she was all right.

Looking back, he should have persuaded Faith not to do it. He was as guilty as she was. He knew it made no sense to dredge up old history. If he told Hope the truth, knowing Hope, she would probably shrug it off and tell him she was better off. It wasn't in her to play the victim.

"Can you come out and have coffee with me?" he asked when the receptionist took him to see Hope, who had her own office. He was impressed. She stood, obviously delighted, hugged and kissed him, and took him in to meet Martin.

"This is Tommy Rowland," she said, holding on to his arm. "He's from my life with the Simpsons. He saw me through a lot of trouble. His mother probably saved my sanity."

"Hello, Tommy Rowland," said Martin with a big smile. "Happy to meet you."

"Likewise," said Tommy. "I see Hope has her own office. That means she's doing OK."

"She's doing better than OK," said Martin, looking at Hope when he answered. "She's my partner."

When they were out on the street, Tommy said, "I never told you this, but my mother and I never believed you were involved in that business at Seawatch. You would never have done that to Asa."

"I'm sure there was plenty to talk about after I left. Mrs. Coombs was suspicious of me from the start."

"She thought you were always just looking for opportunity. For a way to make it better for Hope."

"Was that the impression all around?"

"I'm not trying to be mean. It's the way you were seen. My mother always defended you."

"Well, thanks for telling me that, Tommy Rowland. I finally understand my personality," she said.

"Don't be mad, Hope. I didn't think that, but so what if you had a little ambition? Look where it took you. Martin called you his partner."

"He took a chance on me. I'm not really his partner yet, but we work closely."

"Are you and Martin together?"

Hope laughed. "Not in the way I think you mean. We like each other as friends."

"Hmm. I'm not so sure about that on his part."

"Why?"

"The way he looked at you."

Hope shrugged. "I like it the way it is, although I do get a little lonely on weekends."

"I know plenty of men who would be happy to keep you company. Just say the word."

"I'm going to confess something, Tommy," she said, looking down at her cup. "Remember Robert Trent? I sometimes think of him."

"I not only remember him, I just saw him last week at the Simpsons' apartment at the Dakota. You know Mr. Asa's living in New York, right? My mother and Mrs. Coombs are living in the apartment to help, but there's really not that much to do. I go over there to visit my mother, and Trent's been there a couple of times."

"Maybe he's seeing Faith."

"I don't think so. Faith lives at the college. He's there to see Mr. Asa on business. If I see him again, I'll mention you. Just a little nudge, nothing obvious." Tommy didn't really know if Faith was still pursuing her old crush, but in the moment, he wanted to do something for Hope. He'd let Trent decide if he was free to look her up.

A few weeks later, when he saw Robert Trent at the Simpsons', Tommy made it a point to mention Hope.

"Do you remember Hope Lee?"

"I remember Hope Lee," said Trent, and Tommy took note of how quickly he responded.

"I saw her recently and she mentioned you."

The look on Trent's face was unmistakable. He was interested. "What's she doing now?" he asked.

"She works for a financial firm, Beck and Company, down on Franklin. No surprise there. Mr. Simpson thought she was a genius on that score." Tommy didn't say any more. He had planted the seed, and if there was going to be any follow-up on Trent's part, he had enough information. Trent had been a cool number, but he wasn't cool when it came to Hope. Many times that summer at Seawatch, Tommy had seen him staring at her.

Tommy hoped he'd made reparations for not lifting a hand when Faith had put her best friend in harm's way. Faith was the sole heir to Asa Simpson's fortune. Hope had nothing. She had no real education, no background, no . . . polish. That was Hope in a nutshell. He wanted to help her, even though her disregard for convention frightened him. She didn't act out of rebellion; it was just the way she was. He wondered if Trent saw it, or did lust blind him? He couldn't believe that the man who had so carefully structured his career could marry someone like Hope. It would be interesting to see how it played out.

Chapter Thirty-Six

Robert Trent, his law degree in hand, had solidified his position at Wentworth and, because of his association with the Simpsons, was the natural liaison with Asa in business matters. He often walked contracts over to the Simpson apartment and had developed an easy relationship with Asa.

"Thank you for bringing these." Asa never took the accommodation for granted. "Saves a lot of time, and you always bring interesting news."

Robert was in the habit of saving bits of business gossip to get Asa's commentary. "It's really self-serving. I want to know what you think."

Pleasant as it was to have a spot in the firm, Robert Trent had very specific plans for his future. He didn't want to be just another good lawyer. He wanted to work toward a position that would be both public and respected. He wanted to put to rest any lingering doubt about his father's character. He also wanted to financially and socially overshadow the narrow-minded grandfather, who had never wanted to meet him.

Asa Simpson was an obvious avenue toward that end. Asa had a daughter of marriageable age who was already his friend, and he liked many things about her. She was whip-smart and had a sense of humor that he liked to play against. He didn't have to adjust his personality to be at ease with her as he did with some women. She wore her status well and never traded on her father's stature.

For all those reasons, it would be plausible for him to court Faith Simpson and ask Asa for her hand. But that was not the union Robert wanted. He felt a tenderness for Faith that gave him pause. He remembered those first awkward days at Seawatch. He had seen firsthand her determination and grit on the tennis court and in swimming. She was afraid of the water but swam every day, even though he could see her trembling with anxiety. But a marriage of convenience had no appeal to him. His mother had risked alienation and loss of a sizable trust fund to marry his father, and she had never been sorry. They were in love. Faith deserved nothing less.

For the past two months, they had been seeing each other, and his reservations were weakening. He had not kissed her yet, but he often wanted to kiss her. Her breasts were a constant distraction. They were round and unrestricted. It looked as if she wasn't wearing underwear, and that thought excited him. She had begun to hold his arm when they walked, and he liked to have her hand resting there.

Now Tommy's mention of Hope had stopped the march to Faith. *Wait. Don't I want to see Hope? What about Hope?* Upon hearing her name, he felt anxious, as if he had already made the mistake of not choosing her. Then came relief that it was not too late. He thought of the loneliness she must have endured when she left Seawatch. He had heard the gossip of the breach perpetrated by a girl at the Simpsons'. The tycoons had lost a lot of money. He had never believed Hope was involved. He could have found her and reached out. Not that she would have shown him any weakness. Not Hope.

◆ ◆ ◆

The tempest that had plagued him every day of that feverish summer returned and blew apart the fragile alliance he had so carefully constructed with Faith. There was nothing he could do but go to Hope.

Chapter Thirty-Seven

For many days after she saw Tommy, Hope replayed their conversation. Her cheeks got hot when she remembered what Mrs. Coombs had said about her. Was she always after something? She had heard the word *chiseler* used recently by Martin regarding a broker who always needed to take a few extra cents commission. "He's a chiseler," said Martin. "He's always after something extra for himself, and it makes me uncomfortable being around him." Was that her, too? Hope was seldom self-reflective, but after the conversation with Tommy, she monitored her behavior to see if she was chiseling her way through life.

Something else troubled her. Asa and Faith had moved to the city. It was just the two of them. When Faith had told her that she had never gone on a special outing alone with her father, had Faith been sending her a signal to leave some room in Asa's heart for her? Hope replayed the months she had spent alone with Asa, heads together, happily sharing ideas while Faith remained outside the inner sanctum. She had behaved like a smug, selfish girl. She wanted to tell Faith how sorry she was to have taken her father away from her.

Tommy's comment about Hope being out for herself was harsh, but it was a turning point. There was no need to be always hunting for the edge. Life had ceased to be a struggle for survival. She had sold half of her old furniture polish business to the woman manager and received a monthly check. She had a cushion of money and a decent apartment. Her job with Martin had given her the opportunity to be as successful as she wanted to be. It was the perfect place to learn and develop her skill for taking those dollars Martin had spoken about and using them to make more dollars. He had taught her how to be cautious and how to take chances. He taught her about risk.

"Everything you do is a risk," Martin said, "but there's a way of hedging your risks so that the downside is minimized. One way to do it is through puts and calls. There are other ways. Remember one rule: there are no sure bets, in life or in business."

The firm had accumulated clients, some from Martin's colleagues in London and others from his contacts in New York. His father had gone on to get a law degree and specialized in immigration. He was able to send the new arrivals to Martin. They managed funds from as little as a thousand dollars to several million. They also had the firm's house account, which Martin managed very conservatively and kept as a cushion to protect the few stocks he bought on margin.

Every day, the work was a challenge and always thrilling, right up to the minute the market closed. The excitement of it never diminished, and Hope remained at her desk many evenings plotting the next day's transactions.

Martin invested most of the money in blue-chip securities: oil, sugar, transportation, and steel. He didn't churn accounts, a practice of selling and buying often to induce commissions. He followed politics avidly because laws were passed that either hurt certain stocks or helped. He covered all his bases, kept it clean, and refused to act on emotional hysteria that seemed more and more to grip Wall Street.

Six months in, Martin had put Hope on the penny-stock desk. She would buy large lots of a stock that traded at a few cents, and when it gained two or three cents, she would sell. She repeated this maneuver throughout the day. It didn't take her long to discover a bundle of stocks that fluctuated all day long, and she concentrated on those. One was a company called Magnetic Devices, which she bought and sold at least five times a day. She traded for the firm's account and kept 20 percent of any profits. The penny-stock desk was a moneymaker and perfectly suited for Hope, who quickly developed a knack for getting in and out quickly and not being deterred from diving in again.

It was a laborious way to make money, and you had to have youth and daring on your side. Hope had both, and it excited her anew each time she bought ten thousand shares of a 50-cent issue and made a profit of $200 when it went up 2 cents a half hour later.

Some days, there was extreme volatility, and the market churned up and down. On those days, she increased her trades, but the discipline was always there. Three cents was her trigger to sell and she never deviated. She had learned this from Sen. If something was going up too quickly, there was a manipulator behind it 90 percent of the time. It didn't matter if she missed a few cents. The game was played with caution, and that's how she won.

After several months of penny-stock trading, Hope graduated to a new category—stocks priced at $1 to $5. These stocks had less volatility, but they were safer. She learned the rhythm of her new list and continued to make small but reliable amounts of money.

When Hope had been in the partnership a year, she stopped worrying about her livelihood and keeping her life together. She turned to her personal life.

Martin was dating an attractive woman doctor who had inherited $100,000 and given it to Martin to manage. He kept insisting it was very casual, but it reminded Hope that she didn't have an emotional life. She spent so much time in the office with Martin that most days there was no room for anything else. It would have been so easy to turn to Martin. There were moments when their faces were inches apart, and she would see a softness in his eyes that was possibly directed at her. It wouldn't have been fair to either of them. She didn't think of him in that way. Besides, Martin had no problem attracting women, and he was content playing the field.

On weekends, she would go out and see young men and women in pairs. Everything she saw summarized what was missing in her life at the moment. Even old men and women gathered together and played chess or chatted on the benches in Seward Park. The streets she loved so much were a reproach. There was no one for her.

Love was a new concept for Hope, and it took her by surprise. She needed someone who knew where she was, how she was doing, and if she was happy or sad at the end of the day. She thought of Robert Trent. She had never forgotten the kiss at Seawatch. Lips were the smallest place to touch and yet the result was chaotic. She wanted to test that chaos, but only with him. She thought of looking for him but always pushed the idea into the future. In the end, she didn't have to look for him. He found her.

One evening in June at the end of a warm spring day, she walked out into the street thinking of how best to walk home, and there he was. A low wall made of schist, the stone that they had excavated to make room for the subway, surrounded a small rectangular spit of grass. He sat on the wall with his arms propped on his thighs, looking up at her with a quizzical expression. He wore a beige linen suit and a white shirt. He had loosened his tie, and that small detail made him look vulnerable and questioning. She felt as if her blood had been rerouted and was rushing to her chest and the front of her head. Her first thought was to run, but she was unable to move.

They stayed still and looked at each other without speaking. They had both known this moment would come. "Hello, Robert Trent," she said, already frightened by what was going on inside her. "What are you doing here?"

"I'm here to get you," he said softly. He was certain. Why had it taken him so long to look for her? Tears rolled down her cheeks. He stood and took her in his arms.

He pushed back her hair and held her face in both his hands so he could kiss her fully. The palm of his hand unintentionally grazed her breast, and he pressed down gently. She pushed away. "Wait. What happens now?"

"You come with me. You come with me."

A moment later, as dusk enveloped the street and the figures, Martin Beck saw them as he came out of his office building and realized for the first time how much he loved the girl and how much he had lost from his fear of scaring her. For now it was too late.

Chapter Thirty-Eight

He lived in a brownstone building on Charles Street, a little mews that ran for only two blocks. Carved at the entrance was the name "Docevilla." They arrived there after a dinner that had been a blur, and they left their meals uneaten. She hardly saw where they were going and was surprised to reach a destination.

"I'll take you home if that's what you want," he said.

She shook her head. "I want to stay with you." She felt fragile, as if she could splinter into a million pieces. The kiss, the way he held her arm, guided her, put his arm around her waist, and brought her to him; it was all new. One moment she was just an ordinary girl standing on the street, and the next she was part of someone else. The most startling thing was that she hadn't known she needed this, and now it would be unthinkable to have it gone.

"I remember that first day at Seawatch. You came late in the afternoon and we were coming up from the beach. We cleaned up and went to dinner, and there you were. I remembered you from the poetry class. I was so nervous. I didn't know where to look."

"I didn't know where to look, either. I wanted to look at you for a long time, but Asa would have sent me right back to the city. I would have run away with you right then and there."

"And now?"

"Now we're grown-ups. Now we can decide what to be to each other."

What they both knew with some relief was that they didn't have to decide anything for a while. They had this period of grace.

◆　◆　◆

She loved everything about his apartment. She loved his furniture. She loved the wide sleigh bed with a feather mattress that gave willingly to their forms. She loved his clothes. She loved the feel of the fabrics against her skin. He had photographs from his boyhood and his time at St. Paul's, and they depicted a solemn, thoughtful young man in an ice hockey uniform.

He didn't approach her that first night, even though they slept entangled in each other's arms. The intimacy was difficult. She would reach a point and then was too frightened to continue. It took her a long time to trust the ritual, and he didn't rush her.

"We can stay this way forever," he told her. "It's enough to be with you."

She held on to herself as long as possible. Each night, she tried to push a little further. She stayed alert through his sighs and groans of pleasure. Then, when she thought she'd managed all of her feelings, she let him travel her body with his lips, until one night he could not stop.

"I love you," he murmured over and over. "I love you." It was hard for her to trust. It was impossible to let go. She stayed vigilant through all of his lovemaking, but it was too frightening to let go.

One night, he said to her, "Open your legs. Open them wide," and then he placed himself in that niche and covered her body. She was slim, but her hips and legs were muscular. "This is where I want to be. Be with me. *Be with me.*"

It was that day that Hope rose above all her fears. When he was inside her, she called out, "Don't move." Then she wrapped her muscular legs around him tightly and held him in place.

He couldn't move, and it both shocked and excited him. "Hope, for God's sake, let go."

"Wait," she said and held him tighter. When she finally released him, he entered a new rung of sensation, and they stayed together without speaking for a long time.

Afterward they were in a different place. When they looked at each other, it was different. They had arrived at a dangerous plateau. Robert Trent forgot his future. Only the moment mattered. He was obsessed with Hope Lee.

Her days became unreal, and only the nights mattered. She didn't know where it was going or how it would end. It never occurred to her that it might not end. All she knew was that life had become fluid. It didn't stop and start like before. It was a continuous ribbon of sensation and lightness and a blindness to everything but her beloved.

There was a mindless compulsion that transcended lust. It transcended fear and consequences. Finally, they were together, and the relief of fulfillment was almost more than they could absorb from minute to minute.

"We waited too long," he said. "This is what I wanted from the first day I saw you."

Her work life continued as before, and if Martin was more reserved and less likely to chat with her, she didn't notice. Robert came by to get her at the end of the day, and they stopped to eat dinner before going home.

One night, they were lying close together in silence. She sat up and looked down at him. "I was thinking how I wish my mother was here to meet you."

"That's odd," he said. "I was thinking about my mother, too. She married an outsider, and her parents never spoke to her again."

Hope was surprised by this revelation. Was he telling her this because of the disparity between them? "Do you want to do something important to avenge your mother?"

He didn't respond right away, and there was a moment where his consciousness pushed away awareness to keep him from focusing on the future. Finally, he said, "Probably. That's part of it."

After he told her about his mother, Hope asked him to take her to Agatha's grave. "You have access to the city records. Please help me find where they've buried my mother." She wished many times that Agatha could have spent time with Robert. The next best thing was to sit together at her grave.

It didn't take long to find the records. The Triangle fire had held a mirror to the shameful working conditions in the sweatshops, and the tragedy was the standard-bearer for reform. Because of Hope's story in the newspaper, Agatha's information was precise. When Robert found the records, the clipping was also in the archives. He understood why Asa took her in. The look of terror in that beautiful face was heartbreaking. "I've found out where your mother's buried."

"Are you sure it's her? She has a gravestone?"

"Yes. They had records of her at the factory. They also had records of her marriage certificate. It was a cross-verified identification. There was a clipping there with a picture of you."

Hope stiffened. "In that awful first year, Emma Rowland, Tommy's mother, took me. She was the one that stuck with me. I should have stayed with her."

"It didn't end well at Seawatch?"

"It ended perfectly well. I was released from the mausoleum. I still love Asa Simpson, though, and I always will. He gave me everything I needed for a long time. I can't imagine how he must have suffered when Billy died. I wish I had been there to help him. He was an orphan, too, you know."

"What about Faith?"

She didn't answer for a long time but looked steadily at his face. "I miss Faith. She was my second real friend." She thought he would react, but his eyes were centered on her, and Faith seemed very far away.

"The second? Who was the first?"

"A little street girl named Gloria. She taught me how to beg on the streets when my mother was in the hospital and I was alone."

Robert looked alarmed. "How long did that last?"

"A few weeks. Then she left without saying good-bye. I wanted to kill her. Faith lasted much longer." She thought he'd want to talk about Faith. He must see her from time to time when he went to the apartment. He was finished with Columbia, but they must have connected while he was there. She was sure that's what Faith had had in mind. He changed the subject.

"Would you like me to take you to your mother's grave?"

Maybe Faith was still in love with him, and now he was with her. She didn't want to know any of it. She was happy and she felt complete. She would hold on to him for however long it lasted. "Yes. Please take me. Where is it?"

"After the fire, the bodies were taken to Charities Pier over on Twenty-Sixth Street and the river. Relatives took many of the bodies and buried them privately. The others were divided between the Hebrew Free Burial Association and the Mount Richmond Cemetery, and the six unidentified victims are at the Cemetery of the Evergreens in Brooklyn."

"My mother wasn't Jewish. Are you sure she's at the Hebrew cemetery?"

"Yes. She's there. Twenty-three bodies from the fire are there. Maybe not all of them were Jewish."

"Where is the cemetery?"

"It's on Staten Island, near the ferry."

They took the ferry to the Saint George Station and hired a car to take them to the cemetery. In less than half an hour, the driver pulled up to the entrance. Hope was quiet the entire trip. She was in her own reverie.

Robert asked the driver to wait for them. The caretaker walked them to the grave and gave them some background. "They buried all of the factory girls in one section. They're in a nice spot where they get the river breeze," he said. "I'll help you find your mother."

She was at the end of a row. The tombstone showed Agatha's name and how she died.

AGATHA M. LEE, 1879–1911, VICTIM OF THE TRIANGLE SHIRTWAIST FACTORY FIRE

Hope sat on the grass next to her mother's grave and ran her fingers across the tombstone. She rested her head at the base of it and then lengthened her entire body so that she was fully stretched over her mother's grave, her face pressed to the ground.

As she lay there, Robert wondered what his mother's family would think if they saw this scene. He wondered what his own mother would think. Hope was different. She offered a vigorous, irresistible reality, one that was not for the timid.

He heard her murmuring, talking to the grave. He sat on a bench nearby and gave her privacy and time. There was nothing he could do for her here. She was far away from him in a place he could not reach.

On the way home, she sat away from him with her face pressed to the window, looking toward the cemetery long after it was out of view.

Chapter Thirty-Nine

Faith was aware of a deep melancholy overshadowing her life. She tried to convince herself there was a good reason for Robert's absence, but there was no scenario she could summon that had a happy ending. For almost two months, they had been meeting at least once a week at the little Greek restaurant on Columbus. The dinners passed with talk and laughter. The silences were comfortable, and when they looked at each other, there was a new understanding. She felt beautiful because she felt wanted. They had been on the verge of love, or at least an accommodation.

Then Robert had evaporated, and there had been this horrible long silence. She had called Tommy and asked him to meet her at a coffee shop near campus. She needed him to investigate.

"I need your help," she said. "Robert and I had been seeing each other regularly and it's stopped. I need to know if he's seeing someone else. I need for you to investigate."

"No investigation needed," he said. "Robert is living with your old friend Hope Lee. They live down in Greenwich Village. My new office is down there, and I've seen them together, but they were far down the street. We didn't talk."

"Why didn't you tell me?"

"I didn't see any reason to tell you. I didn't know that you and Trent were serious or even semiserious."

"You've seen him at the apartment." There was accusation in her voice.

Tommy put up his palm. "Faith, stop. I've seen him there with your father. If you and Robert Trent were having a serious relationship, why would he be with Hope? And how should I have known that their relationship would interest you?"

She looked at Tommy as if he were talking gibberish, then she squared her shoulders and took a breath of acceptance. "They're living together?"

"I can't say for sure, but I think so."

"Thank you for telling me. Sorry for my tone."

"It's all right," he said. "Sorry it worked out this way."

"It hasn't worked out any way," she said crossly. "This is temporary." She threw a bill on the table and got up to leave.

When Tommy left her, he felt guilt and confusion. Had he known he was taking Faith's beau? Had he conveniently ignored their history and obvious signs just to do something nice for Hope? It was too late now to undo what was started. What had she meant that it was temporary? She had said it with certainty, and he believed her. In his heart, he, too, felt it wouldn't last, but for different reasons. Robert Trent was ambitious, and Hope had nothing to offer.

◆ ◆ ◆

Faith's redemption script, charming as it was, had lost its footing, but she convinced herself it was temporary.

Now that Robert was unavailable, her need for him was almost unbearable. What hurt the most, if you could characterize Faith's emotional frenzy as hurt, was the humiliation she had to face. She was easy to leave. Maybe it had been a relief. Was he relieved to be rid of her? Conversely, his attraction to Hope was worth all the money and prestige and long-term social gain that he was throwing away. Hope was magnetic; without any effort, she had lured Robert away from a fortune so large it set the bar for other fortunes. Just as she had lured Asa away. If you stripped it down to the crass truth, that's what it was.

Faith had no heart left for Barnard or New York, but she remained at school and even began to see a quirky boy from her economics class. His name was Henry Cole, and he engaged her interest when he told her that his life motto was "Like everyone else, I am being tortured to death." His black humor sustained her until the semester was over.

During the summer, Faith worked full time for her father's firm and became so proficient at analysis that she didn't want to return to Barnard. She had her father's full attention. He depended on her, sought her advice, and included her in every aspect of his business. It was that summer that he finally divorced Alice. Faith wondered if one of the beautiful gold diggers who were always infiltrating the social scene would go after her father. She hoped not. She hoped he would meet someone who truly loved him and took the time to understand him.

Out of the blue, she got her wish. An attractive woman from Muttonville, Margaret Fellows, who had occasionally cut Asa's hair at Seawatch, began coming to the Dakota. She still cut his hair, but that was just an excuse he used to see her, then she stayed overnight. It was obvious that they made each other happy.

Margaret was a late-in-life gift for Asa. She came from an upper-middle-class family and had studied medicine. She had begun cutting hair in Muttonville when the one barber died. When the new barber came and set up shop, she continued cutting Asa's hair, and he admitted to her now that many times he had wanted to kiss her but was afraid she would take the scissors and stab him. Margaret smiled and said, "That might have happened."

When they were together, Asa touched her arms, her shoulders, her face. He sometimes covered her hand with his at dinner. Faith could see that he had absorbed all that had befallen him and gained some peace.

Seeing her father happy after so much pain, Faith herself regained her optimism and looked to the future. That didn't mean she abandoned her pursuit of Robert Trent. Her pursuit of an acceptable outcome was still in place.

Chapter Forty

Hope sat on the bed in the early morning, her hair spilling over her forehead. Her nightgown was just a simple silk slip with thin straps. One of the straps had fallen over her arm and the top of her breast was visible. A slant of morning sun highlighted her face that was still pale from sleep. Everything about her that he found irresistible was there. She filled all the unvoiced needs, desires that only she aroused. He knew what he had to give up for her. He also knew what he received in return.

He went to sit next to her and took her hand.

"I love you being here with me," he said. "I want to make you happy."

"I'm happy," she said.

"No. You're thoughtful. You're thinking about all of this."

"I'm so used to being by myself, and now I have you. I think about it all the time."

"How can I make you stop thinking and just be with me?"

"Give me a little time. It will happen."

Her constant evaluation lessened but didn't disappear. He was what she wanted. The sight of him crowded out all else. When she brought him to that senseless abandon, it was a triumph and a source of wonder but also a source of worry for a time when it would diminish. She didn't trust this state of nervous excitement. It had to be temporary because people couldn't live their entire lives like this. When would the sensual disappear and calmer emotions take over? And would that be enough for him? He was oriented in a different direction. He led an entire other life that she found hard to share.

He took her to plays she didn't understand and made references to books she had never read. She felt her lack of a classical education. The classes at Seawatch had taken her just so far. There were other things. He had his suits tailored to order—even his shoes were made by hand—and all the materials were chosen with care. She had good clothes and accessories, but they didn't have that extra patina, the special seams, the suppleness of select fabrics tailored to perfection. Every time she saw his initials embroidered on the breast pocket of his shirt, it reminded her that though he wasn't wealthy, he was wellborn, and those lessons had deep roots. Faith and Billy had the same roots and so had their mother, Alice.

Sometimes he would practice addressing a jury in the mirror. He would speak without notes. Beautiful, concise ideas would pour out. He framed his arguments in emotional word pictures that often brought her to tears. It wasn't just that he could present a persuasive defense, it was his use of language and the thoughts and ideas that showcased his character.

Asa had always remarked that she was a raw thinker, whatever that meant. And maybe that was good for evaluating stocks, but for any other profession, she would have been at a loss. These concerns rose up from time to time, and no amount of reassurance on Robert's part made her believe that she was an adequate partner for him.

One morning, as he was getting dressed and she was still lingering in bed, he said, "We're going to a grand party. It's the firm's end-of-year celebration, and they make it into a charity ball."

"You mean with dancing? I don't know how to dance. I learned a little at Seawatch, but it doesn't come naturally. I think you should go alone."

Briefly, his face relaxed. It would be so much easier to go alone. Introducing Hope into the conservative culture of the Wentworth firm would be risky. Her stark honesty might not play well with this older crowd. Her face was beautiful but obviously biracial, and there were bigots who could be patronizing. Then, of course, there were Asa and Faith. Did Asa still feel she had betrayed him? Would it upset him to see her there? Despite the risks, he had to do it. She had to be part of *all* his life, not just the evenings. "I want you to buy something fancy to wear and go with me. Not too fancy but fancy for a ball. I can go with you to buy it if you like."

He continued to dress, and they were both silent, contemplating the many pitfalls. Hope knew it made him nervous to take her. How could it not? Asa and Faith would be there, and it would be awkward. It would probably be devastating for Faith if she still longed for Robert. She felt strange about that. On the edge of consciousness, a thought formed of a future without Robert. Even now, before it was fact, she could feel the sadness of it. The moment held all the open questions they had put aside for a later time. Now the time was here.

He came and sat next to her on the bed to put on his socks. He reached over and kissed her first on the cheek and then on the mouth. His hand found her breast.

She took it away. "It's late," she said.

"I can't get dressed," he said and reached for her again.

"Wait." She lay back on the bed, pulled her nightgown up around her waist, and exposed her thighs. She parted her legs. She wanted to be bold. If this was the only hold she had on him, she would use it.

The lovemaking was different that day. It was slow and deliberate. When he finally bent over her, they were both racing forward, reaching for a closeness that would crush any doubt.

Chapter Forty-One

Faith asked Tommy Rowland to meet her in a luncheonette near Barnard.

When he arrived, Faith stood and embraced him. Tommy felt nervous, unsure of what she wanted, but he no longer felt guilty. It wasn't his fault that Trent lusted after Hope and only liked Faith for her money and social standing. He had probably done Faith a favor. Who would want to marry a man who only wanted to use you?

"Thank you for coming way uptown to meet me."

"Sure. Why not?"

"I ordered coffee for both of us. They have a bottle here for me if you want something stronger."

"Coffee is fine," said Tommy. "Was there a particular reason you wanted to see me?"

"It can wait. I want to know how your job's going. Papa can help if you want a change. Just say the word."

"Thanks. That's nice to know. They had a job fair at the college and all the firms came looking. They interview you right then and there. I got something before school ended, and it's worked out."

"That's wonderful." She stirred her coffee and took a sip. "I have a proposition for you," said Faith. "A business deal, really. You do something for me, and I will pay you well to do it."

"Sounds interesting," said Tommy, "although I could just do you a favor for old times' sake. No payment necessary."

"That's very gracious, but I want to pay. This is more than a small favor and will require some skill. As you told me a while back, Hope is living with Robert, a man I want to marry."

Tommy was surprised to hear her lay it out so simply and honestly. You had to hand it to Faith, she didn't waste time with platitudes. She had definitely grown up and left the sensitive, awkward girl behind. He noticed how pretty she looked and was a bit surprised he hadn't seen it before. "Are you going to ask me to kill Hope?" he said and laughed.

"Not at all." She didn't miss a beat. "I want you to go to the firm where Robert works and speak to the managing partner, Mr. Paul Wentworth. You know him—he was president of the board of the Muttonville Neighborhood Association. He may even remember you. Set up an appointment with him. I've written a speech that I want you to give him." Faith handed him an envelope. He opened it and saw five $100 bills and the neatly handwritten message that he was being paid to deliver. He read it twice. He had to admit it was a stunning move. "Will you do it, Tommy?"

Tommy handed back the money. "This isn't necessary for me to do you a favor."

"Of course. I'm sorry."

"That doesn't mean I'm going to do it. I have to think about the consequences. Not for you and Hope, but for me."

"There shouldn't be any consequences for you."

"How can there not be? You're like my sister, Faith. More than anyone, I'm a witness to everything that happened to you. You have every right to fight for happiness. Every right. But I have to think about this."

He walked away, leaving her there with the money and a new respect for Tommy Rowland.

She had no misgivings over what she had set in motion. Choose happiness, Billy had told her. *Just take it.* However he had meant it,

229

this is what she had to do. Robert Trent had disengaged from her and taken up with Hope. She was betting that as much as he may have been attracted to Hope, he loved his future more. She was going to remind him of that in gentle terms. As Josie often said, "Men are dolts and you have to save them." If he chose to remain with Hope despite the consequences, she would have to accept it. The loss of Robert's attention had created turmoil for a while, but now she would give it one more try. She was going to fight for happiness.

Chapter Forty-Two

In the end, Tommy did what Faith asked. He loved Faith Simpson, and she deserved to be happy. What he could not admit until much later was his suspicion that Trent was using Hope without good intentions. If he was wrong, Trent would stay with her regardless. Either way, it would be the right outcome.

The firm of Wentworth, Blanchard and Grunwald was located at the southern end of Park Avenue on floors three and four of an imposing limestone building. The lobby floor was marble and echoed each step, as if you were tap dancing. The upper walls were papered in dark-maroon silk and sat atop paneled mahogany wainscoting. Rows of etched-glass wall sconces threw off a subdued light. A liveried man stood behind a mahogany podium, lit with a green accountant's lamp, directing those who came in.

Tommy had never had business in such a building. The closest he had come was the bank where he'd gone to open a checking account. But despite all the marble and polished brass in that bank, it was a well-lighted place and business was done on one floor. He considered abandoning his errand. He felt inadequate. He felt the seriousness of the legal profession. Mr. Wentworth was not only a lawyer to many important men and corporations, he was an important man himself. He was a founder of the Muttonville Neighborhood Association and had headed the board of directors for more than fifteen years. He gave generous amounts of money to keep the library fully stocked and the building in good repair. He maintained the tennis courts next to the library. He funded a day camp for disadvantaged children who came out from the city every summer and spent two weeks in tents, enjoying fishing and swimming in the clear waters of Long Island Sound.

Tommy felt clumsy and ill dressed. For one of the few times in his life, he also felt his class. He wanted to leave but he had made an appointment, and Mr. Wentworth had probably scheduled a time slot for him at the expense of his law work.

After a brief conversation with the greeter, he entered the middle elevator. When the attendant closed the door, he said, "Four. I'm going to Wentworth."

"Yes, sir," said the operator and closed the elevator door.

He was carrying information that was of interest to the firm. It was not terrible information. It was just a gentle aside that something was going on that might not sit well with the firm.

Wentworth's office was as somber and imposing as expected. When Tommy walked in, Paul Wentworth rose and shook his hand. After a brief greeting, Tommy looked straight at Paul Wentworth and gave Faith's speech in a strong voice, word for word: "Mr. Wentworth, thank you for seeing me. You may remember me from Muttonville. I'm here to make you aware of a relationship being conducted by one of your employees that could potentially bring unwelcome publicity to the firm. Robert Trent, a man I've know from his visits to Seawatch, is living with Hope Lee, a protégé of Mr. Simpson who was banished because of questionable behavior. If this information is of no concern to you, I apologize for wasting your time."

Paul Wentworth, a thin, elegant man with sharp features, played with a letter opener that sat on the leather-bound blotter on his desk. He took it out of its sheath and replaced it three times. Finally he placed the sheath in its niche and fixed Tommy Rowland with a cold, unswerving stare. "My initial reaction and perhaps my only reaction, Tommy—and I do remember you—is to question what could possibly be your interest in this? Why would you take the initiative to warn me? I can't believe it's just a whim on your part. What is your stake in this?"

Tommy, expecting to be met with gratitude, became flustered. The only answer he had was the truth. "Faith Simpson asked me to do it, sir."

"I see. Am I to understand that Asa has no knowledge of this?"

"I think not, sir."

"Well, Tommy, I know of your loyalty to the Simpson family, and you've carried out your mission. Thank you." He rose, and Tommy took his cue to stand and say good-bye.

"You are welcome, sir. Did you want to ask me anything else?"

"No. I've got the picture loud and clear."

"All right, then, good-bye."

By the time he left Ten Park Avenue, Tommy Rowland had aged to full adulthood. He felt sad and uncomfortable. During the twenty-block walk to his evening job on Second Avenue, he amended his thoughts. He hadn't created this mess. It was Faith's doggedness and Hope's crazy beauty and Robert Trent's lust. Those three were the ones to blame. Maybe nothing would happen. Paul Wentworth might see it as trivial and not worth his attention. If he did reel Trent in and ask him to adjust his lifestyle, then it was up to Trent to decide where his loyalties were placed. Maybe it would turn out better for Hope. Maybe Trent would decide to marry her and keep the whole thing on the up-and-up.

Chapter Forty-Three

One late afternoon after the market had closed, a well-dressed young man came to the office and asked to see Martin privately. Martin recognized the man from Princeton but was surprised to see him there.

"I won't beat around the bush," said the man. "I've been sent by Wentworth to impart some information." He proceeded to relate the story of Hope's banishment from Seawatch and the distrust they felt for her.

"And now Trent's in her grip." His voice had a high pitch, and this last came out as a screech. "He's one of the fair-haired at Wentworth, and they've invested a lot in him. Now his job is in jeopardy. They don't want bad publicity."

Martin said nothing throughout the hysterical outpouring, but a rage began to build in his chest.

"How dare you make such baseless implications, you bastard! How dare you libel a young woman without a shred of proof. Tell your superior and all of the pale cowards at Wentworth to do their own dirty work. But if they continue on this path, we will sue for libel. Hope Lee is a heroine in lower New York. Her mother died in the Triangle fire, and her face in the newspaper did more for workplace reform than any politician. Am I clear?"

The young man left, but the rebuke from his classmate stung. He needed revenge and he had a target. He was not done with Miss Hope Lee. He was waiting for her when she left at the end of the day.

"You little half-breed tart. Does your boyfriend know what you did back at Seawatch? He's going to lose his job taking up with the likes of you. You've tainted everything."

The attack was so sudden and so concise she didn't take it in right away. She had to pull the words apart to fully understand what had been hurled at her. *You little half-breed tart.* A tart? Is that what she was? But wasn't that when you wanted money in exchange? The worst part was that she could see it from an outsider's point of view. What was she doing, after all? Giving herself freely to a man with no stated intentions. However it looked to that man, his words were not true. She was not a tart. Her relationship with Robert had begun many years ago. They had loved each other from the first day. Her only regret was over the order of it. Love should have progressed step-by-step. She thought of Faith. Faith would never have agreed to the arrangement Hope had with Robert.

Buried in the man's insult was a kernel of truth. She had fallen into Robert's arms like a rag doll, without will or demands. There should have been a clear definition of what they expected and a plan to reach it.

Chapter Forty-Four

That evening, she brought up the charity ball to Robert and convinced him to go alone. "It's too soon," she said. "I'll go to the next one. Promise."

The night of the event, she found it difficult to be in his apartment by herself and she went to the office. Martin was still there but getting ready to leave.

"I was about to go to dinner. Want to join me?"

"Did you have a date? Are you changing your plans because of me?"

"A little. I was going to ask someone else, but how often do I get to see you outside of work these days?"

"All right."

"I thought we could go to that little hole-in-the-wall on Mulberry. The food is great, and they know my mother. They'll give us something good."

"I remember your mother. That's how you found me. She wanted to marry me off. I think she had someone in mind."

"Probably me."

"We are kind of married. I see you more than I've ever seen any other man. We're together all day long. It's like being married."

"No," said Martin. "It's not like being married. Let's get that straight. What are you doing here anyway? Isn't the big shindig tonight?"

"Yes."

"Didn't Robert go?"

"He went."

"And you?"

"It's not my kind of thing."

"Well, you had better make it your kind of thing, because this isn't the last charity ball Robert Trent will have to attend."

She remained quiet. She went to stand by the window so she wouldn't have to look at him. "Martin, I was afraid to go. I was afraid I'm the wrong kind of woman to be with their star lawyer. I was afraid for him."

"I hate to hear you talking like that. Don't tell me that coward got to you, too."

"What do you mean?"

"This toady was sent from Wentworth to warn me about you and, by extension, your relationship with Robert."

"This was about two weeks ago?"

"Yes."

"Why didn't you tell me?"

"Because I considered it underhanded and weak and ill considered at best."

"He caught me outside and called me a tart," Hope admitted. "He said, and unfortunately, I remember it word for word: 'You silly little tart.'"

Martin shook his head. "I'm going to report this bastard to the Princeton Alumni Association. I'm going to make sure he is reprimanded for behavior unbefitting a Princeton man."

"What will that do?"

"Probably nothing, but for that kind of person, a reprimand from his alma mater will hurt. Is that what's behind your not going tonight?"

"In part. I'm sure Asa and his daughter, Faith, will be there, and it will be awkward on many levels. Faith was in love with Robert."

"Hmmm. The plot widens." He was silent a moment, gearing up for a hurtful truth. "Robert should have insisted that you go with him."

"But it was my decision."

"No. It was not your decision. It was his, and he decided to take the easy way out. You might be angry to hear me say that, but as your friend, it's my job to tell you the truth." She had no answer. "Do you still want to have dinner with me?"

"No. But only because I need to be alone for a while and think things through. You said you were going to ask someone else. A girl?"

"Rebecca."

"That poor girl thinks you're going to be her steady."

"It's very casual between us."

"Maybe to you."

"She'll be all right."

"I wouldn't be all right."

Martin shrugged. After he left, she thought of the peevishness in his tone. He as much as said that Robert was not the man he wanted for her. Still, he wasn't above reproach, either. She didn't like that he was using Rebecca for company without intending a lasting relationship. Martin would argue that Robert was doing the same thing. The difference was that she was ready for it. Their attraction had been gaining strength all these years, and it had been irresistible. Now it might turn into a tawdry thing. She would end it. She had already ended it. Now it was about finding the day to let go.

Chapter Forty-Five

Tommy couldn't stop thinking about his visit to Wentworth and was glad he was going back to Muttonville to help with the annual book sale. Maybe he'd tell some of it to his mother.

When the estate people gathered at the library the day of the sale Tommy went over to Emily, who'd married one of the local boys and was very pregnant. She knew all the participants, and it was a relief for Tommy to spill some of the thoughts that were whirling in his head. When he told her that Robert Trent was living with Hope Lee, Emily almost dropped the stack of books she was carrying.

"Tell me you're fibbing. Please. I can't stand the idea."

"Why does it make a difference to you?"

"First, this girl lives with your mother as if she were an important guest instead of the penniless orphan that she was. Then she sashays over to the mansion and begins to behave as if she owns it. She charms her way into Asa and Billy's affection and shuts out Faith and makes her the outsider. And now, good Lord, it makes me want to smash these books right on the ground, she has stolen Faith's only love away from her. I don't want to get upset, because it's not good for the baby but I *am* upset. I'm very upset. Does Faith know?"

Tommy looked at Emily with alarm. He wasn't ready for the complete history of Hope's mistakes. He was already frightened by Emily's enormous girth. She had made him feel the baby kick, and he had jumped as if he'd been scalded. If Emily knew that he had a hand in the whole mess, she would probably give birth right in the book stacks.

"Faith knows."

"What is she going to do about it?"

"She's already done something, and I don't want to talk about it anymore. I've had a really stressful week."

Chapter Forty-Six

A few things helped Hope make the break. Martin sent her to New York University to take a course in statistics two nights a week, and it was easier to go back to her own apartment because it was closer to the school.

"I'll go there with you," said Robert. "I can't sleep when you're not here."

"Let's do it this way for now," she said. "I've got studying to do. We'll be together on the weekends."

There was something else. One morning, she was eating breakfast bought from a vendor and her stomach rebelled. She vomited without warning. Something was off. "I'm ill," she said to Martin. "I need to go home." She slept for the rest of the day and all of the night. Robert came around to see her and brought her food, but the sight and smell of it set her off again. She began heaving and couldn't stop. He was alarmed and wanted to take her to a doctor, but she dismissed the idea. "If I'm not better tomorrow, I'll go."

The constant nausea continued to plague her, and after two weeks, she finally went to the clinic at Bellevue Hospital and told them her symptoms. "Sounds like you are pregnant, my dear. Let's have a look." Shortly after they put her in the stirrups, the nurse had a verdict. "From the look of your cervix, it's almost certain, but we'll do a test and be sure. Best to prepare the father." Even before the test results came back, she knew it was true. She was carrying Robert Trent's child, and she knew that everything had been decided for her. She would not tell him. Pity or duty would force him to stay, and that was not a life she wanted.

She had already begun to pull away. It would just take a little more discipline to end the long good-bye.

On the last day they saw each other, he looked so dejected she wanted to open her arms and reassure him, but it couldn't be done. "I love you," he said. "Please don't push me away."

"I'm not pushing you away," she said. And then, with sadness, "Is it just the physical with us? Is that what holds us together? Because that won't last."

He was not ready, and he struggled to find reassuring words that did not come. "I don't know," he said. "I don't know."

"It frightens me. I don't want to wait to find out."

He put his hand on her face and there were tears in his eyes. She had already made her decision. "I love you, Hope Lee." Then he walked out.

◆　◆　◆

She would not allow herself to relive any part of it. Would she ever know such closeness again? She knew there was nothing like it in store for her. She was twenty-three years old and her life was already done with love.

She saw it as an episode of illness with a high fever, one in which you are delirious and nothing is real except your need to stay still and heal the body. You get better and the everydayness of life helps you, and you continue as you were.

The nausea finally went away, but she never felt like her old self. When the baby kicked for the first time, it was an affront. The movements startled her. It was as if the baby were jostling her for attention. She had to face the fact that she was tied to Robert in the cruelest way. He would not be the same man if his future were taken away. A child out of wedlock would probably ruin his career, and the two of them would be tied by misery and regret. She wanted a clean break with no strings or recriminations. For both of them.

Chapter Forty-Seven

Tommy shared an office with three other young men. While the others went carousing after work, he had always headed to his second job. Since the Prohibition Act, it was now at a restaurant where he waited tables. After the Wentworth encounter, Tommy began joining the boys for a few beers after work. He needed time joking around and laughing with the carefree young group. He needed to forget about Faith and Seawatch.

His office was a few blocks from Hope's company, and he sometimes spotted her in the street. In late spring, he had seen her ahead half a block, but she quickly was lost in a crowd. He became obsessed with looking for her at the end of the day. Twice he had followed her at a distance and was concerned by the way she walked. Every few feet, she would stop, hold on to a building's wall, and wait to gather strength to continue. It was obvious she was alone and not going to Charles Street. He would tell Faith that her plan had been accomplished, and then step away from the Simpsons for a while.

"How can you be sure there's been a real break?" asked Faith. She had come downtown and met him at his office. They walked arm in arm along Broadway. Tommy bought some fish and chips from a street vendor, and they sat on a bench and munched on the chips.

"I've followed her home several nights. She seems ill. She stops every few steps and hangs on to a building. I can see there's something wrong. As far as her entanglement with Trent, that appears to be finished."

That was the last time he saw Faith until he went back to Muttonville for Christmas. It was not the last time he thought about Hope. He worried about her. He remembered the first few weeks when his mother had taken care of her. They had trudged together back and forth to the Neighborhood House. She hardly spoke in those early months, but she often grabbed his arm. She followed close wherever he took her. She trusted him to teach her how to be buoyant in deep water and how to use the simple breaststroke to swim in the sound. He heard her pitiful, private crying at night. Now he feared there was something wrong. It worried him.

He had a hand in starting the affair between Hope and Trent, but the decision to end it had been theirs. He was almost certain it wouldn't have ended in marriage. Trent was on a path that needed a different wife. Now beautiful Hope was left ravaged. A disease had taken over her body. Maybe she had been driven to prostitution. There was plenty of that going on downtown. The one time he had approached her, she had rushed away with vague excuses. He could see that she didn't want to talk. He knew also that Martin would make sure she was all right.

Chapter Forty-Eight

Faith had expected to feel satisfaction, but it didn't come. What she felt was unease, an unspecific sadness. Twice she had interfered in Hope's life, and even though Tommy had said rightly that if Robert had wanted to stay, he would have stayed, she could not absolve herself. She took her dilemma to the unlikeliest person, her roommate, Josie Klein.

She had gone to Josie for solace when Robert had disappeared. "The man I love has taken up with a girl," she had told Josie during a massage session at Arden's.

Josie immediately sat up, upsetting a bowl of oil on the table. "Ditching good money for a romp in the hay with a girl? I wouldn't worry. Help him come to his senses. Men are dolts. You have to show them the way or they'll go to ruin."

"I took your advice about that man," she said now to Josie. "It worked."

"He came crawling back?"

"Not yet, and I don't feel good about what I did."

"Why not?"

"I know the girl he was seeing."

"Really?" Josie was surprised. "Took him from a friend, eh?" Josie shrugged.

"Sort of. We haven't been friends for a while."

"So what's the problem?"

"I don't know. Now that we're talking about it, I honestly don't know what the problem is."

"Oh wait," said Josie. "I know. Now that you have him, you don't want him anymore. That can happen."

"I still want him, but he also has to want me."

"I can't believe what I'm hearing," said Josie. "You have eighty million reasons to be wanted—and don't cringe and say that's not the way you want it to be, because that's the way it will always be for a girl like you. Even if somebody adores you. And, by the way, you don't really want somebody adoring you. Usually they are weak individuals who can't hold an important job. What I'm saying is the money is too hard to separate. That's why the rich go into arranged marriages. They have contracts and all that stuff, even if they're in love. That's the way it is. Have your father arrange it. He'll approach it like a business deal, and your man will take the deal."

"I'm not so sure."

"Believe me," said Josie. "He'll take the deal."

"That was exactly my friend's advice when I first met this man."

"The friend you snatched him from?" Josie's eyes were as wide as she could stretch them. "This is turning into a fabulous tale. What has she got? More millions?"

Faith stretched out on the narrow bed, closed her eyes, and thought of how to describe Hope. "She has no real money. I would say she's exotic, but that's not really true. She's beautiful in a unique way and completely oblivious of her powers of attraction."

"Wow. You are lucky he left her at all. But that should work in your favor. If he was able to detach himself from this love machine, he's looking toward the future and will be open to your father's deal."

Faith went to Josie and kissed her on the cheek. "You're so smart, Josie Klein. You cut everything down to size and make it surmountable.

I'm lucky that I landed you for a roommate, and I'm going to buy you something glittery from Tiffany's."

"Just invite me to the wedding."

◆　◆　◆

Faith wasn't completely aware of how compelling it was to be Asa Simpson's daughter or how much that aura would play into her success with Robert. Any psychologist could have told her that the aura was more important than the actual details. She came with a promise of not just rising above the ordinary but blasting through it to unimaginable heights. It was like stepping up on a platform where the air was rarified and the possibilities stretched out into the ether.

Behind the gates at Seawatch, surrounded by servants and villagers who had known her all her life, she was just Faith. Her father wanted to keep it that way. In New York, the financial capital of the world, she was Asa Simpson's single daughter and sole heir. Because of Billy's death and Alice's departure, she had not gone the route of coming out as a debutante. She was relieved that she had escaped what she saw as a parade of flesh for eligible upper-crust lazy males.

She bumped into Robert on Amsterdam, the street that ran in back of Columbia. She suggested they have coffee and catch up. She wanted to satisfy herself that he was really separated. He was subdued and thoughtful and kept stirring the coffee and looking up to examine her face. "You look beautiful," he said. "Being a city girl suits you."

She thanked him but wanted to continue her investigation. "The little group from Seawatch has moved to the city. Tommy is working for a big accounting firm and has a couple of other jobs because he's determined to buy one of those tract houses and be a regular commuter. Hope works for a financial firm and is doing well."

At this, Robert turned and she could not see his face, but that turn told her everything. Hope was not out of his system. Never mind. She had the resources to wipe his heart clean.

She had stopped reviewing the past and made some decisions about her future. With another year looming, she was done with Barnard and would convince her father to let her leave.

"I'm ready to join you at the firm, Papa. I don't see any value in continuing with the soft curriculum I'm getting at Barnard. I know about the Lake poets and Henry James and the Hegelian dialectic."

"Those are all good things to know," Asa said. "Take it from someone who didn't go to college. You have your whole life ahead of you. This is the time to get to know yourself. Make some friends and connections."

"Papa, let's face it. I'm not good at making friends. I have one friend, Josie Klein. She says you're worth eighty million dollars, and that makes me a good catch. Is that true?"

Asa laughed. "You're definitely a good catch, but I have no idea how much I'm worth. It would be too tedious to add it up and a silly way to spend my time. After a certain amount, it really doesn't matter. With your mother and Billy gone, you're too solitary. I want you to have more friends."

"Most of the girls are at college to meet the man of their dreams or become communists, neither of which appeals to me. I will stay if you insist, but I hope you don't, because I don't see any purpose in it."

Asa knew that although what Faith was saying about Barnard wasn't true, she would never back down. "Finish the semester, and we'll talk about it again." They both knew that meant he would let her do whatever she wanted.

◆ ◆ ◆

Asa wanted to ease out of the day-to-day management of the firm and pursue his new interest in real estate. The market had become a playground for the unscrupulous and the greedy. Sound principles went by the wayside. For almost a year, he had turned his focus to residential real estate on the west side of the city. Many of the big old buildings west of Central Park were turning into cooperatives, which meant the tenants could buy shares in the building and own the apartments in which they lived. If you bought a rental building and then sold off shares to the tenants or new buyers, you tripled or quadrupled your money when the entire building sold out. He often walked the streets identifying neighborhoods that had potential.

What better time to ease his daughter into the business? Faith had been managing her own portfolio and doing better than the Dow list. She knew all the traps. More important, she was at ease with the entire glossary of investment options. She had definitely done her homework, and she was ready. Asa had two high-level employees with steady hands who would guide her. There were rules and a philosophy in place and as long as she didn't stray too far, she would be all right. Asa would continue to be a presence if not a participant.

Like all men who had never gone to college, he felt stigmatized. He knew that while life experience could substitute for much of a college education, there was a lot more to it than that. Barnard was teaching his daughter about world history and philosophy and art, and making her interact with some of the smartest young women in the country. The experience had transformed her. Despite the double blow of losing her brother and her mother, she had taken control of every aspect of her life. She looked wonderful and had more flair and confidence than he ever remembered. Faith was blossoming into quite the woman, and he was impressed. He believed she was the best person to evaluate her capabilities, and he trusted her. Asa's attribution for his daughter's transformation was not quite correct. Despite the lofty academics and exposure to the best and the brightest, it was not Barnard that had transformed Faith but her relentless drive to attract Robert Trent.

A few days later, during dinner, Asa brought up the subject of Barnard.

"It's hard to admit it, but you are now a grown woman with an excellent work ethic. If you want to leave Barnard, I won't interfere. It would be beneficial to have you full time in the office. All I ask is that you finish the semester and make sure a move is what you want."

"Thank you," said Faith. She put her fork down and took a sip of water. "There's something else I want to talk to you about. It's about Robert Trent. I've decided he is the man I want to marry."

Asa put both his hands on the table and shifted in his seat to attention. "Really? This is a surprise."

"Do you have objections?" she asked.

"Not at all," said Asa, recovering. "He's a wonderful choice. Have you been seeing him?"

"I see him once in a while, but not yet as a beau. I was hoping you might approach him and feel him out. You can tell him he's a good candidate for my hand. You have a lot of influence, Papa. Besides, I come with a generous dowry. He would have to take you seriously."

Asa looked at his daughter with some concern. "My influence doesn't stretch that far." He could see that despite her businesslike presentation, her eyes flickered and she was unsure about what she was proposing.

Faith wouldn't let him off. "You were going to offer him Hope that last summer." There was the barest quiver.

He understood immediately. He reached over and cupped her face in his hand, feeling a new tenderness and responsibility. "Have you any indication that he is falling in love?"

"I didn't say anything about falling in love. Very few people marry for love, and those who do quickly find out they're not in love at all. A marriage between us makes sense. You already know what kind of a man he is, and I do, too. His father had some bad business a long time ago, but he was cleared. He even went to jail, but it was a setup.

His mother has very good lineage, but her family cut her off when she married Robert's father."

"You've done your homework on this man."

"I have. More than you know. On top of everything else, he's a brilliant lawyer."

"Paul Wentworth agrees with you. He's thrilled to have him at the firm."

"Does that mean you approve?"

"I'm the last one to give advice. Look at your mother. Her father was the one who approached me and floated the idea of marriage. It seemed like a good idea, but Alice was a sheltered young girl, and she only saw the glamour and getting away from that boisterous and competitive bunch. Almost immediately she wanted to be back with them and never was happy at Seawatch. I don't blame her at all. I was selfish and wanted to get it done. Look what happened."

Asa looked at his daughter and studied her face to find some similarities that bound them. There were few. Until recently, he hadn't felt a visceral connection to Faith. The dual tragedies of death and desertion had driven them together. They were finally a solace to each other. She had a steeliness that was foreign to him, but he admired it and had leaned on it during the worst days. He knew that once she joined the firm full time, she would be a formidable partner. He was sure that she had given this proposal a lot of thought, and now her decision was final. He had no doubt that whatever else Robert Trent had decided to do with his life, he was also going to marry his daughter. Asa would do his best to help her. He owed her some happiness.

"I'll ask Robert to come and see me," he said.

Chapter Forty-Nine

Martin knew what had happened long before she told him. At first, he was furious with Trent and wanted to show her how stupidly she had behaved. His anger passed when he saw her struggling to get through the days. Her face was wan, and she often looked bewildered. He never asked her any questions. What good would that have done? Obviously, Trent was unaware of what he had left, and she didn't want to tell him.

When she became ungainly and could not hide her condition, he placed her in his inner office so he could keep an eye on her or take her home if she was too fatigued. Even though her figure had changed and her face had a different cast, she appeared more beautiful to him.

He saw how difficult it was for her to move, and he wondered how she was able to take care of herself. Toward the end, when she could no longer come to the office, he made her move into his house. He had bought a brownstone on Sullivan Street and rented out the two upper floors, keeping the lower three for himself. He had plenty of room for her, and when the time came, he would be close by to take her to the hospital.

She obeyed him like a child. Every night, he came home with food he had bought for the two of them, and they ate together. He would recount the day's affairs on the Street, the ups and downs. The market was robust and, outside of the shenanigans being perpetrated by the manipulators, stocks on the Dow list were going up.

He had managed a return of 14 percent for his clients for the year. A Republican, Warren Harding, was in the White House, but it hardly mattered. There was a giddiness in the country that didn't depend on political parties or government. The big news was the automobile. Henry Ford's assembly workers could put together a car in ninety-three minutes, and they were selling faster than he could build them. When you could get in your car and take off under your own power, who wouldn't feel giddy? It was a different America, and the biggest winners were women, who now had the ability to vote and also join the work force and go out into the world if they chose. Hope's baby would come into the best possible America.

In the last few weeks of Hope's pregnancy, when movement was awkward and often painful, Martin helped her dress and brushed her hair. She let him do it. Her arms became too fatigued to comb through the tangles in her hair. She couldn't reach her back to fasten buttons or hooks. She needed help to get out of chairs. She felt more secure if she walked holding on to his arm. She let him do as much as he wanted, and he did many intimate things that would have meant more if she had not been in the total grip of a full-term child getting ready to come into the world. She cried often. She thought she was crying about the baby, but she was also mourning the loss of her beloved. Twice she was ready to tell Robert about the baby. He would be hers once again. But it would not be the same. He would be hers out of duty.

Through it all, the clumsiness, the crying, the fatigue, and the fear, Martin stayed by her side. When he combed her hair and made a braid down her back, she cried and then kissed his hand. "Thank you. I feel so clumsy. The baby kicks all the time, and I don't know what to do."

"It's all right." He didn't know if it was all right, but he would make it as all right as it could be. He felt responsible for her, and this was not the time to examine the reason too closely. In the last few weeks, she was always uncomfortable and often in pain. Her ribs hurt; she was plagued with a stuffy nose and found it hard to breathe at night. Her legs were swollen and the doctor told her that if she retained too much water, he would have to take the baby through cesarean, a risky procedure.

Martin's old anger flared. He was angry with her, but primarily with Trent. The golden boy had taken what he wanted carelessly and left Hope in danger. In time, he calmed down. Hope admitted she was the one who ended the affair.

"Does he . . . does Robert know?" he asked Hope.

"No. He doesn't. I made that decision, too. It would muddy everything. I want it to be a clean break with no strings. No recriminations. We both will have a clean start."

He knew that although she was saying that, there were no clean starts after something like this.

Chapter Fifty

Asa decided that the office at Seawatch, with its serious paneled walls and heavy drapes, was the best place to have the meeting with his future son-in-law. He had carefully outlined the three components of the contract—emotional, professional, and financial. He wasn't just trying to pretty up a simple cash-for-services deal. Faith was a valuable asset. The proposal that Asa Simpson offered to Robert Trent was philosophical, comprehensive, and irresistible. He mentioned longevity and compatibility in place of impulsiveness and short-lived thrall. Once he had set that foundation, Asa clothed the rest of the proposal with the reward. The figure that came with a partnership with Faith Celeste Simpson was $10 million. To Asa's credit, he presented the offer as completely advantageous even without the money. He had considered that perhaps the figure was too generous and that he could have bought Faith her husband for half the sum, but he wanted the outcome to be certain, and he didn't mind overpaying for a guarantee.

At the start, Asa asked a question. "Before I begin, let me ask you if you are currently romantically involved?"

Robert was surprised. He immediately thought of Hope and wondered if Asa was asking what seemed like a frivolous question because he knew of the relationship. *Romantically involved* was such a superficial phrase. It did not represent the feverish need that still plagued him when he allowed himself to think of her. "I am not."

"Good. I can continue." Asa proceeded to outline what at first seemed a hypothetical scenario of a path to financial glory with details of holdings, global reach, precise figures, and predictions of growth. There followed a provocative personal offer, the first tier of which was a union with his daughter, Faith, but reached far into the future and included the entire Simpson legacy. Asa segued into specifics. "I'm offering five million up front to show you how pleased I would be with this union," Asa said. "The up-front sum is a celebration for what I consider a joyous marriage. The rest of the money, an additional five million, is what any good father sets up for his son. It will keep you steady during those trying first years and will be deposited on your fifth anniversary."

"Am I to understand, sir, that you are offering me Faith's hand in marriage?"

"That is an important part of it," said Asa.

"It's the only part of it that is important to me," said Robert. He walked to the multipaned window and looked at the beautiful brick apron abutting the circular driveway. It reminded him of Saint Paul's, where a similar brick pattern stood near the old chapel. He thought of the morning prayer murmured in that chapel that extolled truth, kindness and unselfishness. He was satisfied that he could meet those virtues.

"You don't have to give me an answer right away," said Asa. "Take some time."

"There's no need to think about it," he said. "It would be an honor to marry Faith. If you don't mind, though, I'd like to be the one to tell her."

It cost Asa Simpson $5 million to repay his daughter for twenty-three years of neglect and lack of parental love. The additional $5 million was to make sure Robert Trent stayed married to her. The telling phrase in the proposal had been *keep you steady during those trying first years.* To a cynic, it might have sounded as if he were expecting Trent to bolt once his $5 million was safely in the account. Robert Trent had turned it around. He'd taken any callousness and avarice out of the proposal and made it all about Faith. He had said yes to a simple agreement for Faith's hand in marriage. He was sincere. He put away what he still felt for Hope and turned wholeheartedly to Faith.

A week later, Robert Trent asked Faith out for a dinner date. He took her to the Plaza Hotel. As they faced each other, the flattering light bouncing off the polished wood of the Oak Room, he was surprised at how beautiful she looked. The supple silk chemise skimmed her body, hugging her breasts in a provocative way that made him want to touch her. Few would have believed him, but Asa Simpson had made a decision for him that he would have eventually made for himself. Perhaps not with Faith but with someone like Faith. The money was not the big factor. The union made sense. He knew Faith. He knew what to expect from her. She would be someone he could depend on, and ultimately, although it was not the carrot one would suppose, he would have the fiefdom of Asa Simpson to manage. That night, after a dinner of beef Wellington and an excellent crème caramel, he asked her to marry him and produced a five-karat emerald-shaped diamond solitaire, nestled in the little blue box of Tiffany & Co. Faith did not shed any tears. She took a deep breath as if she had completed an arduous task. "Of course, I'll marry you," she said. "You're the love of my life."

◆ ◆ ◆

Despite his desire to escape the sheltering arms of Seawatch, Tommy Rowland knew the rhythm of the estate and he could sense when something important was going on. When he came home one long weekend, he sensed a shift, and his mother confirmed it. "It looks like Faith has a serious beau and it's that nice young lawyer."

"How do you know he's nice?" Tommy was unhappy with this news. He hated the idea that while Hope seemed ill and struggling, Trent had switched over to Faith without hesitation.

"Asa likes him, and he's always polite."

"That doesn't mean he's nice. It just means he puts up a good front."

"Tommy." His mother was surprised at this reaction. "Be happy for Faith."

Tommy was not completely happy for Faith and went in search of Emily. He knew she would have more information.

"Remember when I told you Trent and Hope were living together and then Faith did something about it?"

"Why? I just saw them together in the village. Whatever she did, it worked. My mother thinks they might already be engaged."

"I don't like it. He barely skipped a beat trading Hope for Faith. That was a callous thing to do."

"You know I didn't like that love story one bit. I'm glad it's over. Hope was always an odd girl, and he has a big future. He's not going to mess it up with a girl like that."

"What do you mean 'a girl like that'?" He didn't like Emily's being so dismissive.

"That girl was always looking for what she could get."

"I don't know why everyone thinks that. She never pandered to anyone to get things. And, by the way, you could say the same about him. What do you think he wants from Faith if not her money?"

"I think he wants the right partner for the kind of life they lead."

"Really? And you don't think Hope was good enough for that life?"

"No. I don't," said Emily. "It's as simple as that. Hope doesn't have the polish for it. It's all about social connections and money and getting more of it, and nobody seems to love anybody. Has anything happy ever happened to this family? Mr. Asa's finally found someone, thank goodness. I guess he doesn't have to go to your parents' house anymore for sociability."

"He still comes to our house. Margaret comes, too. She and my mother get along really well."

"Maybe, but all those millionaires are lonely and bored in their big castles. The butler over at Laurel Hall says they drink themselves into a stupor most nights."

"Emily, I wouldn't be repeating those rumors. You don't know that they're true."

"Since when did you get so much above it all?"

"Mr. Asa's not like the others. He's as regular as they come. I used to drive him home many nights, and he struggled out of the car, he had so much wine in him. When I asked if he wanted me to go in the house with him, he would always say, 'No, Tommy. I need to keep some of my dignity.' He was embarrassed in front of the groundskeeper's son. I can't speak ill of him. I just can't."

"Nobody's asking you to do that." Emily hated it when Tommy became sentimental over the family. They weren't his family, but sometimes he talked about them as if he were responsible for their happiness. She would say, "They'd sell you down the river if money was involved," but Tommy would always refute it. "They wouldn't. Mr. Asa loves my mother. And he loved Hope, too. He didn't consider her a street girl."

"If it makes you feel better, you and I probably wouldn't fit that life, either. And I wouldn't want it, for heaven's sake. And you don't, either, Tommy Rowland, so don't say you do."

"No, I suppose not."

Tommy kept rethinking the part he had played in the affair between Hope and Trent. He knew one thing for sure. It would never be possible to cut all ties to the Simpsons. When he had helped Asa out of the Packard and had been sure he made it into the house safely, some emotion passed between them. In one way or another, Asa, Faith, Hope, and Billy, too, had depended on his help, and it made him feel satisfied and connected. His plans had always been to escape the estate, but something had changed in Tommy. When he saw how happy and natural Asa was with Margaret, he realized it was the same natural affection Asa felt for his mother and father. He *chose* them to be his friends. If Tommy was in need, Asa would help him as much as any natural son. That's the way it was, although it had taken him a long time to see it.

Chapter Fifty-One

Her labor pains came in the middle of the night. Martin brought the car around and drove her to Saint Vincent's Hospital on Eleventh Street. Hospital staff thought he was the father, and he didn't say otherwise. What he didn't know and what she told him when they arrived is that she had already decided to give the baby up for adoption, and the adoption agency would claim the infant immediately. Martin was shocked and tried to dissuade her. "At least wait a few days. Your emotions are not reliable now."

She refused. She didn't want to see it. She didn't want to know the sex, and she didn't want to know about the people who adopted it. Not that they would tell her. It was a closed-adoption process. Nobody knew anything.

"It's such an irreversible decision."

"I want it to be irreversible," she said.

She wanted to give up the baby and continue her life with a new purpose. A purpose that didn't involve love. When Martin saw that he couldn't change her mind, he became agitated. It was inconceivable to him for a person to give up a child. He was sure she would regret it. When they wheeled her out of the delivery room, groggy and sleepy, he made her wake up and begged her to reconsider. "No, no, no," she screamed at him. "No."

He followed the nurse holding the small bundle down the corridor. He couldn't let it go. It was too important. On a hunch, he asked, "Is it a boy?"

"Yes," she said, "a perfect little boy."

He continued to follow the nurse. "May I have a look at him?"

"No harm in that," she said and pulled away the swaddling. Hope's face was replicated with a wisp of reddish hair. Freed from the swaddling, the baby waved his arms and opened his eyes. Martin was certain he looked directly at him.

"Are the adopting parents here?"

"Yes, sir."

As the nurse walked through the corridors, Martin continued after her. Having seen the baby, he rebelled at the idea that this was the last they would know of this person. He wanted to take the child from her arms and whisk it out, but it was not his. He had a feeling that any further questions would be met with silence. But he was a Rhodes Scholar; surely he could maneuver a few clues from this pleasant young woman.

"I wish he could grow up in the country," he said. "City life is so unhealthy for children."

"Oh, he will," she said brightly, before she could stop herself. "Harrisburg, Pennsylvania."

"Wonderful. The father must be a farmer."

"A mechanic," she said. "Fixes automobiles."

"I don't suppose you can tell me his name."

"No, sir. It's against the rules." She walked away, and he repeated the information to himself. An auto mechanic in Harrisburg, Pennsylvania. At least he would know where to start looking.

◆ ◆ ◆

The first thing Hope did was to look for a new apartment, even though Martin had offered to let her stay. She could now afford a doorman building and some luxury. She found a spacious one-bedroom on West Eleventh Street near Fifth Avenue. There was a living room with a coffered ceiling, a large windowed bedroom, a kitchen, and a complete inside bathroom—inside the apartment, not a shared one in the hall—with intricate black-and-white tiling. The rooms had been newly painted, and the floors were a light oak with a pretty inlaid ribbon border. The long windows looked out to a beautiful tree-lined street. She chose the second floor so she could hear the noises from below. She still didn't like silence. She went to Kamen and had him send a decorator to outfit the rooms with new furniture and a good large bed. The only things she kept from her former life were her mother's pots and the threadbare sheets and comforter that she continued to use.

She also bought herself new business clothes at Lord & Taylor, where they had stylists who helped ladies create a wardrobe. She patronized her first beauty salon and had her hair cut, her eyebrows shaped, and her fingernails trimmed and polished. She bought new silk underwear and a robe to wear in the mornings. She had been through an upheaval, both emotional and physical, and now she was going to take care of herself and make a lot of money to cushion her life and insulate her from any hardship and need.

Often she thought of Faith. She thought of those months of closeness and sharing and knowing what the other felt. She had known Faith wanted Robert with all her heart. It was different from what she felt. With her it was a physical need, whereas Faith wanted him to fill her life. Maybe that had happened. Faith would help him achieve all that was important. Hope wouldn't mind if he was safely with Faith.

When Hope returned to work, she spoke to Martin about the future and a little about the past. She told Martin her parents' story so he could understand her new resolve and take it seriously. But there was another, more pressing reason. She didn't want to forget a single detail. Now that the baby was no longer inside her and she was alone again, she wanted to remember the long-ago past when she had heard her parents talking amiably in the late evenings and early mornings. Those moments had been the most comforting of her life, and she needed to talk about them and try to re-create the solace. She had loved going to sleep to their murmurings and waking up to them, too.

When she got to the part in the story where she and her mother began getting letters from Sen, she looked Martin straight in the eye. "The letters were decorated with Chinese symbols and we hung them over the fabric like art. There wasn't one inch of that room that was plain," she said, "but it was beautiful. It was a bold stroke that assured me my mother wasn't ordinary, and that's all that mattered to me. I'm extraordinary, too. I'm telling you all of this to assure you that I'm going to succeed here. I'm going to succeed in a very big way."

Martin listened to her speech and said little. He knew how emotionally raw she was. Her new look, although beautiful, bothered him, too. Her hair was cut in a short bob. It was still curly, but it was shaped to lie softly around her face. She had a new wardrobe of formfitting jackets and matching skirts that she wore with silk blouses. She was using cosmetics to enhance her eyes and her lips. She looked beautiful and serious.

"I will never forget your kindness," she said and embraced Martin.

They continued as before, but he had many private thoughts. The child was frequently on his mind. He was still drawn to Hope but knew it wasn't the right time to approach her. She was locked up tighter than the vault in his office. He both liked and feared her new zeal for success. He knew without a doubt that she had a unique talent for the business and would do well. And she did—both with him and on her own. Within the next twelve months, they bought a seat on the Exchange and drew up papers to be real partners. She was a one-third partner, but she participated in the profits, and the profits in the decade of the 1920s were plentiful, even if you weren't astute.

◆ ◆ ◆

Hope's will was not enough to keep out the little creature she had given up. The child was on her mind every day, and sometimes her yearning to hold it became so strong that she had to go out into the streets and walk briskly until her emotions quieted. Sometimes she thought she heard it crying, and there was a recurring dream in which she came upon a lost little boy in the park, sitting quietly on a bench. When she passed, he asked her name. She never allowed herself to think of Robert. The only path she had to reclaiming her life was to seal off that episode.

Chapter Fifty-Two

They seldom went to Seawatch, except for the big holidays and the month of August. Even then, it was a forlorn little group.

At Christmas, the staff decorated and put all the holiday paraphernalia out, but when there are no children, the stockings mean little. On Christmas Eve, all the estate workers came to the mansion with their children, and Asa gave them gifts and a generous bonus. He and Faith thanked each one, shook hands with the men, and kissed the women. Mrs. Coombs had an enhanced role in the house, and Margaret, the new Mrs. Simpson, allowed her to do as much as she wanted. They had known each other in different roles but fell easily into the new relationship. Trask had gone back to England, and Asa had hired an estate manager who came once a week to look over the ledgers and keep an eye on purchases.

Faith lived full time at the apartment in the city. Robert had passed the bar and was flourishing at Wentworth, where he worked long hours. Two or three times a week, Faith would meet him at his office, and they would go out to dinner.

Faith had taken a full-time position at her father's firm, in charge of what they called "private equity accounts." Asa had always been a money manager for many of his wealthy friends. He invested for them and took a small yearly percentage. He also managed his own account.

Some of the long-standing workers at Seawatch had asked to put some of their savings into a fund of dividend-paying issues that had very low risk. Most years, the fund made 9 or 10 percent. Faith took over the fund part of the business that was now a full division and included big investors, not just the estate workers. They called it the "working fund." Faith was a confident manager but still sought advice, almost daily, from her father. It was ironic the way it had worked with them. Now that they both had partners, they were closer than they had ever been and needed frequent contact. Most of the time, Asa agreed with her tactics, although he was always more cautious. It was telling that though she was getting married in a matter of weeks, Faith kept her schedule at the office. Her father's firm was a revered institution, and she guarded it.

On her last night as Miss Simpson, Faith spent the evening with her father in his office at Seawatch. Margaret made sure they had the time alone. Although she was not Faith's mother, she sensed that this last night would be emotional, and both father and daughter should voice the last of their fears.

Faith looked around Asa's office and thought of all the times she had come here in apprehension or fear. She remembered the day he had told her and Billy that he had invited a girl to come and live with them. She had feared the girl would be a bully like Steven Butler, but Hope had needed comfort and support instead.

Tonight she was saying good-bye to the first part of her life, and she felt melancholy. There had been only a handful of occasions when Faith had wished for her mother's presence, and this was one of them. It troubled her that Alice had disappeared so deliberately and completely. What can a person think when a mother leaves with her lover and doesn't try to find out how her daughter is doing? "Why does Mother never get in touch with me?" she asked Asa that night.

"I truly don't know. I can't answer for your mother."

She hadn't expected an answer, but this was her last chance to present all the unspoken questions that needed to be aired.

"Do you wish it had been me who died and not Billy?"

Asa looked alarmed. "Faith, don't voice a thought like that. When Billy died, it broke my heart. When my parents were killed, I thought that was the worst thing that could happen, but I was wrong. Billy was such a jolly little boy. Everything delighted him, and he was everything I wanted. I loved you in a different way but no less. My biggest mistake was with your mother. Your mother didn't fit into this life. She was lost here and I was blind to it. I wasn't fair to her at all. I married her for all the wrong reasons—she had a good background, good manners, beauty. Your mother was a beauty. But I neglected her and never tried to understand her. We were too formal with each other. She was right to leave me. We had the most honest conversation the day she came to tell me she was leaving."

"It's so hard for me to think of Mother doing something so decisive," said Faith.

"This was the new Alice. She said, 'I'm not blaming you, Asa. I was in love with the idea of marriage and had no thought of what came after. When Billy died, I knew it would only get worse here. I feel as if I'm escaping. Forgive me, but I feel as if I am escaping and will soon be free.'"

Her speech had been so enlightening, he had even memorized parts of it. Often, as he was getting dressed or sitting alone in his office, a snippet would play in his head. *I feel as if I'm escaping. Forgive me, but I feel as if I am escaping and will soon be free.* Her honesty had freed him to examine feelings and intentions that had been dormant since he lost his parents.

"Don't make that mistake with Robert. Take his situation into account. I think with Robert, it's all about order and rightful place. He would not have agreed to marry you if he didn't think this was his rightful place. But look at him outside of yourself and see what kind of man you have."

◆ ◆ ◆

Asa had it right with Robert Trent. Robert saw his alliance with Faith as just that—an alliance, and a solid platform for creating an orderly and satisfying life. He would always keep his end of the bargain. He would respect and value her. Happily, she excited him sexually, and if his ardor reassured her of his love, so be it.

The entanglement with Hope had been the opposite of order. It had been tumultuous. His attraction for her was so strong, it overshadowed normal thinking and normal behavior. His life would have taken a different direction and in the end, he might have awakened one day as if out of a long sleep and realized he had lost himself. That's not to say he forgot about Hope. That was impossible. She was as near as his breath. She was his heart.

Everything went exactly as planned. They were married at Saint John's, the limestone society church in Lattingtown, by the Reverend Charles E. Hinton. The beautiful country church had a rich history. It had been the first place of worship built on the north side of what was then Pudding Lane.

The church was filled to overflowing. The nave was decorated with white and pink peonies, delicate anemones, the tiniest tea roses, and baby's breath. Every estate worker attended with his or her spouse and stood side by side with the gold coast tycoons. Old Mr. Guthrie, who had been J. P. Morgan's lawyer, sat in a back pew. His estate bordered the church, and he had donated the stone and funds for the facing of the building.

The reception was at the ultra-exclusive Creek Club, on the coastline next to Seawatch. The Lanin Brothers Orchestra played all of Faith's favorite songs, and she did the very modern thing of changing out of her wedding dress into a seductive satin slip gown for the lively reception. Many of the guests were from Robert's law firm. Paul Wentworth, of course, was there. There were others whom Asa still saw, the younger Bakers, the Coes, the Doubledays, the Aldreds, and the Guthries. Right alongside were Chester and Emma Rowland, Joe and Ginny Stokes,

Mrs. Coombs, and Trevor. Robert danced with his bride. Asa, who had hired a coach to learn the foxtrot, danced with his daughter and even kissed her in a rare public show of affection. He also danced with his wife, Margaret, and Mrs. Coombs could not get over seeing her long-time employer in such a giddy mood.

When it was over, the newlyweds left for New York City to spend the night at the Plaza Hotel. The next morning, they would sail on the *Mauritania* for an extended honeymoon, motoring through England and France.

The bridal suite at the Plaza was everything Faith had wanted: an oversize canopied bed, chilled champagne, flowers everywhere. Robert had purposely not had a lot to drink at the reception. He had been subdued but had done all that was expected from a groom. He had kissed her for photographs, lifted her veil back gently, held her around the waist with his hand firmly on the small of her back. He had made a sentimental toast. "To my lovely wife. My chosen companion, the light of my life. I toast her with a full heart."

That night, he made love to her in a slow, deliberate way, kissing her softly as he went, murmuring how happy he was. The marriage was consummated in the proper way, but Faith couldn't help but think, *This better be good. It cost Papa ten million dollars.* It might be true that Robert loved her, and it might even be true that she was his chosen companion, but there was something vital missing. She knew it right away. Robert loved her and would be a good husband, but he didn't want her beyond all reason. He would never pursue her with the mindless passion of a man who couldn't live without her. He could live without her, and that's what she knew on the first day of her marriage, and she carried it with her every single day. It had the effect of forcing a formality in their relationship that had its own intimacy. She told herself that she loved him enough for both of them, and after all, she had never been able to inspire intimacy in anyone.

The picture of the happy newlyweds took up half the front page of the society section in the Sunday *New York Times*. Faith looked beautiful, and Robert looked like a film star. "The newlyweds have known each other since the bride was a teenager," noted the article. "The groom, who is a graduate of Columbia Law, spent a summer at Seawatch playing polo for the Simpson silks." The one thing the article failed to mention was that while the newlyweds ate their first breakfast together in the canopied bed of the Plaza's bridal suite, the groom's son was crawling, unattended, on the cold linoleum floor of a modest kitchen on the outskirts of Harrisburg, Pennsylvania.

Chapter Fifty-Three

The flapper era of the 1920s was a time of unbridled excess, affluence, and social upheaval. They called it the "fabulous decade." In the aftermath of the great world war, America was now the financial capital of the world, and the citizens were turning to a carefree pursuit of pleasure. Skirts were getting shorter and so was ladies' hair. Those in the know thumbed their nose at Prohibition and guzzled the gin supplied by the underworld. The economic postwar boom was making ordinary citizens slightly rich, and it was making bankers like Charles Mitchell—now the president of old Mr. Baker's bank—very rich men. The bankers and brokers who had swollen their bank accounts to unbelievable profits had tempted even the prudent to put their life savings into stocks.

Every business conversation Asa had with Faith was laced with words of caution.

"When you were eight years old," he told her, "there was a struggle for control of the Northern Pacific between Harriman and Morgan. Shares went from under a hundred to over a thousand in a couple of days. Investors sold all their holdings to raise money to buy into Northern Pacific. The short sellers were ruined. I wanted no part of it and sold everything in the eight hundreds. Even though I made a profit, I was dismayed by the gullibility of the general public. Don't be suckered in, Faith. Erring on the side of caution is never wrong."

It was hard to think of things going wrong amid the euphoria. Two miracles had permeated every aspect of life: the automobile and radio. Almost anyone could save the $250 it took to buy a Model T off the assembly line. Ouija boards, mail-order miracle remedies, and popular stocks with unreliable dividends were bought without a thought. It didn't take much to convince the gullible that the stock market could go up indefinitely.

Over twenty million Americans had bought Liberty Bonds and were introduced to the heady business of investing. Joe Stokes had bought Liberty Bonds, as had Chester Rowland, Trevor Kent, and Julia Coombs.

It was into this robust new Wall Street that Beck & Lee had bought their seat on the Exchange, and they had thrived.

With the war's end and America ensconced as banker to the world, the traders' curb became more respectable. Back in 1921, over the vigorous protest of some old-time members, it had moved into a building off Broadway, behind Trinity Church. The boisterous group that had operated happily on the curb didn't like the solemn indoor space. The crowded outdoor arena where Sen had spent so many months with his young daughter was no more. Hope had taken a walk to the familiar blocks, tracing the steps she had taken with Sen so many times. There were stragglers but no crowds, no telephones dangling on window ledges. The Exchange was meant to be sedate and businesslike, but the sucker bait got worse because there were a lot more suckers. Paying the piper was still several years away. The prudent had some time to make money and insulate themselves against disaster. Martin Beck, Hope Lee, and Asa Simpson were insulated. Others who should have known better were sucked in.

Chapter Fifty-Four

After their honeymoon, Faith had wanted to move into Robert's apartment downtown, but he discouraged her. "It's small. There's not a proper place to eat, so we couldn't entertain. Let's be realistic: it's not good enough for the entertaining we will be expected to do." He could not imagine Faith lying in the same bed he had shared with Hope.

"And what lifestyle is that?" Faith had asked.

"We will be sucked into what they call 'café society,' although why they call it that is a mystery. And whether we want it or not, we are part of society's Four Hundred, thanks to Mrs. Astor. That's what happens when your father is the famous financial genius."

"You think my father's a genius?"

"Most definitely. And you're probably a genius, too. In fact, I know you are, where analytics are concerned. It's an amazing trait, and I've heard your father mention it."

She loved having these chats with her husband, even though she never knew if it was just banter or if there was a tinge of irony in everything he said. He was wealthy in his own right, and even though there was a $5 million carrot waiting for him if he completed five years with the winsome Miss Simpson, she thought perhaps he was not her husband just for the money. Something unexpected had colored their life together. He cared for her in a gentle way and habitually took her in his arms. He never failed to kiss her upon leaving and when he saw her again. When he kissed her, he always put his arm around her waist and drew her to him. She loved his attentions, and when she realized they were spontaneous and not likely to evaporate, she relaxed into the role of a contented wife. They had settled on a luxury duplex in the Kenilworth, a building a few doors from the Dakota, also overlooking Central Park. After more than a year, Robert still had the place on Charles Street.

"Why do you keep that apartment?" she asked him when they were fully settled in their new place.

"Too lazy to go through all the stuff. All my Yale stuff is there and law-school papers. The rent is negligible and cheaper than renting a storage locker."

"You could move everything here now or out to Seawatch."

"I'll do it one of these days."

She could guess that he kept it for sentimental reasons, but it didn't bother her. They had all been through an upheaval, but he was solidly hers now, and if he needed the apartment as a symbol of something, she didn't object.

She had a far worse secret to keep. In the second month of marriage, she had become pregnant. Coming so soon after winning her prize, it scared her. Pregnancy brought with it a host of unattractive problems. She would gain weight, bloat, become clumsy. Her hard-won good looks would be reversed, or worse. She was a new bride, and the intimacy was still new, too. She couldn't give that up just yet. Never for one moment did Faith consider that having a child would have the opposite effect of cementing their marriage. Never did she consider that giving birth would be fulfilling for her. On the contrary, she saw pregnancy as debilitating and imprisoning. She had heard her mother say once that all her teeth had gone bad because of pregnancy. She had also said that her hair had thinned and her feet had swollen to the point where she could hardly walk.

For all of her sophistication, Faith was afraid of pregnancy. For her, the bearing of children was not the miracle every woman prayed for. She panicked. For her, it was a trap that immediately narrowed her options and her ability to control her fate.

The day she confirmed her pregnancy, Faith made arrangements to have an abortion. Through a family doctor, she gained access to a safe "medical" abortion that was recorded as a uterine scrape due to endometriosis, a buildup of uterine tissue. The fact that the buildup was the embryo of a baby boy was never recorded. After the procedure, when she returned to the doctor for a follow-up visit, he told her something that was like an absolution.

"I want you to know the baby would not have reached term," he said. "There was a fatal discrepancy in the formation of his heart. This information might help if you experience guilt or regrets."

The information should have helped, but she still felt guilt over withholding the pregnancy from Robert. She even wondered whether the doctor was telling her that to protect himself.

She and Robert continued to have a robust sex life, but she secured a diaphragm, and although he must have known, it was never mentioned.

Faith was not a person on intimate terms with guilt, but the abortion and her lack of candor created a mental squirm that tapped at her consciousness for many months. She could not shrug her shoulders at having killed Robert Trent's son as if she were just selling off a block of stock that she no longer wished to have in her portfolio. The knowledge that the child would have been stillborn was of no help. Her intention had been to kill a healthy baby.

Chapter Fifty-Five

In the spring of 1925, Martin Beck went on a business trip that took him to Philadelphia. When his business was over, he looked at a map and noticed that Harrisburg was only about a hundred miles away. It had always been his intent to look for the little boy, and now he was within striking distance. He decided to make a side trip.

He didn't know a lot about Harrisburg except that it had been home to steel mills, iron foundries, and machine shops up until the first decade of the century. The Pennsylvania Railroad and the Pennsylvania Canal ran along its eastern border, making it an ideal industrial hub. It had been important to the military effort and in the last days of the war, the American naval ship USS *Harrisburg* had been named in honor of the town.

About ten years prior to Martin's visit, there had been a population shift to the suburbs, and industry had declined. When the automobile made travel so easy, workers could live outside the city. Times were hard in this once-populous and important city; he could see the evidence as he drove through the downtown streets.

Martin began to construct a scenario. Maybe the parents were destitute? Maybe they had to give up their adopted little boy? He decided to make a few stops and ask some questions. He checked into a hotel in the middle of town and asked the clerk for a directory so he could look up the local auto-repair shops.

"I'm trying to find a lost relative, and the only information I have is that he works for an auto-repair establishment. Do you know any nearby?"

"There are two right in the center of town and one about eight miles west." The clerk gave him a local map and marked all the spots where the stations were located.

The first two stops yielded nothing. There was little activity at either of them. He asked a few questions. His story was that he was looking to settle an estate, and the only information he had was that the man had a son who would be about four years old. No one that worked at either shop fit the description. The third place looked deserted. An old man sat in a torn leather chair behind a partition. The cars in the yard were mostly carcasses. Martin told his story and the man rubbed his chin.

After a pause, he pointed to the yard that had all the earmarks of desertion. Tall weeds grew around discarded automobile parts, and playing among them was a pale thin boy.

"The parents moved to find work. The father is my son. He's not well at this time. They couldn't keep him, and I can't keep him much longer myself. This place gets no business except for a few locals."

"What will you do with the boy?"

"Put him in the Odile Home. It's not like he's my own blood. He was adopted."

"What's his name?"

"William. William Fuller."

"Do you mind if I talk to him?"

"Go ahead. He won't say much."

Martin went out into the field and crouched down a few feet from the boy.

"Hello." The face was still Hope's face, and he had to control his emotions. He didn't want to scare the boy.

The boy looked at him but didn't respond.

"Do you like playing around the cars?"

He nodded.

"What's that part called?" Martin pointed to a fender lying in front of the boy.

"Fender."

"Thank you," said Martin.

When the boy opened his mouth, Martin could see how little care he'd had. His teeth were discolored. He was dressed poorly and not warm enough for the day. His shoes were so worn it was impossible to tell their original color. His instinct was to take the boy immediately, but that wasn't possible. Whatever the situation, it was all the boy knew. Even if he could take him, it wasn't his child. Hope had to want him, and she hadn't expressed that wish. Sometimes he'd catch her looking at children in the street who matched William's age. Her eyes would narrow and she'd pause. She never spoke of it, but he was sure the whereabouts of her child was always on her mind.

The second visit he made to Harrisburg was just four months after the first. He had had a dream that the boy was gone and the old man was gone and there was no way to find them. He drove straight to Harrisburg the following day and went to the repair shop. The old man was still there but no sign of the boy.

"Where's William?"

"He's at the church school on Tuesdays and Thursdays."

"I think I should tell you the truth," Martin said. "It isn't that I meant to lie, but the mother didn't know I had found him. Please promise me you won't put him in an orphanage. I'll come as often as necessary and pay you for his keep. No strings attached. I can see you are a caring man, doing your best in a bad situation. On top of that, your son is ill. I would like to help you, but you must promise me that you won't move away or give the boy away."

"That's a fair deal," said the man. "I would do it for nothing if I could."

"I know that," said Martin. He handed the man an envelope with five hundred dollars. He also left his card. "Please call me if anything changes."

"I surely will," said the old man.

It remained that way for a year, during which Martin made the trip three times, and each time, he left money with the grandfather. He also spent several hours with the boy and brought him a toy. Soon he would bring up the subject with Hope and see if she was ready to take back her son.

Chapter Fifty-Six

One afternoon after a hectic day, Martin and Hope stayed at their desks, waiting to unwind before heading home. They had made a heavy investment in the Radio Corporation of America. Martin was nervous. He had never put so much money into one stock. He, like Asa, had a varied list of barometers that guided him in selecting what he bought. He always looked for the next big sociological shift. Mass communication was the next move in the country, and radio was the vehicle.

He had talked it out with Hope as they sometimes did when planning a big move. This time, it was Hope who pushed for a big purchase. She was convinced that broadcasting would turn out to be as big or bigger than the automobile. More than once, she had made the case to Martin. "The automobile depended on paved roads to succeed, and the railroad needed passengers. Now the 114 million Americans in the forty-eight states need a way to experience big events as a unit, and the new National Broadcasting Company is going to provide that service. Remember what happened when they broadcast the Rose Bowl? Eighty percent of the country was glued to the little brown box. Imagine what else the country can experience together. It's a miracle that is only going to get more miraculous."

Years earlier, Martin and Hope had bought ten thousand shares of the original RCA stock when it was $1.50. The following year it had tripled and they had purchased ten thousand more shares at under $5 and another ten thousand shares at $6. Presently, the price was $66.87.

Now they had decided to bet even more money on Mr. Sarnoff, head of NBC, the umbrella for all the RCA radio stations, who had already thrilled the country with the Tunney–Carpentier fight. The stock had jumped five points, and although they both felt nervous, they were optimistic about the future of radio. Everybody listened to the radio. It was now an integral part of daily life.

The anxieties of the day and the nerve-racking trades had left them both exhausted. What Hope had not shared with Martin is that all along she had been purchasing shares of the RCA stock on her own, and when the stock hit $66, her private account jumped by a couple of million dollars. After the market closed, Hope sat at her desk unable to move. She looked at the confirmations for their trades scattered over her desk.

She began to talk almost in reverie. "I'm doing exactly what my father did. He was a cook, but he also was a prospector. I'm a prospector, too. I just realized it. My mother was self-motivated, and I am, too." She was quiet a moment and then, out of nowhere, she said, "Thank God she didn't burn up. She jumped, but she didn't burn up." She still missed her mother and often talked to her out loud in the early morning. *Can you see me, Mama? Do you know all the things that have happened?* "I wish my mother could see how well I'm doing. I have no one to share it with."

Martin came to her and took her in his arms. He knew this melancholy and reflection was emotion that had been held back since the baby was born, and the fatigue and tension of the day had weakened her defenses. She talked of her father and mother often since the baby.

He whispered in her ear, "You haven't lost everyone. There is one person left, and I know where he is." She jumped away from him. She knew immediately what he meant.

"How do you know?"

Consuelo Saah Baehr

"The day you gave birth, I followed the nurse who took him. She didn't tell me much, but it was enough for me to find him."

"He's here in New York?"

"No. Harrisburg, Pennsylvania."

"You've seen him?"

"Yes."

"How is he?"

"Looks like you. The situation is not the best. The father is dirt poor, probably because of the downturn in those industrial towns. The boy stays with his grandfather while the father looks elsewhere for work."

"Why are you telling me this now?"

"I know you think of him. All this about having no one is not true. You do have someone, and it weighs on you."

"Martin, what can I do?"

"It might be possible to do something. I don't want to say they'd be glad to be rid of him, but the father is ill, and we might be able to get him back. I think they might be relieved. And we could certainly give them some money if it came to that."

"We would need a lawyer to help us."

"That's easy enough. Are you saying you want to do it?"

"I want my boy." After she said it, she looked stricken. "Maybe I won't know how to take care of him. Maybe I'm not fit to have him."

"That can't be. You will love him, and that's really the most important thing."

The next day, Martin contacted the best lawyer he knew, Harvey Whitaker, another Rhodes Scholar he had met in London who now practiced in New York. Harvey heard him out and told him it was not a complicated case if all the parties were in agreement. It was a matter of drawing up a reversal of the adoption, having the family sign it, and having it approved by the courts.

Martin and Hope were both so excited, they forgot their bold stock purchase of the previous day. When Hope happened to look at the closing price of National Broadcasting Company, it had jumped to $101. All told, from their first purchase at $1.50, the firm had made $17 million. As a principal of the firm, some of that $17 million went to Hope, and her private account had jumped by another million, too.

"Should we sell some of it?" Martin said.

"Not yet."

"All right," said Martin, not quite convinced. "Don't come crying when it dips."

"It's not going to dip," said Hope. "We still have a ways to run. I've done my homework, and the market is not even close to being saturated with the little brown box. Millions of immigrants are still pouring onto our shores. We'll see RCA triple or more."

Chapter Fifty-Seven

Martin traveled to Harrisburg, and this time he told the grandfather the complete truth. "The mother was young and she thought she couldn't keep the boy. I wouldn't bring this up, but I see you are struggling in these hard times, and perhaps it would do good all around to relieve you of the responsibility. We would do it all legally, and we would compensate you for the years you took care of him. You don't have to answer me right now, but I'm going to leave you my card and you can contact me anytime. In the meantime, here is something for you. It isn't meant to influence your decision. It is just a small sum. I'm doing well, and I'm aware of the downturn in the area."

The old man said nothing. He took the envelope.

"My boy, the father, is not getting better," he said. "It's only a matter of time. It was always his idea to adopt. His wife wanted no part of it. Let me talk to him. He barely sees the boy these days, and we sure could use the money."

The call came a week later. "If you are still of a mind to take him, we are ready to turn him over. You mentioned a sum, and I don't mean to sound hungry, but could you tell me what you had in mind?"

Martin could hardly breathe. He was so happy he wanted to shout. "What sum would you want, Mr. Fuller?"

"We were thinking a thousand dollars."

"Mr. Fuller, that is a modest sum for the sacrifice you're making. You are an honorable man, and I'd like to make it five thousand for all the years you've taken care of William. I'll come to the shop with a cashier's check and the legal papers within a day or two."

"That will surely help us out. Five thousand. That will surely help us out."

◆　◆　◆

He told Hope not to come with him. "I don't want you to see him in that context. It will color everything you feel about William, and I think you should start fresh. He's a resilient boy. You stay here and I'll bring your son to you."

The transfer was not very complicated. They met in a local lawyer's office in Philadelphia that had been contacted by Martin's lawyer. They all sat around a conference table, Martin on one side with the lawyer and William and his adoptive father on the other side. The father was thin and weak but well aware of what was happening. He kept his hand on the boy's shoulder the entire time. Martin could see the hand going back and forth across William's shoulder blades. He was so full of emotion, he had to look away. William had been loved and that was all that mattered, but Martin could see how hard this decision was on Daniel Fuller. He was glad he had given them the $5,000 and thought he should make it more, although he knew money would not alleviate the man's agony.

Martin had seen William enough times to be familiar to the little boy. This time, he brought him a car with wheels and a small steel tractor with a hinged moving hauler in back. He sat with the boy in comfortable silence while he played. When his father bent down and told his boy that he was going to go with Martin and it would be OK, William nodded and didn't cry. The father's face was crumpled in sadness, and Martin could not keep the tears from rolling down his face.

He embraced Daniel Fuller and whispered in his ear, "You will always be welcome to visit. Always. If money is needed for expenses, it's yours for the asking. I will talk about you to William as long as I'm alive." The father nodded and left the room. Martin took William by the hand, and they got in the car.

Before he brought the boy home, Martin took him to a fancy hotel for the night. He had bought pajamas and a change of clothes. He ordered dinner from room service, and when they had finished, he ran a bubble bath and brought out a little boat and a duck to put in the tub. William didn't want to get in and hung at the bathroom door. Martin told him to put the duck in the water, which he did. Then he told him to put the boat in the water. Then he said, "Look, the boat and the duck are sailing along. Wouldn't you like to play with them? Get in. It's all right. Get in the warm water and play with the toys."

The boy was so thin, his bones stood out. His eyes, Hope's eyes, were large and vigilant. Martin sat on the edge of the tub and watched the little boy play for an hour. First, he pushed the boat. Then he put the duck on top of the boat and pushed them. Finally, he took the boat in one hand and the duck in the other and pushed them both until they collided. By accident, he squeezed the duck, and it squeaked and he began to laugh. Martin laughed also, and they looked at each other and laughed some more.

Hope's apartment was on the south side of West Eleventh Street, between Fifth and Sixth Avenues. It was a serene residential block of townhouses, anchored at the Fifth Avenue end by the beautiful Gothic mass of the First Presbyterian Church. Number 22–24 was one of the small buildings with six floors. The elevator was slow and clunky, and when it began to ascend, William was startled and clung to Martin. "It's all right," he said and held his hand. "We're going to meet someone who will be glad to see you. Don't be afraid. She's going to like you a lot."

When they knocked on the door, Hope called out, "It's open. Come in."

She was standing near the window, and he realized she had watched them as they entered the building. To her credit, she wasn't crying. "Hello, William," she said. "I'm so glad you're here."

The boy said nothing but looked at Martin, who nodded. "It's all right."

He realized he couldn't just hand the boy over to Hope. "He's seen me several times and would probably feel better if I stuck around. Maybe I should just sleep on the couch here. Until he gets used to you."

The three of them sat side by side on the couch. Hope had bought a train set. The engine had a whistle, and each time it passed the midway spot, it whistled. William watched from the couch. Martin put his hand reassuringly across the boy's back. Hope put her hand over Martin's, not daring to touch the boy directly. After a few minutes, Martin slipped his hand away and Hope's hand was touching her son. She could feel the outline of his bones. He was frighteningly thin. She wanted to take him on her lap and hold him, but she knew that would scare him, so she kept her hand on his back until his eyes closed and he slumped against her. When he was safely asleep, she carried him to her bed and cradled his body until morning.

Chapter Fifty-Eight

Tommy had a week's vacation in the month of July, and he had come back to Seawatch to help his father reroof the house. Asa and Margaret were spending the summer at the mansion, and his mother was back at Seawatch, too. Emma was like a mother hen having her Tommy home and took every opportunity to pamper her boy.

"Do you ever see Hope?" she asked him one morning as they sat in the kitchen finishing their breakfast. "Faith is doing fine, and I'm wondering if Hope's all right?"

"I haven't seen her lately," said Tommy. "I went to her office once, and she was on her way to being a partner in a Wall Street business. Maybe she's done it by now."

"Thank the Lord," said Emma. "It could have gone the other way. Is she still so pretty?"

"Very pretty. I think her boss likes her, but you know Hope. She wasn't taking notice."

"If I hadn't sent her up to the mansion, she wouldn't have learned all of that business that Mr. Asa taught her."

"You did a lot for her. She's still the little stock genius. I think that's the part that Faith couldn't swallow."

"Faith's got the whole business now, and she married that nice lawyer. I would say Faith did all right. Do you see her at all?"

"I see her a couple of times a year, and if she's out here, we usually find some time to talk. That didn't go away."

His mother looked at him with one eyebrow raised as if she wanted to ask other questions, but then thought better of it and began to take the dishes to the sink.

What Tommy didn't tell his mother was that the last time he had seen Hope, she might have been in trouble. She might have been ill. He had never forgotten how she appeared that day, and the image had stayed with him. Recently he had had a breakthrough. He had figured out what might have been wrong with her, and he wanted to share it with Faith because it was really important.

One of his coworkers had a pregnant wife, and several times he had seen her walking with him down the street. The woman had to stop and hold on to a car or a lamppost because something had caused her body to revolt. She called it a *stitch*.

"Harold, wait. I've got a stitch," the woman had said and stopped in her tracks.

She looked exhausted, and her face had a vacant expression. There was something about that look and behavior that nagged at Tommy. It made him think of how Hope had looked when he had seen her on the street. He had not forgotten it all these years. Could Hope have been pregnant? That would explain her behavior. But what had happened to the child?

His mother told Tommy that Faith was around, and he called the mansion and asked her to meet him for lunch. She said yes without questioning him, but she knew if he asked her to a private lunch during a family gathering, it had something to do with Hope, and it made her apprehensive.

She decided they should meet at a small restaurant near the railroad depot, away from the prying eyes at Seawatch. After a quick hug and a kiss, they looked at each other for an appraisal.

"You look beautiful," Tommy said.

"And you are the same handsome man you always were. It's really good to see you, Tommy. You seem more relaxed than the last time I saw you."

"I'm doing fine. Thank you."

"Please come over to the house with your parents. I know my father would love to see everyone."

"I'll tell my mother."

Faith sipped her water. "I suspect this meeting has to do with our friend. By the way, she's doing very well. Miss Hope Lee now has her own seat on the Exchange. We do business with her partner from time to time." Tommy was glad to see Faith say this with some pride for her old friend.

"I think I've figured something out that troubled me back then and still nags. I told you that Hope seemed ill after she and Robert parted company, and I now think she was pregnant. Watching the physical difficulties of my coworker's very pregnant wife reminded me of how Hope moved and looked. The child would be about six."

Faith knew instantly that Tommy's hunch was correct. Of course. She had been surprised at the rapidity with which Hope had let go of Robert, and now it made sense. She didn't want him to know about the child and stay with her out of duty. She knew that independent streak in Hope would not allow anyone to stay with her out of duty.

"I think you're right. But what happened to the child? I could hire someone to look at birth records for the year. It's not that hard, but she could have used another name."

Tommy looked stricken. The idea that Faith would now interfere in Hope's life was unthinkable. "Leave it alone, Faith. Leave the girl alone. What's to be gained? She deserves some peace. I don't even know why I brought it up except that it was such a shock."

"Don't worry. I'm not going to do anything. I have more to lose than you know."

Faith became clammy and started gulping water. She thought of her own pregnancy and the clandestine abortion. To find that there was a child from Robert in the world was hurtful. She was being punished for her own selfish actions. Although he hadn't mentioned it, she knew Robert would be delirious to have a child, and that was the one thing she could not bring herself to give him.

Hope Lee still had a hold on her. She would forever be entangled in Faith's life. There was another feeling that was unexpected. She wanted to see the child. She wanted to see Hope as a mother.

Chapter Fifty-Nine

For several months, Martin had been nervous over the euphoria that had gripped Wall Street. No one seemed to care what a company made or how stable their finances were. If the stock went up, people bought in. The manipulators were having a field day. Each day, he and Hope would sit down and write out two scenarios with plus and minus columns. He would bring up all the historical signs that preceded a frightening down market.

"The signs are all there and then some," he said to Hope after each day's list. "Are we going to kick ourselves for not acting?"

"Let's at least get rid of our margined stocks. We don't want to be caught in a squeeze."

Martin agreed. "That's an easy one. We'll sell all of them systematically during the next day or two and wait on the sidelines." The margin requirements were so low that any significant downturn elicited margin calls. Margin calls could ruin you in a matter of hours. "What about the short sales?"

"I would get rid of those, too, but you're better at calling that one. Maybe get rid of half? I don't know."

Throughout September of 1929, Martin's nervousness became outright dread, and he scheduled systematic selling of his holdings and all of his clients' holdings and turned to an all-cash position. He didn't want to be exposed when prices were falling, and he knew as sure as he knew his name that prices were going to fall. The euphoria was frightening and unfounded.

By the third week of the month, he held only a few blue-chip stocks, less than 5 percent. What singular trigger had pushed him to liquidate at that particular week was a mystery even to Martin. One of the events that raised fear was that RCA stock, some of which he and Hope had bought initially for $1.50, had hit $500 a share, netting them millions. There was no sound reason why RCA should have catapulted to that number, and it turned on a switch in Martin. What was the saying? *Pigs get slaughtered.*

Hope also felt discomfort at waking every morning to higher numbers. "I told you I would tell you when to pull the trigger on RCA," she said. "Today's the day. We've made more than enough money. I don't mind losing a few points." Martin didn't need any coaxing. He sold their shares throughout the day. Hope did the same with her private account. At the end of the day, she wished she could talk to Asa and share her success with him, but she had never heard from him in all these years, so she settled for a glass of champagne with Martin.

Knowing they were no longer exposed didn't keep Martin and Hope from the anxiety of what was to happen. Was this the day the market would start to slide? And if it went down, where was the fun that everyone assumed would last forever? Therein lay the dilemma. The kind of childish reasoning that had brought all the newcomers into the market would just as quickly turn them sour when a downturn came. They were too inexperienced to know there was always a downturn. Hope remembered Asa's story of the stock that had taken Sen down that fateful day. Asa had watched it go up several hundred points in an hour. A runaway train was always dangerous.

By September 27, the firm of Beck & Lee was sitting on $90 million in cash for their clients' accounts, $6.5 million in Hope's personal account, and $11 million in Martin's account. There was a cash reserve in the firm's account of $30 million.

On September 28, they had little to do but monitor the tape. The next day, the horrid carnage that would soon engulf most of the world began to play out in London. The London market crashed, and the damage immediately seeped across the ocean. Martin received a telegram from his friends in London urging him to liquidate. *Things are even worse than they appear,* they cautioned.

Investors all over the country were losing their savings, but in New York, the financial capital of the world, it was as if a tornado had upended everything and there was no place to hold on. With all of that, Martin and Hope were too stunned to feel relief that they had escaped. The whole thing began to feel unreal, and several times Hope had to check the bank statements to be sure they were protected. The winnings brought no euphoria for either of them. The devastation was everywhere, and it was hard to feel anything but fear.

The beautiful marble building bounded by Broad and Wall, with its six Corinthian fluted columns, was a hell of misery. The mahogany paneled dining room, where members ordered beef Wellington, was deserted. The baths on the third floor, where members could soak in sybaritic splendor, were dry. The only place to be was on the floor of the Exchange watching the quotes.

Martin and Hope had already alerted all their clients of their decisions, and although a few balked at having their portfolios liquidated, Martin assured them that if the inevitable decline was temporary, they could buy in again at lower prices. A few refused to liquidate, and then it was too late. Martin's friend from London who had been his first investor made a transatlantic call in tears to thank him. "You saved my life, old chap. It's grim here. Grim beyond words. There is no dignity left. Grown men weep openly and then leave for the bars, or worse."

It was fully a month later on a day designated as Black Thursday that the market lost 11 percent at the opening bell. The tape was hours late because of the heavy selling, making it impossible to quote prices. The presidents of the big banks met and chose a designated buyer to place large bids on steel and other blue chips well over the market price to stem the selling. A designated buyer placed similar bids on other blue chips. The slide halted, and a rally continued through the half session on Saturday, October 26. Few knew that the bear was just rearing back for its final assault on Monday and Tuesday. William Durant, founder of General Motors, who was known as the Bull of the Bulls, tried single-handedly to stop the market crash. He was unsuccessful and lost millions.

Martin called Hope, who ordinarily didn't come in on Saturday, and told her he was liquidating the last few issues and taking advantage of the short rally. It was the single most important act he ever made in his career, and it not only saved his clients and his company losses, but it created a cash reserve for the firm of over $50 million. Still, there was no joy at the offices of Beck & Lee. Even those who had survived were too stunned to feel anything.

Chapter Sixty

October 24, 1929

Faith monitored the tape all day, stopping only for a cup of tea at one o'clock. The slide continued, and the market was off by 11 percent. When she saw all the blue chips at historic lows, she wanted to buy. This was an aberration and prices would continue their rise in the morning. She wanted to put in orders before the close and beat the bargain hunters in the morning. She committed 50 percent of the firm's cash and went on a fifteen-minute buying spree, spending $15 million. A great deal she bought on margin, which meant she put down 10 percent. At these prices, that did not seem risky. The next day, the market did recover and it seemed that she had acted properly. She was elated and called her father at Seawatch to tell him the good news. He didn't seem particularly happy.

"I don't like it. This doesn't seem like the usual tidy seasonal correction. There's too much exuberance. Half the estate workers are playing with stocks. There are two brokerage offices opened in Muttonville. I would keep a healthy cash reserve until we see how it's going to settle."

Faith didn't tell him that she had already used their reserves to bolster their portfolio against margin calls after the first downturn and had bought new issues on margin. What Faith didn't notice until much later was her uncharacteristic behavior. If a close friend had been watching, she would have urged her to stop. What Faith was doing defied good sense. She couldn't stop buying. She was putting in orders as fast as she could write them, choosing stocks indiscriminately. She was in the grip of a compulsion that was beyond conscious thought. She was compelled to ruin everything to see if she, Faith Celeste Simpson Trent, had any real value by herself. Everyone had worth as a human being, but no one had ever extricated the human Faith from the heiress. What would happen if she destroyed the heiress and only the woman was left?

The rally continued into Friday and the half-day Saturday session. On Monday, margin calls sank everything, and the Dow lost a record 38 points. The next day, Black Tuesday, October 29, the ticker did not stop running until 8:00 p.m., and the market lost $20 billion in the space of two days.

Seventy-five million of that figure belonged to the firm headed by Faith Simpson Trent, the shell-shocked daughter of the financial genius. Faith could barely stand or speak or comprehend what she had done. She had ruinous margin calls, and unless she met them, her father's firm, which had operated firmly in the black for almost thirty-five years, would be no more.

She could not move or speak or even lift her hand. She sat still, facing a window in her office and seeing nothing. Her mind shut down.

When her husband went looking for her late in the evening, she was sitting in her dark office. "Tell me you're all right," he said. He had to shake her to get her attention.

"I can't. I'm not all right."

"What's wrong? Tell me."

The numbness that had protected her for a few hours was broken. "We're on the brink of bankruptcy. I did all the wrong things. In three days, when we have to settle the margin calls, we will lose sixty percent of the value of our investors' portfolios. The firm will go bankrupt."

He went and stood by the window and looked out into waning light. He could still see people on the streets. They were walking and talking and seemed oblivious of the carnage that had taken place in downtown New York. If he turned around, he had to say something and he really had nothing to say. To offer platitudes would be cruel. Unless he had real help, he could not say a word.

After a half hour of silence, something caught his eye in the street. Two friends met and greeted each other so warmly and with such delight, it was a jolt. How could there be any joy at a time like this? What, if anything, could he do for Faith? He could offer her the money her father had given him. It was intact, and he had some more of his own. He turned around.

"I have almost six million to give you. Is that enough?"

"I need thirty to cover the margin calls, and then we can wait for recovery. I have ten of my own in gold mining shares that have held up. I can liquidate."

"That's sixteen," he said excitedly. "We only need fourteen more. Can't you ask your father?"

"Never. My father will be devastated when I tell him. I refuse to go to him. Not with this. I'd sooner ask Hope Lee than I would ask my father."

He knew what she meant. Both Hope and her father were equally forbidden sources. But Hope was not a forbidden source for him. As hard as it would be to approach her, he had no choice. He would do it to save his wife.

"I can ask Hope," he said. "I will ask her for you."

"Let's decide tomorrow," she said. "We'll gather all our money and use it. If you still feel this way in the morning, we can ask Hope Lee to save the business she was accused of sabotaging, that resulted in her leaving Seawatch in disgrace. If you ever need a definition of irony, look to this situation."

Chapter Sixty-One

They met at her office, which was now in a limestone building on Wall and Broadway. He had to prepare himself to see her. On the way, a deep melancholy overtook him. It wasn't regret over a lost love. Now that he was going to see her again, he realized he had missed her. She was and always would be part of him. He had felt it from that first day in the community room of the Neighborhood House. Now he felt it in a different way, and he couldn't even define it.

She had never looked more beautiful. Her face had grown into its adult version. The old impulsiveness was gone. She was calm and thoughtful. She greeted him with a quick embrace and a kiss on the cheek.

"I'm glad to see you," she said simply, and he grasped that she meant it. He took a seat at her desk, and they inspected each other quietly. Many emotions passed through him, but the strongest was one of connection. He was connected to this person and it would always be so.

"Was there something specific that brought you here?" she asked softly.

"I have a favor to ask and it is not a simple one," he said. He was a trial lawyer, he reminded himself. He had faced killers and thieves and grieving parents and kept his composure. He could do this. "Before I ask it, I want to go back a bit to when you and Faith were still adolescents. Faith once told me that you were the first person in that family to help her see how she could gain independence. There were many instances, but one she particularly remembers had to do with mashing some potatoes. Does that make sense? You were the first person to save her from timidity."

"Yes. I told her she didn't have to ever mash potatoes again."

"She needs you to help her today."

Hope was genuinely surprised. "What could she possibly need from me? She has the money, the business, and you. She has you."

He ignored the last sentence, hoping to keep his emotions from bursting through. "The firm's in danger, and she needs a loan to stabilize it or it will go under. I've put in all my resources, but she can't meet the margin calls. She needs an infusion of cash until things right themselves or she'll lose it all. We have two days."

Hope was shocked. If she had learned anything from Asa, it was that you did the cautious thing at the first sign of trouble, and there had been a thousand signs of trouble. How could Faith be so exposed? You could never be exposed. That was the golden rule. She needed a moment to recover; she stood up and went to the window.

"Do you love her?" she asked. Her back was to him.

"It seems a betrayal to answer," he said. "Married love is more complicated than a simple yes or no. Married love is based on different criteria than any other kind of love. You have complete and precise knowledge of the other. You know better than anyone how to hurt them. Every day, unconsciously, you add it all up and make a decision to cherish the union. Yes, I cherish our union. It works better than what most people think of as love."

She understood what he had said because she did that every day with Martin. Right there, in front of the window, she ignored Robert's presence to take in this new thought. Every day, she cherished her union with Martin. Robert's phrasing and analysis had opened her eyes to her own situation. Did she love Martin?

"By the way." He began talking again. "There's another kind of love that is beyond reason. It overtakes you like an illness and keeps you suspended in a kind of frightening abyss. That's what I felt for you. The months we were together were like being suspended over an abyss."

She turned around. His eyes were glistening. She could see deep into his heart. She could trace the entire emotional journey and the will and strength it had taken him to arrive at this place. He opened his arms and she folded herself into him, placing her face in the crook of his neck and letting the sadness flow out. She wanted to make him happy. She wanted to shout with joy, *We share a child together!* That abyss produced a perfect boy. She said nothing. She could not afford that emotional upheaval.

Hope stepped away and walked back behind her desk. "How much?"

"At the very least, fourteen million. We'll pay it back at five percent. That's a point over the current rate. I can draw up the loan agreement and let you add your provisions, if any."

"I personally have about six million that I can liquidate without loss. I'll transfer that today. For the rest, I have to ask my partner. We were fortunate to weather this downturn. I want Faith to weather it, too." She meant what she said. She did not want Faith to fail.

When Robert Trent left her office, Hope felt at peace. It had been the right thing to do, and she knew without a doubt that Asa's daughter would pay back every cent. In reality, lending money at 5 percent was a good risk-free move. She had no doubt that when they met their margin calls, the stocks under pressure would rebound enough to keep Faith in business. She knew also that the lesson had been learned.

There was something else. Without intending it, Robert Trent had uncovered a truth she'd been too close to see. That talk about marital love perfectly described her feeling for Martin. They had shared so much anxiety, grief, triumph, and laughter. She was always happy to hear him come in every morning. It started her day. *Oh, he's here!* He had taught her so much. He had found her son and brought him to her.

The totality of his generosity and caring hit her hard. How could she have been so blind? He had brought her to this point and never asked for anything in return but her presence. He came into the room and found her crying softly.

"What? What?"

She rose and went into his arms. She had sought refuge in his embrace countless times. His arms were ever open for as long as she needed.

"Martin," she said, "Robert Trent was here."

"Oh. I see. Tears of regret?" He stepped back. "You didn't tell him about William?"

"No. And these aren't tears of regret. He made me realize something about you and me. He made me realize that I love you, and now I'm afraid you don't love me back in quite the same way."

"And what way is that?"

"In every possible way. I love you in every possible way and have been too closed off to realize it. Robert Trent opened me up enough to see it, but it may be too late."

"Too late for what?"

"For us. Maybe our time has passed."

He brought her close to him again. He took out a handkerchief and dried her tears. "I think you should blow your nose," he said. He was smiling.

"Oh, Martin, I'm serious."

"Is it because I'm so rich now?" he teased.

"I'm rich, too."

He held her face in his hands. "You stole my heart on that very first day when you took me to your operation center, where you made your purloined furniture polish. Remember? You could hardly find a spot to stand that wasn't already occupied by a rat. I loved you that day and didn't want to let you out of my sight. And, to my credit, I didn't. By the way, I could have prosecuted you right there and then, but did I?

No. I kept you close to me. You have stayed by my side all these years, and we will keep it that way." He realized that Robert Trent had made possible the two loves of his life, Hope Lee and her son. "Thank you, Robert Trent," he said.

"Oh," said Hope, "I almost forgot. I promised we would lend him fourteen million dollars."

Chapter Sixty-Two

In the midst of one of the worst events of her life, the possibility of losing her father's firm, Faith also experienced one of the most important insights into herself. She realized that all of her adult life she had not ever thought of loving someone but only of being loved. She had never asked "Do I love my father?" She'd only asked "Does my father love me?" She had never considered being the lover to Robert; the concern was "Does he love me?" Yes, she had wanted him for her husband, but love? Now that he had offered her all the funds her father had given as her dowry, she had to examine herself and take stock of the root of her struggle to be lovable. It would have been so easy from the beginning if she had thought of it in complete reversal. *Faith loves.* She knew that Robert had surrendered all to her. When he came back from Hope's, they had looked at each other with complete understanding and found the courage to continue. He had withstood the most humbling act to get her the money she needed. The realization made her feel fragile. In the days that followed, Hope kept intruding into her thoughts. Hope was standing tall amid the carnage and, without any fanfare, had given her the funds to save her from ruin. Hope had learned to live and prosper without Robert beside her. Hope had learned her love lessons well. She had sacrificed her child for the man she loved, while Faith had denied her beloved a child. She wanted to go to Hope but was afraid. Maybe she could do it at another time, when the business stabilized and she didn't feel so open and raw.

Robert took the money to his wife and added his six million to it. He had initially done it to prove to her how much she meant to him, but in the days that followed, he realized he had wanted to prove it to himself. Seeing Hope had pushed him right back into that conflagration. That was not what he wanted. He did not want to live so close to the fire. He wanted his life to mean something else. He wanted the precious camaraderie, the humor, the order. He had chosen the right woman. He loved her and could not imagine life without her. When he came back with the funds, they both knew it.

After a one-day recovery on October 30, the New York Stock Market continued its fall. The bottom came on November 13, 1929, when the Dow average closed at 198.60. Faith's firm survived, and in the new landscape, that was remarkable. Their clients suffered paper losses of some of their profit, but their principal stayed intact. She even managed to take advantage of some currency swings and build up her cash reserves.

Robert and Faith were at their breakfast table on a sunny Sunday morning. The *New York Times* was opened to the society page and right in the middle was a beautiful photograph of a newly married couple. Miss

Hope Lee had married Mr. Martin Beck in a civil ceremony presided over by the groom's father, who was a municipal judge.

Beside them, holding his mother's hand, was their nine-year-old boy. Faith saw Robert inspect the picture for a long time. He looked at the boy. "I had no idea Hope had a child. I have to assume it's Martin's. He looks just like his mother."

"He does," said Faith and continued eating her breakfast.

Chapter Sixty-Three

In the fall of 1930, fifteen million Americans were out of work. President Herbert Hoover didn't do much to alleviate the crisis. Self-reliance, he said, was all Americans needed to get them through what he called "a passing incident." It wasn't a passing incident to millions of suffering citizens. The stock market had not rebounded, but it had stabilized. Those who were going to go bankrupt or throw themselves out of windows had already done so, and the drudgery of poverty was just an everyday occurrence.

When her personal turmoil had died down and her firm was past danger, Faith continued to focus on her old friend. For several days, she geared up to do something difficult. She had one more favor to ask of Hope Lee Beck. She had faced corporate heads and foreign leaders, but this meeting filled her with dread. She had no right to ask for anything and certainly not this. Was it preordained that this girl who had come into her life by chance would always have something she needed?

When Robert had come back with the funds to save the company, she had wept with relief. She had wept for the love it showed from her husband, but also from Hope. He had told her that Hope had said she could not let her fail. Without hesitation or any word of recrimination, she had gathered the money needed. It was a lot of money, and some of it had come from her partner, a man Faith had never met. Hope had wanted to keep her safe from harm.

Hope had something else Faith needed, and this was for Robert. He, too, had acted without hesitation. He, too, would not let her fail. She had repaid him, her sole love, with deceit and withholding. She had brought him to the brink of disgrace in order to tear him away from Hope. She had persuaded her father to coax Robert into marriage—there was no other way to describe what had happened. When he gave her his loyalty, his companionship, his respect, and finally his love, she had repaid him by killing his son. Even though the pregnancy had been doomed, it didn't absolve her, and now she had to try to make things right. He should know about the boy he had given Hope. He needed to know there was someone to carry his name and his ideals and his lineage. All of that was so important to him. Now she had to pay the piper. Faith had to convince Hope to let them share her little boy.

She made the trek downtown by car. She had learned to drive, but she asked Trevor to take her, hoping to compose herself on the drive. They were going to meet at the famous Crook, Fox & Nash restaurant, a landmark.

When Faith entered, Hope was already seated and sipping a glass of wine. She was wearing a wide-brimmed hat that was the perfect backdrop for her face. She was a beautiful woman; there was no doubt anymore.

She half rose when Faith came toward her, and she reached out to kiss Faith's cheek.

"Now that we're together, I can't imagine why we didn't do this sooner. I'm glad to see you, Faith."

"I never thanked you in person for the loan. It made a tremendous difference. It saved my father's firm. There will never be words to express my gratitude."

"No need. We're getting a nice return on our money. It's business as usual."

"You must be wondering why I'm here. Don't worry—it's not for more money. I have something difficult to talk about, and very personal, and the outcome will disrupt many lives. But I feel so strongly, I'm willing to risk my dignity and suffer complete humiliation to do it." Before Faith said anything more, Hope knew what it was about. She said nothing.

"When we were first married, I got pregnant. I was so insecure in my marriage and so deeply in love with Robert that I feared all the ills of pregnancy. I feared looking fat and ravaged. I feared the ungainliness of it. I didn't want to risk his love, and I had an abortion. I've never forgiven myself for it, and I haven't been pregnant since. Now I have to say something else that will shock you perhaps, but it must be said. I know you have a boy, and I know that Robert is the father."

Hope took the butter knife and made deep lines in the tablecloth. After a long silence, she said, "I knew why you were here before you said it, but I won't help you. I won't speak to you about this. I can't risk any more heartbreak for William. When he was born, I gave him up. He spent six years with another family. But dear Martin was determined to get him back, and he did. William is just now accepting that he was mine before his adoptive parents. He loved that father. He loved that grandfather, and then they were gone. Both are dead, so he can't even visit them again. He's accepting the reason I gave him away, which makes no sense to him. 'You gave me away so my father wouldn't stay with you?' You see how that sounds to a child? Senseless. False. He's only now beginning to realize that humans, even nice humans, make terrible mistakes. And he's willing to forgive. It would be horrid to put him through any more trials."

"Does he know that Martin is not his father?"

"Yes, but he adores Martin. Martin went often to make sure he was all right. And he wasn't all right. He was malnourished, and his teeth were in terrible shape. He wasn't abused. He was just neglected because of circumstances."

"Does he look anything like Robert?"

"There's a lot of Robert in him, but he has my coloring. I think when he grows into manhood, he will look very much like his father."

"I understand," said Faith. "I understand. Thank you for seeing me." She was about to get up, but she settled in for something that had to be said. "You're an extraordinary woman. I want to thank you and beg your forgiveness for the mess I made in the end. Papa was hell-bent on marrying you off to Robert. He and Mama were thrilled with the idea. I had just begun to gain Robert's interest, though maybe it was only in my head. But Papa made a decision to give him to you. His indifference made me furious. By the way, Papa knows you weren't the one who betrayed him. He follows everything you do. He loves you like a daughter. We're sisters, Hope Lee. We're sisters to the end."

Hope looked at her friend for a long time, trying to remember the girl she had been. "You had every right to be furious. It was a terrible miscalculation on your father's part, and I was oblivious, too. I should have told him that you wanted Robert."

Faith said nothing more. She rose and left the restaurant. Back in the car, she sobbed helplessly, and Trevor, who had known her since the day she was born, reached back and grasped her hand.

Chapter Sixty-Four

When the Packard took the turn off the highway onto Piping Rock Road, Hope's heart seemed to stop. Tears slipped down her cheeks, and Martin reached over William's lap and placed his hand over hers. "It's going to be all right," he said. "You've lived through worse than this."

The decision to visit had been festering since the luncheon with Faith. Even before that, she had struggled with the idea. Robert Trent had a right to know about his son. He had done nothing wrong. He had loved her well, and it had been her decision to withhold the pregnancy from him—out of pride, but mostly fear. She had had a long talk with William, and to her surprise, he took all the information in stride.

"I knew it had to be someone nice," he said, "and I would like to meet my father as long as Martin doesn't mind."

Now the moment was here, and she steadied herself for the accusations she knew might come. Robert had had a right to know, and she had denied it. There was no excuse strong enough to counter the pain he was sure to feel.

Faith told Robert he should meet Hope and William by himself. This was a matter for the three of them, and it required privacy so they could say what was on their minds without fear of hurting the spouses. She took Martin, whom she had never met, for a walk to the pavilion by the beach. Mrs. Coombs had set up a table with iced tea, lemonade, scones, and butter. Martin took Faith's arm as they walked over the uneven grounds.

"Hold on to me," he said companionably, and Faith, relieved to find goodwill, slipped her arm through his.

"I'm so glad you came," she said. "I've wanted to meet Hope's husband for a while. I also wanted to thank you for saving my business. There's no other way to put it. You did me a great favor, and we had never met."

"It turned out well," he said. "That's all that matters." They continued arm in arm to the pavilion, and when they got upstairs, they sat silently, in their own reveries, looking out over the water to the shores of Connecticut and beyond.

As for Hope, she had little to say or do during the meeting in the sedate and intimidating library of Seawatch.

"This room is where I first met Faith," she told them. William nodded, but he was eager to meet his father. He approached Robert with an outstretched hand, which Robert took, and it quickly became a tight embrace. Robert Trent held on to his boy, and she could see his face crumple and tears roll down his cheeks.

The two of them seemed to know what was needed far better than Hope. After a moment, she slipped out of the room. Let them decide how it would go. They were the main participants, and anything she could add would be superfluous. She trusted William. She trusted Robert. What more was there to do? Leave the boy with his father and let them decide what they would be to each other. As she walked into the hall, she took the familiar right turn to Asa's office. She had to see it once more. It had loomed in her mind as the most exciting place of her young girlhood. The door was open, and Asa was behind his desk.

He rose and came toward her. He took her hand and held it in his. "My dear, dear girl." His eyes were filled. "How can I—"

"Hush," she said. "I'm so glad to see you. There's nothing to say. We were partners then. We are partners now. You're my Mr. Asa. You're my Mr. Asa."

The Becks stayed at Seawatch until almost evening. They talked a little about the economy and the state of the country, but mostly they reminisced about Tommy and Joe Stokes and Emma Rowland and Chester and Billy. Even Alice. They treated it as a normal family visit, one in which all the relatives take stock of each other and are satisfied that all is well. All was well.

Afterword

In December of 1932, Hope and Martin went to the Music Box Theatre to see the musical *Of Thee I Sing*. The female lead looked and sounded familiar to Hope. Her inflections were unique, and they kept replaying in her head. The actress's photograph was in the theater lobby, and during intermission, Hope stared at the image for a long time. Her name was Grace Malraux. She didn't know anyone named Grace Malraux.

The following day, the voice and the image nagged at her, and she went to the theater and waited at the backstage door. The cast arrived in twos and threes, but none of them looked familiar, and she wondered if she had missed Grace Malraux. Then she saw her. She knew that face, and without thinking, she called out, "Gloria? Is that Gloria?"

The woman turned instantly and stopped to look at who was talking. "Who is it? Who is calling me Gloria?" She saw Hope and walked toward her. "I would know that hair anywhere. Holy Mother of God, it's little Hope. You survived. You were just a little one. I didn't believe this could happen, but look at us. We made it. We made it."

Hope had often searched the faces in the streets of the old neighborhood, hoping to see Gloria once again. Twice she had been so certain, she had almost embraced total strangers. At last, dear Gloria was standing before her.

"I've been hoping to see you again all these years, and here you are."

After that meeting, Hope realized there was one missing piece that still puzzled and haunted her. She had spent all of those years at his side, much of the time in his arms. She had known his features, his touch, the scent of his newly laundered shirt. He had loved her. He had to have loved her, yet all these years without a word. How could that be? Hope went to see her old landlady, who was still at the same address. "Tell me," she asked when they were seated and sipping a cup of tea, "were there any letters from China after my mother died? Any letters from my father?"

"There were many letters. I didn't know if I would see you again. I sent them back to the post office. You should go around. They have a dead-letter office. They might still be there."

She went to the main post office on Thirty-Fourth Street and inquired. The man took her form and was gone for about twenty minutes. When he returned, he had a small canvas sack.

"All these," he said. "From the dates, you can see they came regularly for a long time. There are a couple of small packages in there, too. We wouldn't have kept them much longer. It's good you came."

The letters were in English, written in beautiful calligraphy and illustrated with small sketches. They spoke of remorse, declarations of love, a request for a photograph to keep. The two packages held dolls, little cloth dolls with oriental faces, but with bright copper hair. Pinned to their silk robes was a note: *From your papa.*

She read every letter, and then put them away. Knowing her father had not forgotten her gave Hope the gift of emotional release. She let go of the last bit of armor. She could feel herself soften. Her heart opened fully. Later that year, she found that she was pregnant, and the following spring she gave birth to a little girl. Martin was overjoyed. Hope had a photographer take a formal portrait of the four of them and sent it to Sen.

Dear Papa,

I received all of your letters. In each one, you ask if I am in good health, if I am all right. I am all right, Papa. Sadly, Mama died but she had many good times before her death. She always wanted her own restaurant and she got one. It was a big success and appeared in the newspaper. You would have been proud to see her using all the cooking lessons you taught her.

I don't cook at all, Papa, but I am in the stock business that you introduced to me so many years ago. I remember everything and I use it with success. Even though you left us and express remorse in your letters, you gave something valuable to both Mama and me. You taught Mama how to cook and you made me fall in love with the stock business. We needed that help to do the work we love.

I'm sending a picture of my family for you to have. The man is Martin, my husband. The boy is William and he is eleven. The girl, who looks like both you and Mama, we named Agatha Sen Beck. We won't forget you and please don't forget us.

Your daughter,
Hope Lee Beck

About the Author

Fortune's Daughters is the most recent family saga written by Consuelo Saah Baehr, bestselling author of *Three Daughters*. Her previous novels include *Best Friends* and *One Hundred Open Houses*. She is also the author of the novella *Softgoods* and the romantic comedy *Nothing to Lose*. Saah Baehr was born in El Salvador to French-Palestinian parents but soon moved to Washington, DC, where her family owned and operated the upscale boutique department store Jean Matou, a favorite of Bess Truman and Jackie Kennedy. A former copywriter for Macy's, and contributor to the *New York Times*, Saah Baehr lives in a cottage close to the Atlantic Ocean and writes about the everydayness of life at www.consuelosaahbaehr.com.